D0665779

COMING IN HOT

SEAL EXtreme Team - Book 1

Kimberley Troutte

Coming in Hot
Copyright © 2014 by Kimberley Troutte

All rights reserved. Except for use in any review, no part of this book may be reproduced, stored in or introduced into a retrieval system, or transmitted in any form by any means, electronic or mechanical, including photocopying, recording, scanning to a computer disk without prior written permission by the copyright owner of this book.

The characters and events portrayed in this book are fictitious with the exception of the brief mention of historical figures woven into the story fictitiously. Any resemblance to persons, whether living or dead, is strictly coincidental and not intended by the author. The author acknowledges the trademark status and trademark owners of various products referenced in this work of fiction, which have been used without permission.

ISBN-13 978-1496002389
ISBN 1496002385

Cover by The Killion Group

PRINTED IN THE UNITED STATES OF AMERICA

Look for these titles by Kimberley Troutte:

SEAL EXtreme Team

COMING IN HOT

LOCK AND LOAD

DOWN AND DIRTY

GOD WHISPERER

CATCH ME IN CASTILE

SOUL STEALER

Middle Grade Fiction by K. Troutte:

SAVING MINER'S GULCH

Dedicated to Anne Marsh.
Thank you for loving Mack as much as I do, and helping me to bring him to life.

CHAPTER ONE

The Harmonds were late. Nail-chewing, stomach churning, where-in-the-heck-were-they late. Didn't they understand how dangerous it was to be a rich American family in South America? They couldn't just wander around out there. It wasn't safe.

Jenna Collins had hired reputable guides and posted undercover employees on the highway to escort the Harmond family to the yacht club. But she worried it wasn't enough. The Harmonds were unpredictable, the weak link. They were still poking around buying trinkets in Otavalo, the Ecuadorian outdoor market, instead of boarding a yacht to the Galapagos.

Jenna rolled her neck, stretching out the kinks, and glared at the phone on her desk. She hated being out of control with a white hot passion. "Ring already!"

Being Admiral Jeffrey Collin's daughter meant that being prepared for every scenario was embedded in Jenna's DNA. It was also a job requirement. As the top travel agent for EXtreme Adventures, she arranged exciting and sometimes dangerous trips for her wealthy clients. Want to trek to the top of the Himalayas and parachute-ski down? Call Jenna. Care to kayak the Amazon River to lunch with native tribes? Jenna's your girl.

She loved her job, even if the rich and famous were notorious for spur of the moment changes to her carefully planned itineraries. Andrew Harmond, recently retired CEO of North America's largest bank and lover of all things spontaneous, was turning out to be one of the worst offenders.

"They're in the car now," Kat, her assistant, reported from her desk. "The driver says they want to take the scenic way."

"Of course they do. Tell the driver not to veer off the mapped route. Our guys are in place on the road."

Her phone rang.

"Andrew. Everything all right in Ecuador?" *Get on the dang yacht!*

She was surprised when a little voice came on the line. "Hey, Jenna, it's me, Jacob. My sister got you a gift, but she didn't want me to tell you. It's a surprise. I don't think you're gonna like it. It's too girly. I'm getting you something way better, so don't worry."

Jenna couldn't help but smile. Ten-year old Jacob was a freckle faced sweetheart. His sister, Anna, was thirteen and more of the "all adults are lame and why do I have to go on this stupid vacation anyway?" variety. "Ah, that's nice. I'm sure I'll love whatever you and Anna get me."

The phones her company had given the Harmonds to use were so clear she could hear him let out a breath thousands of miles away.

"Good, 'cuz Dad said I could send you a lizard from the islands. They sneeze salt water out their noses. Do you think they shoot blood out of their eyes too? That'd be cool."

"What?" She bolted up. Blood nearly shot out of her own eyes at the impending international incident. "Jacob, tell your dad that the animals on the Galapagos Islands are endangered. No touching."

"All right." He sounded bummed. "No salty-snot lizard. But what about a penguin—?"

A loud crash cut him off. The screech of tires and subsequent crunching of metal and glass made Jenna death-grip the phone. A series of loud pops exploded through her ear piece.

"Kat! Pull up the satellite." She punched a button to put the call on speaker and cranked it up so that Kat could listen, too.

"He's been shot!" It was Andrew's wife, Marcella. Her normally silky voice grated like nails on glass.

Shot? Who? Jenna grabbed her cell phone and called her man who was supposed to be tailing the family out of the market. "Roberto! What's going on?"

"Don't know. The driver went off course. Luis, Franco, and I are on the way now."

"Hurry! It sounds like they're being robbed." The screeching of tires drowned out Roberto's next words. "Jacob! Can you hear me? I need you to tell me what's happening. What can you see?"

Jacob didn't answer.

A man coughed in the background, a wet, choking sound. The driver she had hired mumbled, "Gunmen... They...are...CRAF."

Jenna's heart went cold. The Colombian Revolutionary Armed Forces, or CRAF, was a guerrilla militant group notorious for kidnapping the rich for ransom. The Harmonds were in serious danger.

"OhGodohGod. Is he dead?" Marcella shouted while young Anna screamed over and over, making it impossible for Jenna to decipher what was happening.

"Holy Lord, Jenna, what's going on?" Kat pounded computer keys, trying to get a satellite lock on the family's location. Her blue eyes were wide with fear. Straight out of college, Kat had never been in a crisis at EXtreme Adventures before. Jenna had been involved with a few doozies but nothing like this.

Breathing sounds, fast and shallow, came through the phone followed by a whisper, "Men with guns. All around us."

"Jacob?"

"I've got satellite!" Kat called.

Jenna raced to Kat's desk. She had to see, had to know. More loud pops followed a series of military-style Spanish commands that had her heart jackhammering her chest.

"They're surrounded." Kat pointed at the grainy picture on her monitor. "Three cars. All unmarked."

"Who are you?" Andrew's voice exploded out of the speaker. "What do you want? Take your hands off me!"

More shouting and gunfire.

"Roberto! Are your men there yet?" Jenna's cell phone threatened to slip out of her sweaty hands.

"We don't see them, Jenna."

"Dammit!" She looked at Kat. "Our helicopter. Can we get it there in time?"

Kat shook her head, nervously chewing her thumbnail. "Half an hour at best to get it in the air."

"Call the police in Ecuador on your cell. Give them the satellite coordinates. Tell them to hurry!"

"Let go of me!" Marcella wailed.

"Touch her again and I'll—!" Andrew's commands were cut off when three large men slammed him up against the car. As he fought back, Jenna scanned the satellite feed. Where were Roberto and the others?

"The *policia* are on the way." Kat's voice had a tremor to it, but Jenna didn't glance her way. She couldn't take her eyes off the monitor as if looking away would break the connection. And she'd lose them.

Anna screeched bloody murder when her little figure was yanked out of the car.

Don't think about a thirteen-year-old girl in the hands of guerrillas. Focus! Squinting hard at the scene, she tried to make out every dot, every figure. The satellite feed blinked and was intermittently delayed. Jenna bent over the computer screen, willing the horror to stop.

A gun went off and a body slumped forward. *No! They shot*

Andrew Harmond! They didn't kill him. She wouldn't let it be true.

The men dragged him and tossed him into one of the unmarked cars. It sped away from the picture, getting lost under a thick canopy of trees.

Jacob's deep breathing shuddered over the phone. "They grabbed Mom and Dad. Anna."

She swallowed the lump in her throat and made her voice as calm as she could. "Listen to me. They're going to grab you too, Jacob—"

"No! I don't want to go." His cries ripped through her.

"They're going to grab you too. But I'm coming. I promise. I'll get you out of there."

The line went dead. Helplessly, she watched the last two cars on the satellite image disappear into the jungle. Seven minutes later, Roberto and his men arrived. Twenty minutes after that the Ecuadorian police showed up.

They were all too late.

***

Mack's legs itched to scout a perimeter, his eyes longed for night-vision goggles, his fists desperately needed to rearrange something—preferably a bad guy's face—and his gut...He patted his belly. Shit, his gut was huge. He needed action and combat, not this sitting-at-a-desk torture.

The phone rang.

Some little old lady probably lost a cat again. A guy might think finding missing persons (and cats) was a perfect job for a Navy SEAL on extended leave. That guy would have to be thinking out of his quickly spreading ass. He'd also have to give a shit about cats. This job just wasn't him. He was Lieutenant Commander Mack Riley, Gold Knight, premier assault expert, and a leader of warriors who had real balls and guts and would die for one another. DEVGRU, commonly known as SEAL Team

Six, was more than a job—it was the skin that fit him perfectly, in all the right places.

He was on extended leave due to a blowout with the Commanding Officer. The CO was not exactly thrilled to catch two of Mack's guys in bed with his daughter during an overnight in Kuwait. Mack tried to reason with the CO but instead got a verbal thrashing for not keeping his men on a tighter leash and the entire team got a "vacation" out of the deal.

Shit, he hated being inactive. Once his term was up, he'd re-up again. He couldn't wait to get back out there.

The phone rang again.

His squadron nicknamed him Riles because he never got riled about anything—not organizing covert strikes, combat, hostage rescues—it was all good. But now? After coming home because of a bunch of political bull crap he had no role in, he was pissed off. His skin felt too tight, especially around the ass.

Another ring.

He grabbed the phone. "What!"

"Uh, Mack? Mack Riley?"

"Speaking. What'd you lose, lady? Your purse? A cheating husband? Fur-ball?"

There was a long pause. Too long. He didn't have time for this. He needed to go for a ten-mile run, pound the punching bag in the garage, or get a life.

"Mack?" The way the caller softly repeated his name turned a screw in his gut. A long spike-covered screw.

He bolted to his feet. "Jenna?"

"I need you."

It was as if a cold hand grabbed his balls and twisted. *Jenna Collins?*

"Are you there?"

Barely. "What do you want?"

There was a pause. She'd heard the anger in his voice. Good. She let out a breath. "My clients from the travel agency are missing in Colombia. CRAF took them hostage. Do you know who CRAF are?"

That's why she was calling? Troubles at *her* job? It was pretty ironic given their history. "Of course I know who they are."

"I figured you would. I've contacted the Chief of Police and Mayor in Quito, the U.S. Embassy in Ecuador, the Red Cross in South America, and a missing persons hotline in South America. No one seems to be able to help."

"And?"

"The U.S. government won't get involved, either. Something is going on behind the scenes. Political crap that could get my clients killed. The administration said they can't send in the SEALs yet, but they won't say why."

"And?"

She groaned. "And I need your help, Mack. Please. It's a family with two young children. We have to get them out of there!"

We? "So pay the ransom when CRAF call. It's not that hard, Jenna." He was being heartless, but he couldn't help himself. His insides were a ball of hot electric wires. She'd virtually gut-shot him and left him for dead. How could she expect his services now?

"That's just it. There's been no ransom call. Nothing. Total silence. I'm starting to think they took Andrew Harmond for another reason. But then..." she paused. "They shot him, Mack. I saw it on the satellite feed. His body hunched over, dragged away..." Her voice choked with horror. "What if he's dead? What will happen to little Jacob and his sister? Will they kill the whole family?"

Something inside him responded to the sadness and fear he heard. *Shut it down, Riles!* He couldn't go there. He squashed the feeling immediately. "Billionaire Andrew Harmond is your client? Trust me, it's all about the money. CRAF will call. Pay the ransom and you'll get your clients back. Good-bye, Jenna."

"Wait! You won't help me?"

"Shit, no. Why don't you call your daddy?" It was a cheap shot, but he hung up anyway.

He sat motionless for a few seconds, and then he picked up the phone and slammed it down again three times. He hoped he broke the damned thing. Her clients were missing? Who friggin' cared? Not him. After the butt-load of silence—no letter, no postcard, *nada*—she'd called out of the blue. Was he supposed to jump up and do her bidding? Hell, no. She'd have to get someone else to find her lost family because he wouldn't touch this missing persons case with an IED.

The phone rang again. Crap, it still worked. Maybe if he threw it against the wall... Fire flicked behind his eyeballs as he snatched the receiver. "I said no, Jenna! Find some other sorry-assed shmuck—"

"I knew she'd call you." The deep voice rolled with a Southern gentleman's twang. "It had to be one of us, and Jenna is too stubborn to call her old man for help."

"Admiral Collins?"

"You *are* helping my daughter with this fiasco. Isn't that correct, Lieutenant Commander Riley?"

Mack pinched the stress headache burning between his eyes.

"The girl is stubborn and handles things her way. Always been the case. She's independent and mighty proud. Even before her mother passed..." The admiral sucked in a breath through his teeth as if talking about his wife's death still punched him in the balls. "...even before, Jenna demanded to be in charge. But my little girl has no idea how bad this thing is going to get in Colombia."

"What do you mean?" He didn't bother asking how the admiral knew what Jenna had told him. He learned a long time ago that the admiral had eyes and ears all over the damned world. And the NSA had access to phone conversations. Nothing surprised him.

"Civil war is breaking out over there between CRAF and the drug cartels over cocaine rights. It's a bloody turf war that's going to get a whole lot bloodier. Jenna's right about behind the scenes politics in the works. She doesn't know the worst of it. No one does. Yet."

Intrigued, Mack sat up straighter. What could be worse than a billionaire and his family taken hostage by militant guerrillas? "What's happening, sir?"

The admiral chuckled. "That's need to know, son."

Mack rolled his eyes. Just like the brass to clutch information tight and hard against the chest, dragging out just enough bits and pieces to keep men fighting and dying for a cause.

"Right now all you need to know is that Jenna is my life. I'll do everything in my power to protect her. Understand? Get in there and offer your advice, son, whether she wants it or not. There must be dozens of ways to rescue the Harmonds from those damned guerrillas. Head up the team, go to Colombia yourself, and do whatever works for you, but keep her safe until this is all over. And for God's sake, do not let her leave this country."

Every curse word Mack knew rolled through his brain. He clenched his teeth. "Is that an order, sir?"

"Let's just say that I could talk to a certain Commanding Officer on your behalf. I hear he is threatening to bench your whole team for a very long time. Let's imagine eternity, shall we?"

Mack groaned.

"I bet you'd like to get back out there sooner than later. Am I right?"

Blackmail! The sonofabitch would probably call it "dangling a carrot."

"Yes, sir."

"This feels like old times, son. Similar shit, same team members. You should get a better group of friends. Do we have an understanding?"

Mack ground his molars. "She won't listen to me."

"At least she's talking to you. It's a good start. I wouldn't tell her that you and I had this conversation, though, unless you want a wildcat with a burning tail on your hands."

Mack knew exactly what the admiral meant. He'd seen that little kitty in action and had the scratches to prove it.

"Good luck, Lieutenant Commander."

He'd need more than luck.

Jenna Collins didn't get to yank his chain, not anymore. That ship had exploded into thousands of pieces eighteen months ago, sinking his heart with it. But the quiver in her voice when she said she needed him was...intriguing.

Jenna didn't need anyone, especially not him. She'd made that as clear as a nuclear explosion. The Jenna Collins he'd known wasn't afraid of anything, not her tough-as-nails admiral father, and certainly not him. It was one of the things he loved about her. *Dammit! Had loved* about her.

Chain yank.

If he had any sense, he'd run like hell, but the admiral's promise to rescind the extended leave order in exchange for helping Jenna couldn't be ignored. He also needed to understand why Jenna had called him for help. That was a first. The softness in her voice had stirred up memories. He couldn't stop thinking about the way her long curls dripped through his fingers like golden honey before fanning across his sheets. He could almost smell her soft skin and feel her lips blazing a hot trail down his belly before taking him in her mouth, so perfectly he didn't know where he ended and she began.

She needs me? Grinning, he headed toward enemy lines.

CHAPTER TWO

Zoom in. Zoom out. The satellite images on Jenna's monitor didn't miraculously produce a road, a trail, or any damn clue about CRAF's whereabouts. Somewhere in that impossibly thick vegetation, CRAF had a home base. They couldn't simply disappear into the jungle.

"What did the senator say? Is he willing to help us?"

Kat rubbed her eyes, exhausted. They both were. It had been one long hairy day. "Which one?"

"Tonell. The guy who graduated from Vassar with Andrew Harmond. Duncan talked to him this morning. Tell me the senator's going to help us."

"Last I heard, he said he'd get back to us."

"He'd better. What about the field crew? Anything new there?" Jenna had called all the packers and guides she knew in South America.

"They're working on it, Jenna. It might take a little time for the word to get out."

"We don't have time! Why won't anyone help us?"

"Because there's a war on, and no one wants to get shot?" Kat asked sheepishly.

Jenna had never felt so out of control in her life. Time clicked by without any real results, and no one seemed to be able to do anything. In the meantime, CRAF and cartels had started shooting each other in what the journalists had dubbed the Coke War. Bombs were going off in Cali and Bogota with the Harmonds right in the middle of all that mess. It was insane! Jenna didn't do sit back and wait. She didn't do helpless, either. Planning, problem solving, conquering—those were her M.O.s. This day threatened to destroy her.

She needed to get Jacob and his family out of there before they were hurt. She needed...

Oh, God, Mack Riley.

The thought made all the blood rush to her toes. She missed every inch of his lean, tanned, sexy body. But Mack was mulish, strong-willed, and selfish. He'd rather make her suffer for her sins than rescue her clients.

She pounded her desk. "Fine. I'll save them myself!"

"You'll get them out of Colombia?" Kat raised her thin eyebrows. "All by yourself? In the middle of a war?"

"I have to." She'd do whatever it took to save the Harmonds. She had promised Jacob. Her eyes flooded with unshed tears.

"Yeah, I'm thinking it's time for a break. And food! I'm starving, aren't you? I've got a few granola bars in the car. Want one?" Kat was already moving toward the hallway on a mission to stop her boss's waterworks.

Not trusting her voice to answer, she nodded. She hadn't eaten all day and was feeling shaky. Had Jacob eaten anything? Was he still alive? She was tired and an emotional wreck. Kat's heels clicked down the hallway.

You are the boss of your life. You control the outcome. Jenna mentally replayed the self-help CD she listened to before bed and in the car. Nothing worked. No matter how hard she fought them, the tears leaked out anyway. Dammit, crying at work?

Unacceptable. But she couldn't stop any more than she could reach out and strangle a CRAF guerrilla with her bare hands.

Plopping down in the middle of the floor, she sunk her head between her legs and tried to take deep-belly yoga breaths to staunch the flow of tears. It didn't work. She covered her face with her hands and berated herself for losing control.

Footsteps came toward her. Kat was back. She was too embarrassed to remove her hands from her face. "I'm sorry."

A deep voice rolled over her. "It's a start."

Two hands encircled her arms and lifted her to her feet. The world was a soggy, blurry mess, but she'd recognize that incredibly handsome face anywhere. The strong jaw, full lips, and piercing blue eyes all made regular guest appearances in her dreams and played active roles in her fantasies. The scar on his chin, however, was new.

"Mack! You came." She threw her arms around his neck before she could stop herself. Blame it on the exhaustion, or the worry dragging her under, but his strong neck was the only safe buoy in the crashing world.

She kissed him for all she was worth.

***

It was a complete surprise attack, and Mack was fully unprepared. He had no idea Jenna had tear ducts. She'd never wasted a single tear on him. This was not how their reunion was supposed to go down. He'd expected and half-wanted a fight. Not Jenna kissing him like she used to before she'd sliced the heart out of his chest. Muscles have memory, lips apparently, did too. Even as his brain spun in shock, his lips reacted, knowing exactly what they were made to do.

That kiss was no little "happy to see you" peck. Jenna held onto his neck and pulled him closer in a desperation he'd never felt before. She hadn't lied. She did need him. Forgetting he didn't want her anymore, he wrapped his arms around her back and lifted her toes off the floor. A bucket of want, sharp and hot, poured through him. His tongue pushed inside her mouth, tasting, probing.

The guttural sound she made nearly killed him. She ran her hands over his short hair and pressed into him, fitting perfectly. As if she'd never left.

His hands went on a roaming search of their own to touch her neck, shoulders, back. Jenna. No dream. No joke. It really was his Jenna.

The office door slammed open, bringing reality in with it. Jenna backed away quickly. Her eyes, still wet with tears, were filled with a wildness Mack had never seen.

Heels clicked across the floor. "Oh! Sorry. I...um...want me to come back later?"

A freckle faced young woman with spikey red hair stood in the middle of the office gaping at him.

Jenna tugged at her skirt, lining it up properly before saying, "Kat, this is my friend, Lieutenant Commander Mack Riley. Navy SEAL. Kat is my assistant and all-around communications slash IT guru."

Friend? Mack narrowed his eyes. He'd sworn he'd never be her friend.

"Cool! Way to go, Jenna. You have your own SEAL." The young woman handed Jenna a granola bar and a bottle of water. She wore all black. Her short nails were painted dark green, a diamond sparkled in her nose, and she wore a pink rubberband for a bracelet.

"No, she doesn't," Mack growled.

"He's...Mack is...was—" Jenna blinked, clearly not sure what the hell he was. Strangely, it looked like she might cry again. She downed the water as if her sandaled feet were standing in the middle of Death Valley. "Go ahead, Kat. Play the recordings."

"Yeah, sure. Follow me." Kat led him to her desk, chewing on a green fingernail as she went. Then she pulled the rubberband back and snapped her wrist. "Ouch. Sorry. I'm trying to stop biting my fingernails. It's a nasty habit."

Her wrist was red and swollen. "Maybe today is not the best day to beat yourself up."

"Yeah, maybe not. We're all stressed. Our CEO, Duncan Fitz, has completely flipped out," Kat told him. "He calls every half hour demanding updates. If he reminds me one more time about how bad the publicity is going to be from losing a billionaire, I will scream. Seriously. Loudly."

He didn't need to turn to know Jenna was behind him. He could smell her perfume.

"Duncan usually leaves us alone to handle the clients. He thinks I screwed up," Jenna said quietly. "Maybe I did."

Kat crossed her arms. "No, you didn't! He can't fire you if the clients ignore your advice and get themselves kidnapped."

"At this point, I don't care about the job. I'm sick over the Harmonds."

Jenna had tension lines around her eyes. She was taking this hard.

"Duncan is a prick. Here, Lieutenant Commander Mack Riley, take a seat." Kat moved her desk chair out for him.

"Call me Mack."

Kat pulled up the recorded satellite images on her computer, and Jenna played the phone recording. Intent, he watched and listened to the moments when the Harmonds were taken hostage. A few times, he looked up at Jenna perched on the edge of the desk chewing on her lip and marveled at how calm she had sounded on the phone. She handled the crisis better than some of the experts in the field. He was impressed. Very impressed.

With Jacob Harmond's final words, anger and sadness swirled in Mack's stomach. Even though Jenna had promised to get him out of the jungle, Mack knew the statistics. If the kidnappers hadn't called in a ransom demand yet, one or all of the hostages were likely dead. A rescue team might turn into a body-recovery team.

"So will you help us?" Jenna's deep brown eyes probed his face, dipping too close to his insides. He didn't like it.

He stood up and paced, needing to let his legs work out some of the pent-up emotions. "You're asking me to organize a covert intelligence operation into a heavily armed militant camp during a bloody Coke War to rescue a family of four and get them all out safely?" He turned his gaze on her. "Is that all you want me for?"

Her cheeks pinked and she swallowed hard. "Isn't that enough?"

Hell no. Not by a long shot. He wanted her legs wrapped around his back and to be so deeply buried in the woman he'd never come up for air. Damn, he was getting turned on just by looking at her.

The old rage bubbled in his throat and he saw clearly for the first time since he stepped through the doors at EXtreme Adventures. Jenna Collins was his kryptonite. She needed him, she said, but once it was all over she'd toss his sorry ass under the tank. He'd be damned if he'd let that happen again. And yet, he had a direct order. The admiral would go apeshit if Mack refused this mission.

But Jenna didn't know that. What would she do if he left her for a change? Now was the time to find out.

"No, it's not enough." Mentally, he crushed the Jenna-chain in his hands. And took a walk.

***

Mack was leaving? Why'd he come if he was going to turn back around? Jenna swung around to face Kat. Her assistant cocked her head toward the door. They both knew Mack was their best shot at rescuing the Harmonds.

Jenna ran. "Stop right there, sailor!"

She caught Mack in the hallway. His blue eyes raking over her made it nearly impossible to breathe. Or think.

"What?" His feet kept moving toward the parking lot.

"Where are you going?"

"To hell, most likely. Before that? A bar."

"This is important. The Harmonds are my responsibility! They might die!"

He stared impassively at her. "The SEALs will move in when the war is over. Your clients will have to wait it out."

She laced her fingers, determined to hide her shaking hands. "Jacob is only ten years old. His sister is thirteen. You know what those bastards will do to a young girl! And a young boy?"

"There's nothing you or I can do."

"Is it that the Navy won't let you go on this mission? Because I'm sure Senator Tonell could get authorization for you."

He didn't speak.

"Or you won't help because of what happened between us?"

The muscle in his jaw flexed. The fire in his eyes was answer enough.

"Dammit, Mack! This isn't about us!" She poked her finger into his incredibly hard chest. It was as if he wore body armor under that black tee. But no, it was only muscle. Strong. Lean. Impossibly sexy. Lord help her. She poked him again for good measure. "Not you. Not me. It's about a terrified little boy and his sister! You need to do the right thing here, Lieutenant Commander. Do the right thing!"

"Tell me why I should."

Before he said another word, the cell phone rang inside in her pocket. She scrambled to pull it out and was shocked by the caller I.D.

"It's the driver." Horror swamped her and she grabbed Mack's muscular bicep. "But it can't be. He's dead."

"Answer it. This might be the ransom call."

Her heart pounded so loudly in her ears that she wasn't sure she'd be able to hear.

He squeezed her shoulder. "Do it."

"This is Jenna. Who...who is this?"

"It's me, Jacob."

He's alive? Relief and terror hit hard. She gripped Mack's arm tighter.

"Jacob," she finally managed. "Where are you?"

"I don't know. Anna and I are tied together in a dark room. I don't know where my mom is..." he broke off, crying softly. "They took my mom and dad."

"It's going to be okay." Her voice cracked. *Liar. Since when was any of this okay?*

Mack wrapped his other arm around her and pulled her in close. "Nice and easy, babe. Tell him to leave the phone on and hide it."

"Good for you taking this phone, Jacob. We'll be able to track your location now. Very good thinking. When we're done talking, leave it on and hide it, okay?"

"I'll try. When are you coming to get me?"

She blinked hard, willing her throat not to close. Mack rubbed her hair as if instinctually knowing she needed more of his touch to calm her down. It did the trick.

"Breathe." His lips touched her ear lobe.

She gulped air. "Soon. You keep being brave. And help your sister, too."

"Promise to hold my hand when we walk out of this place?"

Oh, Lord. "I promise."

"Okay. I'll be brave, Jenna."

A loud commotion on his end meant that Jacob hid the phone, or at least, she hoped that's what it meant.

Jenna tipped her chin up and looked into a face full of steely resolve. Why couldn't she be that strong, that brave? "Mack, please, I need your help."

With the back of his knuckle, he gently wiped the wetness off her cheek. "I'll do it."

She pulled back and looked at him closely. "You'll organize a team to—"

"Yes, Jenna, I said I'll do it." His voice was gruff. "But let's get one thing clear. When this is all over, we go our separate ways. No calling me to take out the trash, or pound something into submission, or find your cat. Got it?"

She swallowed hard. "Yes." She understood all too well. This was payback. Who said it was a bitch? To her it was one long, lean, heart-stealing, chiseled man.

"Fine. I'll call you when the mission is over and let you know where to pick up the Harmonds." He put his sunglasses on. His long legs strode into the parking lot as if he couldn't wait to get away from her.

She raced in front of him, blocking his path. "My company will pay for everything—salary, essentials, private jet, whatever you need. I've been instructed to make this worth your while. Get your team together, and we'll put you up in any hotel of your choosing for the night. Let Kat know which one you prefer, and she'll make the arrangements."

"Don't worry about me. Have the jet ready to leave in the morning. Good-bye, Jenna." He said it like he meant it.

Damn him. "Good night. See you tomorrow."

He gave her one of those looks—jaw muscle flexing, nostrils widening. If she could see his eyes behind the mirrored lenses, they'd be narrowed, intense. "I can find the hangar without help."

"I'm sure you can. I'm going with you." She straightened her back, readying for the coming fight.

He lifted his sunglasses. Those beautiful blue eyes bored into her. "What?"

"These are my clients, Mack, and my responsibility. I will do everything I can to bring them back home."

His voice was dangerously low. "I understand that your boss wants you to take care of things, but this is outside your job description. By a mile. Shit, by thousands of miles. Stay out of the way, and let me do what I do best."

Nothing made her angrier than to be dismissed. Who did he think he was? She planted her feet and fisted her hands on her hips. "I know you're good at your job. That's why I'm hiring you! But get this straight, the Harmonds are *my* job and this is *my* mission. I'm seeing it through. I'm going to Colombia."

"Like hell you are!" He stepped closer, his frame blocking the sun.

"I promised Jacob. I'm in charge here. Got it?" She raised her hand to jab him in the chest again to make her point.

He grabbed the end of her finger. "So help me, Jenna, if you poke me again, I'll tie your hands behind your back."

The sizzling hot vision that sprang into her mind had sweat breaking out over her lip. "I'd like to see you try." She knew her voice was far too sexy for the moment, but dammit, he started it! "I suppose you'd like to spank some sense into me too."

"Don't tempt me, woman." It was a cross between a whisper and a growl.

She was tempted to grab him and kiss him again. He smelled so good—the delicious, clean, fresh, Mack-scent. Her senses were on overload. Lord, being this close to him did all sorts of things to her body. She had missed him so much. "What time should I meet you at the jet?"

"You aren't meeting me. You're staying home where it's safe. I mean it, babe, I'm not bringing my team in unless you do as I say."

She crossed her arms. "Of all the pig-headed...do as *you* say?" Since when had she ever done what men ordered her to do? "Is this how you'd respond to your commanding officers?"

"Babe, you're no C.O. The way I see it, you're out of options here, and I'm doing you a favor. I say how it all goes down."

"A favor? Is that what you call saving an innocent family?"

"Dammit, Jenna. Just this once, would you listen to me? I know what I'm doing. This sort of mission is what I'm trained for."

She knew what she was doing too. If Mack didn't bring his guys, she'd have another team ready to go. They wouldn't be nearly as skilled or capable as Mack's team, but they'd do in a pinch if Mack refused to help. Jenna Collins was all about the backup plan. She bit her tongue to keep from telling him where he could stick his condescending, pushy, alpha-male attitude.

"You act like I'm a liability. I have a few skills of my own, Mack. I've led expeditions in the jungles of Colombia. I have contacts and speak the language. I'm heading this mission."

His dark eyebrow ticked up. "Well, in that case... Make sure the jet is ready to roll by oh-five hundred."

Was he being sarcastic? If not, something was up. He'd agreed far too quickly.

Watching him take off at a jog toward a red Jeep, Jenna felt something twist in her chest. The sweat on her skin had become cold drips down her back. It had been a mistake to call Mack. But he really was her best option. If saving the Harmonds came with a price, she'd gladly pay it to get Jacob and Anna home safely. Besides, her heart was such a small thing to sacrifice. She'd done it before and lived. If she could call it living.

Mack Riley.

God, how she still loved him.

CHAPTER THREE

In the black of night, Mack loaded his Jeep for battle. After calling his team, he'd gotten exactly two hours of sleep in the hotel's far too cushy bed and popped up before the alarm went off. It was the first time before any mission that he'd gone to bed thinking about a woman and woken up still thinking about her. Kissing her had felt so damned right it was scary. Touching her had reawakened the hunger in him that he thought he'd hacked out of his life. Like kudzu, the damned feelings grew right back, covering everything. He needed distance. Lots of distance.

Colombia should be far enough.

Following Kat's instructions, he drove to EXtreme Adventures' private hangars and located the jet. The cabin door and luggage hatch were wide open. Good, the pilot was ready as planned. Kat had arranged everything while agreeing to keep Jenna in the dark about the true departure—two hours earlier than he'd told Jenna.

"Anything you need, ask me, okay? Just get the Harmonds out of there, Lieutenant Commander. I'll take care of my boss."

Kat didn't want Jenna going to Colombia either. It was too dangerous.

He jumped out of his Jeep ready for battle. Well, mostly ready. He'd put on his Nomex aviator gloves, helmet, body armor, and the rest of his gear once he arrived in Quito. There was plenty of time.

Damn, it felt good to be wearing BDUs again. Some guys might feel comfortable in a suit and tie, but for Mack it was Battle Dress Uniform all the way. If a man could love clothes, Mack would be having a committed relationship with his cargo pants. They had lots of pockets to hold his gadgets, and each one was jammed full.

Deep in the leg pocket, he'd sewn in a diamond ring. He should've hawked the damned thing, but he'd hung onto it like a former smoker stashes away his last cigarette. If anyone asked why he had the ring, he'd say it was bug out loot. In times of capture, he could trade the ring for a buddy's life. It was only half-true. He'd never admit the other half, not even to himself.

He unloaded the Jeep. It also felt good to be going in again, proving the point that he wasn't a behind-the-desk guy. He was DEVGRU all the way and would re-enlist after this little jaunt into the jungle. With the exception of Tavon, he was confident that the other guys would re-up when it was their time too. It's what they did.

He and the guys were more like brothers than teammates. Even though the Handly brothers had trouble keeping their pants zipped up, he looked forward to seeing those horn-dogs. They were experts in their fields and he had difficult tactical questions for them that he was sure they'd answer with ease. The Handly boys had hinted that they were bringing something special for the trip. He grinned. What did those lunatics have in their possession this time?

Taking one final look at the quiet, misty landscape, he thought about Jenna. She was...different. When her lips had pressed his with such raw hunger and desperate need, he'd nearly lost it himself. Was she breaking under the stress, or was something else going on?

Tipping his head toward the purple sky, he mentally kicked himself in the ass. *Shut up, Riles. It's not your pig, not your farm.* It didn't matter what happened with Jenna. He had to focus on the mission at hand.

Thankful that Jenna was still safe, warm and cozy in her bed and as far away from him as possible, he climbed the jet's walkway.

The pilot welcomed him aboard. "Good morning, Lieutenant Commander. Are you ready?"

"All set. What's our estimated flight time?"

"Seven hours, fifty-five minutes," the copilot answered from the cockpit.

He set his watch alarm to go off in five hours. He'd get some rest.

"The refrigerator is stocked back there. Please help yourselves." The pilot motioned toward the back of the cabin.

"Will do." Mack stepped inside the cabin. His mind circled back to why the pilot spoke in plural when he got the ever-loving surprise of his life. "Shit."

Curled up in a seat, warm and cozy, was the bane of his existence.

Jenna.

She wasn't in her bed. Neither one of them was safe.

She woke to his stream of curses. Uncurling her legs from underneath her, she rose. "What's wrong?"

He shook his head. "You're here."

"I slept here. I didn't want to hold you up, Mack."

"You aren't going," he growled.

"We discussed this." She crossed her arms.

"Not enough, apparently. I can't let you go. It's too dangerous."

She stepped closer. They weren't eye-to-eye until she tipped her chin up. "*Let* me go? EXtreme Adventures wants me to handle this." Her eyes dipped lower and quickly back up. Heat rose to her cheeks. Apparently, she remembered other things she used to handle.

Good. He wasn't the only one having a hard time with this reunion. The coconut fragrance of her freshly shampooed hair was enough to upset his equilibrium. It seemed only fair that she'd be overcome with hot memories too.

"So do it from your desk. You take care of intel while my team takes care of business."

Through clamped teeth she said, "I hired you and your team, Mack. That makes me the boss! Got it?"

"Dammit! I promised you wouldn't go."

"You promised who?"

Without another word, he slung his backpack over his shoulder, the sleeping bag under his arm, stomped into the cabin, and took a seat away from her.

She sat down and latched her safety belt. "We're ready," she called to the pilot.

Like hell they were. He was definitely not ready for a long jet ride with Jenna. Staring out the window, he shook his head. What was he going to tell the admiral?

The copilot shut the door to the cockpit and the engines started up.

It was close to half an hour before Mack stopped breathing heavily—not in a sexy way, more in a want-to-strangle-Jenna-Collins-boss-of-the-world way—and another ten minutes to find the words to express his feelings that didn't involve four-letters.

He got up and sat next to her. She was scrawling notes inside a book. "Hey."

"Hey." When she looked up, he noticed the dark circles pooling around her brown eyes. "Talk to me about the team. How many guys will meet us at the airport?"

"Four."

"Just five of you! That's not enough. I've got guys ready to go in Ecuador and Colombia. How many do you think we need?"

He looked her in the eye. "*We* don't need any more than the five of us."

"But Mack, that doesn't seem—"

"They're the best, Jenna."

"Maybe."

"No maybe about it, babe. No one better at this sort of mission than a SEAL team. They are the *best*."

"All right. With your men and my guys—"

He crossed his arms. "Your guys. Are they military trained? Cops? Search and Rescue?"

"No. But they have weapons and—"

"We aren't bringing in anyone else to muck up the mission."

She blew a hard breath out her nose. "I don't like being interrupted."

He grinned. "I know."

Cursing, she tossed the notebook into the seat on the other side of her.

His grin widened. Bring it on. He was ready for a fight, relishing the idea of getting it on with Jenna. About time.

"I hate this! Every minute we don't hear from the Harmonds makes me think the worst. I'm scared for them." Her face was too pale.

It was a low blow that hit him right where it counted. Instead of squaring off with her, he fought the urge to rub the chill bumps on her arm. "We'll do our best to get them out."

"But what if..." She white-knuckled the arms of her chair. "What if we're too late?"

That was more than a hypothetical. In reality, one or more of the Harmonds could be dead already since a ransom call had not come in. Those CRAF guerrillas had been far too quiet for kidnappers. Mack didn't like it. Had CRAF changed their M.O?

Were they using the Harmonds as human targets? Prisoner of war pawns? Had the family been shot or blown up during a cartel invasion?

"There's no way to tell until we get there."

"Oh, Mack. Those kids." Her face registered the horror going through her mind.

Mack's insides twisted because he'd witnessed the carnage she was imagining—other children, other countries. But it didn't matter. No child should have to suffer in the ways he'd seen. No one should. It wasn't until his brain registered the softness and the warmth under his palm that he realized he was rubbing her arm. Her gaze followed the movement of his hand which seemed to be slowing down of its own accord, moving up her shoulder, and squeezing gently as it went. She put her hand on his and held on, as if she didn't want him to let go.

"I can't stop thinking about them. My mind won't shut off."

He'd never seen her like this before. Not fragile, but not a tower of strength, either. That hint of vulnerability stirred him up in a way that needed to be shut down. Immediately. He moved his hand off her shoulder and shifted away from her in his seat. He had to keep reminding himself that Jenna was the one who shredded him. The enemy.

But this woman beside him? She didn't seem like that Jenna, exactly. The new Jenna was softer and messed with his head. He was starting to forget why he was so pissed at her. What's worse, he had the insane desire to pull her into his lap, tuck her head against his chest, and whisper that things would be okay. What the hell was the matter with him?

"Get some sleep." The gentleness in his own voice surprised him. "I'll go over the surveillance maps."

She blinked slowly, as if her long lashes were too heavy. Turning on her side, she put her head back on the chair.

Good. She needed rest, and he needed to get to work. He stood and spread the maps on the table and used a magnifying glass to study the terrain. Where was the best spot to set up camp? Launch his strike? Escape to?

"I missed you, Mack."

He didn't turn around. He held very still and listened. Nothing but silence back there. Shit, now he was imagining things. *Get a grip! And get her out of your head.*

Mack went back to studying the maps.

***

Jenna tucked her feet under her and tried to rest, but her heart hurt—for the Harmonds and for herself. It took seeing him again to realize she was still in love with Mack Riley. She'd never met anyone as full of life as he was. The man was smart, funny, considerate, and hot. Very, very hot. Looking at him made her pulse kick up.

He was the perfect man except for that one deal-breaking flaw—he'd never be hers.

She could only borrow him until his next tour of duty or secret mission. Damned Navy. Would she always be fighting against it? It owned Mack, just as it had owned her father. She couldn't fight the Navy, and she wouldn't live that way anymore. It was torture to love a man who'd give his life to save the world, but refused to live for her. Loneliness was keeping his side of the bed warm when he didn't come home. But the real heartbreaker? Knowing he'd choose to run off to fight his wars every chance he got and leave her behind. Mack was a fighter. She needed a lover.

Giving her heart and soul to a SEAL had been a mistake. He'd made his choices long ago, and they didn't include her. No matter how much she loved him, needed him, desperately wanted him, she couldn't be enough for him. Being with Mack wouldn't work. Still, she wished it could.

Curled up in her seat in the corporate jet, she soaked up the beauty and strength of the man before her as he poured over his maps. Doing his job, yes, but he was here. Even though he didn't want to, he came. It meant something, didn't it?

Could it mean as much to him as it did to her?

He was beautiful. Rugged, tough, capable. Before she could stop herself, her gaze traveled from his hard-set mouth, down the cords of his tanned neck, stuttered briefly on his huge biceps, and got hung up on the bulge of his camouflage pants. Her eyes seemed frozen there—riveted to the one place she shouldn't be looking. Her gaze bounced back up to his face and met his eyes.

Dammit.

"I can't sleep," she said softly.

Understatement of the world. Would she ever sleep again?

***

She'd been watching him. Why? What was going on inside that pretty head of hers?

Jenna rose and walked away from him. Slowly, unstable, as if not used to her "air-legs." She leaned against the bulkhead, gazing out the window into the inky sky.

"Jacob and Anna are out there somewhere. What are those monsters doing to the kids? Will they torture them?" Whoa. That last bit came out much too high, not Jenna's voice at all.

In three strides, he was by her side. "Don't do that to yourself. Trust they are all right for now. They are worth more to CRAF alive than dead."

She made a strange squeak when he said the word "dead."

"Look at me, Jenna." Cupping her jaw, he turned her face toward his. "Are you okay?"

Tiny diamond drops clung to her lashes. The instinct to grab her up in his arms was powerful. *Back off, Riles.* Holding her now was definitely not a good idea. It was the poster child for bad idea. He jammed his hands into his pockets.

"How do you do it, Mack? How can you shut down the horrors? Does it all go in a box?"

He frowned. "In a box?"

"That's where my dad used to put mom and me."

"Explain."

"He compartmentalized his life. Dad told me once he had a box for everything that wasn't Navy-related so that he didn't get distracted during the heat of battle. It was the only way he could work. When he stepped out the front door for duty, he left our problems behind. Mom and her alcoholism? Thrown in the box. Jenna Ann, the little girl who clung to his legs and begged him not to go? Dumped into the box. Slam the lid and run."

"When did you eat last?" He studied her face.

"I'm not hungry. I'm sick to my stomach. I keep running through the scenarios, but I have this horrible feeling that no matter what we do, we'll be too late. I hate feeling powerless."

He understood that feeling too well.

"None of this is your fault, remember that. And you're not powerless. You've hired the best the U.S. Navy has to handle this for you. A helicopter load of power and experience will be heading to Colombia. Try to relax."

"How can I relax when there's this big thing sitting on my chest making it hard to breathe? Gunshots and screaming keep sounding in my brain. Oh, Mack. You saw the satellite feed. They shot Andrew. If he dies, will it be worth it for CRAF to keep the family alive for ransom? Or will they...will they kill the kids?" She hugged herself, trying to shut the emotions down. "Dammit, I can't stop shaking. I feel cold inside."

He grabbed her shoulder. "Jenna, you need to sit down."

Her feet were rooted. "I wish I could get the images and sounds out of my head." She pressed her fingertips to her eyelids. "Put them in a box like my dad did. Sweet Lord, I wish I could...Andrew's dead. Isn't he? Marcella too? I won't let them hurt Jacob and Anna. I promised."

"Listen, you might be going through shock. Did you eat anything last night? Yesterday?"

She shook her head. "I can't remember."

"Sit down. Your adrenalin has been pumping for so long that your system's on overdrive. I'll get you something." He eased her back into her seat.

In the small galley he found a carton of milk, premade turkey sandwiches, and chocolate chip cookies. He smiled at the cookies, remembering that Jenna had a real thing for chocolate. Then he grinned in earnest when he remembered he has a real thing for chocolate *on* Jenna.

Had! He corrected. Chocolate and Jenna shouldn't be mixing in his brain. Not anymore.

He watched her eat half a sandwich and a cookie. "Drink your milk too, little girl."

"Yes, sir." She sipped it out of the miniature carton.

He sat down next to her, and with his thumb, wiped off her milk mustache.

"That was good. I feel a little better. Sorry I lost control."

"You have the right to do that now and again, Jenna. It's human."

She didn't respond to that. Instead, she rose to toss her trash in a garbage bag.

He checked her out for himself and noted that her trembling had stopped. And she did indeed still have the cutest ass on the face of the planet.

"Sleep," he ordered.

She chewed her lip. "I can't."

"Go on. I'm right here." He stripped off his vest, fanny pack, knife, and gun holster. He kept them all close in the seat next to him. "We both need our rest."

He stretched out his long legs and closed his eyes. Soft music piped through the stereo system, and Mack felt sleep tugging him down. He was tired too. Being around Jenna was a lot harder than he thought it would be.

A bump against his shoulder made Mack open his right eye. Jenna's head had slid sideways, and she now used his deltoid for a pillow. She snored softly. Her blonde hair fell forward and spread across her face. How could she sleep like that? Gently, he lifted her hair and pushed it back, like he used to do.

Then he did something he'd probably be sorry for later—he pulled her arm over him and wrapped it around his chest. That was better. He always slept well with Jenna wrapped around him. Shit, he was such a sap. Smiling, he sunk into deep sleep.

***

Jenna's heart pounded and terror clung to the edges of her consciousness.

Jacob!

Her eyes flew open. She was sleeping on Mack? Even more startling was how right it felt. How safe and perfect. Sadness tore at her. When this was all over, she'd never see Mack again. How would she survive it this time? What if she couldn't? And if this was the last time she'd be close to him...

Take your chance, Jenna. You might not get another one.

She moved slowing, quietly, not wanting to wake him. Gently, she pressed her lips to his bicep. He tasted and smelled exactly as she remembered—a heady mix of salt and soap and maleness. *More.* She hadn't felt that desire in so long. And now that it was back, she couldn't stop it. Grief twisted up with her need. She wanted Mack and would never have him again. It was madness. She kissed his arm again and again. Moving closer until she was nearly on top of him. His eyes opened, and still she couldn't stop herself. Rubbing his chest, she kissed his neck.

"Jenna..." His voice was deep, but not gruff.

"I need you, Mack." She had no right, and yet she still climbed into his lap. Looking into his blue eyes, she ran her fingers over his hair.

She needed him deep inside her, filling her up and touching her everywhere. Maybe with his hands on her she could stop worrying for a while. Stop hearing the screams. Stop seeing the hurt in his eyes and know that she caused his pain.

He didn't move. Didn't kiss her. He had every right to reject her, but it hadn't occurred to her that he simply wouldn't want her. He wasn't attracted to her anymore? And then she felt his erection through his pants, gloriously pressing hard against her. She'd never been so relieved in her life.

Pressing into him, she sighed, "You want me too."

His hands, so warm on her back, fisted her blouse. "There's never been a problem of wanting you, Jenna."

"Make love to me." She ran her finger over the new-to-her scar that started at the corner of his lip and ran toward his chin. "Please, Mack."

***

Mack was no idiot. Needing him was different from loving him. Jenna Collins wanted to use him to smother the horrors in her head. If she were any other leggy blonde, he might not complain. Hell, he'd go along with sex therapy any day of the week with a blonde, brunette or redhead half as good looking as the one currently in his lap. Blowing off a little pre-mission stress might do him some good too.

But this wasn't going to work. Not with Jenna. She had keys to places inside him he'd locked and bolted. He'd be damned if he'd give her the opportunity to open them up again. Especially if she wasn't sticking around. He wasn't living through that hell again.

He should push her away. *Dump her on her cute ass, Riles!*

But he couldn't. Jenna was his kryptonite.

He ran his hands inside her skirt and up her soft thighs. Grabbing her panties, he ripped them off with a giant tug. Jenna gasped. Her eyes were pinned to his, her lips parted. With one hand, he felt around until he located the button to lower his seat. The other hand gripped her buttocks, not softly, pinning her to him while the chair reclined to horizontal.

Her fingers dove into his hair while her tongue plunged into his mouth. They dueled for dominance. Jenna was all fire and heat, burning him with each touch, each kiss. Holding his face in her hands, she lapped at his tongue, lips, nibbled on his jaw while she rocked slowly, steadily on his hard cock. She knew what she was doing, and oh baby, she was doing it right.

He growled with impatience, gripping her ass, moving her faster along the length of him. She stopped moving altogether and fumbled with his zipper. He moved her shirt and bra aside, exposing one of his favorite nipples. Hers. He lifted his head up to suck her, and the moan of pleasure she made was nearly the end of him. She pushed him back into the chair and kissed his mouth while opening his pants enough so that she could fist his swollen cock. He roared inside her mouth, dying with need.

She rolled a condom on him. It was no surprise that Jenna came prepared. Always prepared.

Opening her legs, she slipped over him like a glove he had no business wearing. A perfect, beautiful, hot glove that felt far too much like home. Like ecstasy. Lifting herself up and down, she rocked him with an abandon and passion he'd never experienced in his entire life. At first, he held on for the ride and then tried to match her pace. Soon they were in perfect sync. When they came together it was like sailing, flying, rocketing into space. All the locked and bolted doors inside him flew open wide. It was as if Jenna reached in and touched his dark places and filled them with exploding stars.

She closed her eyes contentedly and lay on top of his chest as if this is what she'd wanted all along. Him. Jenna wanted him.

Lieutenant Commander Riley was captured.

CHAPTER FOUR

Holy shit.

He rubbed her hair and back while she snored softly in his lap. That was…hell, he didn't know what that was. Exploding stars? That only happened with Jenna. As did coming with a woman in such beautifully perfect…holy hell. What had he done? Why did he let her get to him?

She messed up his neural synapses until he didn't know which end was up. He'd been feeling overly protective, trying to ease her pain and suffering, when wham bam she army-crawled under his defenses and just like that—she owned him. Again. It was a perfectly executed attack. With Jenna he never saw it coming.

Should have dumped her on her ass, he snarled at himself.

One would think hooking up with the love of his life was a good thing. That is, if one was thinking with his smaller head. His bigger head, the one that ached with frustration, knew differently. Jenna would leave him again. Just as soon as the Harmonds were safely home, she'd find some excuse to cut him out of her life.

Jenna was all about control and order. Their relationship was too gigantic to wrap her hands around and fit into her orderly existence. It was wild, blazing hot, glorious, and bigger than both of them.

Hell, it scared him too. Loving Jenna was like lassoing a tornado and hanging on for dear life, never knowing where he'd eventually touch down. Never knowing if he'd survive the ride. He glanced down at her. Jenna's face was a weather map to her emotions, and Mack could read every one. This was how he knew the moment she stopped loving him. Eighteen months ago, she didn't fight, or spark, or cry. She simply walked away.

She might as well have shot him in the chest.

He'd sworn to himself that he'd never see Jenna again, but here he was burying himself in her and wanting to do it again. And never stop. No. Dammit! When the mission was over, old Jenna would be back.

And he'd be gone.

The pilot's voice came over the speaker. "Lieutenant Commander, we're about to begin our descent."

Gently, he kissed Jenna on the forehead, wondering if it would be the last time he tasted her sweet skin. "Wake up, sunshine. We're almost there."

Jenna jerked awake, blinked, and blinked again as if she couldn't believe her eyes. "I fell asleep." She smiled. A real one. Eye crinkles and all. "No nightmares."

"Good. Can you get up so that I can feel my legs again?"

"Sorry." She gave him a peck on his cheek and rose. He stretched out his legs, and his numb feet started to tingle.

"Mack that felt...oh my...it was one of the best."

"I know." What more could he say? He'd felt it too.

A shadow of annoyance flickered across her face. Apparently, she wanted him to say more. Well, tough shit, lady. He was in no mood for talking. He was pissed—at her, the admiral, the friggin' CRAF guerrillas, but mostly at himself for wanting her so bad.

"I'll get cleaned up and change." She walked toward the lavatory.

Stop watching her! Gear up!

He started loading his camo pockets the way he did every time. The blow kit came first. All SEALs put it in the right thigh pocket so that a buddy didn't have to waste time searching for medical supplies while you bled out. The kit contained gauze, bandages, a cravat for a tourniquet to stop bleeding, and a Vaseline-coated dressing for a sucking chest wound. SEALs understood that each new sunrise brought another flip of the dice chance to get shot, or blown to hell. It wasn't so much an *if* as it was a *when*.

Control. That was the issue. In war too many things were light years out of the freaking realm of control. The best way to stay alive and protect his buddies was to seize domination of every damn thing he could. Body protection was something he could do. He slipped the Dragon Skin Body Armor on. It was heavier and more costly than the Navy's standard issue, but shit, it had saved his real hide many times. The Pro-Tec helmet protected his brain from gunfire, shrapnel, or any crap that fell from the skies. The rest of his gear covered his tough skin.

But there was the little issue of his fast-beating heart. How to control that? Jenna was a dangerous factor in the equation. He had little control there, evidenced by his hard-on. Again.

Be on the offensive or the admiral's daughter will kill you. And stop thinking about her!

Rapidly, he folded up the surveillance maps and tucked them in another pocket, along with the infrared chemlights and a couple of grenades. A third cargo pocket was a perfect storage spot for a magazine for his CAR-15 rifle. He turned a breakaway fanny pack toward the front to hold more ammo, a compass, a small red-lens flashlight, a pencil flare, waterproof matches, a space blanket, and a couple flashbangs and fragmentation grenades. It looked like he had a beer belly. Jenna knew that he didn't. She'd always liked his abs.

Slipping his Nomex aviator gloves on his hands, he wiggled his thumb free. He'd cut out the thumb and index finger up to the first knuckle on the right hand of the glove for dexterity and trigger control. Now he'd have two uncovered fingers to touch Jenna with. *Dammit, Riles, stop!* He slapped himself with his gloved hand.

The weapons came next. A holster on his hip held his sidearm, the Sig 226 Navy 9mm. Clipped on his belt was a wicked sharp Swiss Army knife that had gotten him out of a few tough jams. More than once, he'd used the knife to silence a bad guy so that his evil buddies didn't hear gunshots. The suppressors kept things quiet, but to keep the element of surprise in close quarters combat, sometimes one couldn't risk the sound of a silenced gunshot.

Along with the knife, he brought a suppressed MK-14 sniper rifle and a CAR-15 with an Advanced Combat Optical Gunsight (ACOGs) close range point-and-shoot. He kept the CAR-15 loaded with one magazine of ammo. Inside the stock, he jammed a wad of cash in case he needed to bribe his team's way out of the jungle. The diamond ring would work for bribery too, but part of him suspected he'd never give the damned thing up.

He continued checking his weapons. As a sniper, he never went into battle without his bolt-action .300 Winchester Magnum—simply called three hundred Win Mag—and the Leupold ten-power scope. This was his long-range weapon. He rarely missed anything he aimed at with his Win Mag. His best kill shot was close to fifteen hundred yards. It wasn't a SEAL record—that baby belonged to SEAL Team 3 Chief Chris Kyle at twenty-one hundred yards—but it was still pretty damned good.

He was ready.

Or at least he thought he was ready until Jenna returned from the lavatory.

She'd ditched the short skirt and heels for khaki cargo pants. A dark green T-shirt hugged her beautiful breasts. Her long hair was pulled back into a ponytail under a jungle-print baseball cap. The little make-up she wore was gone. He couldn't help but stare. She was beautiful even when she wasn't trying.

"Is this okay?" She tucked a loose strand of hair under the cap and turned around slowly so that he could catch the whole picture.

Her butt filled out the pants perfectly. His eyes took a nice easy stroll across the mounds in her green T-shirt. "Works for me."

Her eyebrow hitched. "I'm talking about the mission. Will I blend in enough?"

With a group of rock hard SEALs? Does a kitten blend in with tigers? "Listen Jenna, you can't go to Colombia. When we land in Ecuador, check into a hotel and wait for the team to return. I'll call you the moment we've rescued the family, I promise. It'll be safer for all concerned." Not to mention Admiral Collins would kill him if he knew Jenna was in Colombia.

She fisted her hips. "We've been over this. Jacob needs me."

"Jacob needs to get out of there. Let me do my job." His voice came out too harsh.

"I thought that we…" She narrowed her eyes. "You don't want me around, do you?"

"Babe, you think *that* after what just happened here?" He touched the hollow of her neck, feeling her rapid pulse. "You make me crazy."

She cocked her head. "In a good way?"

"In a 'kill Mack' way. I can't be thinking about your sweet little body while I'm in the jungle. I need to focus to keep my men safe. To keep the Harmonds safe and get everyone out of there alive."

He didn't like the hardness around her mouth. It usually meant she was plotting.

"I see."

Did she? Did she see the hard-on that was steadily growing inside his camos because she was too close? "Here's the deal. No more looking at me. No touching me. And for all that is holy, no more kissing me until this mission is over. Got it?"

"I can't look at you?"

"Not in the hot way."

"Okay, I'll try not to look at you in a hot way." She bit her lip, which was decidedly hot. "What about after the mission?"

That damned flicker of hope tried to ignite again. He stomped it out virtually with his boot. Jenna was not to be trusted. He'd learned that the hard way.

"One day at a time. First, we rescue the Harmonds."

"I agree. That's the most important thing, Mack. We've got to get them out of there." She wiggled her finger at him. "But I'm not staying in a hotel. I'm coming with the team, and you can't stop me. And if I decide we are under-staffed, I'm bringing in more men. It's my call."

"And she's back." Mack shook his head.

The woman would be the death of him. Best to let her think she ran the show for now to save his energy for the real battle. One way or another, he'd keep her out of harm's way.

The copilot asked them to fasten their safety belts for the landing.

Jenna stared straight ahead, her hands balled, her face pale. The peaceful respite she'd had in his arms was over.

He leaned toward her. "For the record, I'm not anything like your dad. I'd never put you in a box, Jenna."

How could he? The woman would bust out and fill up his life no matter what he did. But he'd be damned if he'd tell her that right now. Instead, he mentally rehearsed what would happen after the landing.

***

After shaking the pilot's and copilot's hands, Mack grabbed his gear and went out the door. He had a pack on his bag and another slung over his shoulders. His hands were full carrying two long silver cases. Jenna scrambled to get her backpack and keep up.

The muggy air hit her like a weight when she stepped out of the jet. She took a second to get her bearings. The airport was on the small side, with lush vegetation just off the runway. In the distance, sharp snow-covered mountains framed the beautiful scenery.

"Let me help. I can carry stuff too," she said.

"Suit yourself." Mack lifted a third case for her. "This one's light."

"Yeah, okay." But when she hefted it, she realized it could rip her shoulder off. Light? How much did those other two weigh?

Mack searched the grounds, as if looking for bad guys already. He started marching toward the immigration station, his passport between his teeth.

Jenna had a plastic manila file full of papers they were going to need to get into Ecuador. She put the silver case down to find the paperwork.

"Careful with that," Mack mumbled through his passport.

Oh God, was it full of explosives? Sweat dripped down her back.

A man in uniform came up to them. "Ms. Collins?"

"Yes. That's right." She whipped her documents out for inspection. "Here is my passport. This is authorization from Senator Tonell, a signed declaration from the White House, and a letter from the CEO of EXtreme Adventures."

"Fine. Follow me." The man didn't even glance at her papers.

"Jenna, it's okay. He's letting us through." Mack nodded his head to the immigration officer waving them on.

"Oh. That was easy."

Too easy. Officials must have paved the way for them to get into Ecuador quickly so they could leave just as fast. The Ecuadorian government couldn't be too happy that Andrew Harmond and his family had been kidnapped on their soil and dragged across the border. Like EXtreme Adventures, Ecuador didn't need the bad press. They'd just as soon let the world focus on the problems in Colombia, not Ecuador.

She blew a strand of hair that had slipped out of her baseball cap and refiled the paperwork in alphabetical order before lifting the heavy case again. Mack kept following the official, apparently not in the mood to wait for her. Fine. Whatever. She didn't need him to look out for her. She was perfectly capable of—*Umpf.* Two men ran by her, bumping her with their backpacks and nearly knocking her off her feet.

"Watch out!" She scrambled to keep from dropping the case that may or may not have had explosives in it.

"Sorry, lady." One glanced at her over his wide shoulders.

"There he is!" The other man cheered.

When she'd stabilized her footing, she took stock of the men who raced past her. They resembled buff California surfers with deep rich tans, long sun-streaked hair, and rippling biceps. Or twin gods. By any standards, they were gorgeous, and they were running toward Mack.

Mack acted like he didn't know what hit him either. They grabbed him in a bear hug and lifted his feet off the floor. Two blonds with dark haired, blue-eyed Mack in the middle? This yummy sandwich could make a girl's mouth water.

"Put me down you, numbskulls!" Mack barked, but he was smiling. "I'm still pissed at you two. You could've had any woman for your party."

"You got that right." The taller of the two blonds had deep dimples.

"And you chose the commanding cfficer's daughter?" Mack growled.

"You would've too, Mack. She was seriously hot. Ten-plus. And she dug threesomes. How were we supposed to know we'd get caught?" The second blondie glanced at Jenna as he spoke.

"Because you were in her father's bed, dip-shits!"

"Again, how were we supposed to know? It really wasn't our fault, Mack. It could have happened to anyone,"the first one responded, doing his darndest to look innocent. It was clear to Jenna that these men were far from innocent. "It's good to see you, Commander Riles!"

They lifted Mack again and swung him around.

They pounded each other on the back, everyone talking at once. Jenna got snippets of conversation, but couldn't make sense of any of it. Gingerly, she put the case down by her leg.

Finally, Mack caught her eye. "Guys, this is Jenna Collins. She's from EXtreme Adventures."

"Hello." She waved.

The one who had glanced at her earlier was getting an eyeful, sizing her up from head to toe. Mack pounded him on the back. "This is Charlie Handly. The best damned SEAL Team Six Black Pirate in the biz. Recon and surveillance are his specialties, but he's an ace with all technology."

"Until the moron-that-shall-not-be-named made me take a break. Being inactive totally sucks." Charlie flashed the whitest teeth Jenna had ever seen. And dimples too? Wow, he was cute.

"Consider yourself active now," Mack said.

"Black Pirate?" She probably didn't want to know.

"Reconnaissance and surveillance. You think your assistant, Kat, is a whiz kid, just wait until you see what Charlie can do."

Charlie tipped his invisible top hat to her. "I'm also the guy who calls in the GPS coordinates to air support to make it rain ordnance on the bad guys."

"Air support won't be available to us on this trip. We're on our own here."

"You can't be serious." Charlie shot Mack a look that Jenna couldn't decipher. Astonishment? Worry?

"Shit, Mack. No air support at all? I should've brought more ammo," the other brother said. His voice had an edge to it.

Jenna sensed tension. "Is this some sort of problem?"

"Nah. I brought extra and my brother's got enough explosives to wipe out three planets," Charlie said.

"So true. Not to mention the Willy Special." The brother stepped forward and offered his hand. "Hey, gorgeous. I'm Willy. Can I show you my Special?" He held her hand for a beat too long. Heat and sex rolled off this guy in waves.

"Um…" she had no idea what to say.

"Stand down, Willy," Mack growled. "Jenna's the boss."

Willy let her hand go. "The boss? Right on. About time we got a boss that looks like her."

Mack rolled his eyes. "Jenna, Willy is our breacher. Without a doubt the best explosives expert on the face of the planet and this side of mentally sane. He's also trouble. Stay away from him."

"Righteous truth, Mack. Like that intro." Willy opened his finger in a mock flash. "Boom."

"Yeah, maybe the other side of sane." Mack grinned.

"Nice to meet you both." Jenna strained her neck to look into their faces. They were all so tall and incredibly buff. Really, really good looking men.

"One question." Willy raised his hand. "How come I didn't get the memo? Did you get the memo, Charles?"

"No, I did not get the memo, William. Which one was it again?" Charlie laughed, obviously waiting for the punch line.

"The instructions to bring a hot chick along. I would definitely be all over that." Willy's green eyes focused on her breasts.

Mack slugged him in the arm. Hard. Hard enough to kill someone if it landed just right.

"Mack!" Jenna said.

Willy flashed his deep dimples and straight white teeth. The Handly boys could be walking dental ads. They should have their own calendars. They'd make a fortune.

"Seriously. No disrespect, Ms. Collins, but you are smokin' hot." Charlie got the same arm punch his brother had received.

"Listen up, Thing One and Thing Two! Jenna is in charge here. We take our orders from her. Got it?" Mack growled.

Jenna looked at him. Did he really say that? Mack Riley acknowledged that she was in charge?

"Sorry, ma'am." Willy dropped his head sheepishly, but when he gazed at her under his long bangs, she saw nothing but mischief in his eyes.

Charlie put his hand out for a shake. "Nice to meet you, boss." His hand was warm and strong, and he held on just like his brother had.

When Mack took a step closer to her, she pulled her hand back. "So? Do we wait here for the others?"

She'd barely got the words out before a man as silent and dark as midnight approached them. Jenna thought the other boys were tall, but this man was enormous. Towering at least six inches over Mack, he was half again as wide and looked as solid as a rock. The man's muscles had muscles. He was amazing to look at with his powerful rock hard body, shaved head, and black beard with the shocking white strip down the chin. Jenna had never seen anyone quite so…impressive.

"Hello, boys." That voice reminded Jenna of thunder as his dark gaze skimmed over her. "And girl."

"Tavon!" Mack's face burst with happiness. He shook the big man's hand. "Good to see you, man."

"Jeesh, Riles, you're getting fat."

"Shit, I know."

The big man leaned over and took a peek at Mack's behind. "You could park a battleship on your ass."

Jenna frowned. What were they talking about? Mack was as lean and muscular as ever. And his ass looked fine to her. Better than fine. Darn it, was she blushing?

"All the more for the ladies to grab. Am I right?" Willy nodded.

Jenna mentally nodded, agreeing wholeheartedly with Willy. She really was blushing.

Charlie high fived him. "When they don't have the Handly endowments, I guess the ladies have got to hang onto something."

"I guess so, Charles. I wouldn't know since I am a Handly. Enormous endowments are all part of the package," Willy bragged.

"Shut up, knuckleheads. We've got a lady present," Mack growled.

"Yeah, Big T. Have you met the boss?" Charlie tipped his head toward Jenna.

"In more ways than I'd like to recall." When the big man looked at her, uneasiness settled in her shoulders. They'd never met. She would remember meeting this man.

"I don't believe so," she said softly.

"No?" Tavon's dark eyes pinned her. "Mack talked about you so much that I just feel like I know you."

Mack elbowed Tavon in the stomach and instantly gripped his elbow. "Ow, Big T. I think I broke my funny bone on your abs."

"Ha. That was funny. To me."

Jenna had never heard a laugh quite like the one Tavon produced. If his voice was thunder, his laughter was the full-blown storm rolling over her, threatening to rattle her teeth. She wasn't sure she liked it.

"Come on, let's go." Mack scooped up his silver cases and started leading them toward the helicopter pad. Charlie and Willy wrestled one another to carry Jenna's silver case. Willy won. He hefted the case as if it was nothing more than a stack of towels.

"Careful," Jenna said.

"Why, what's in it?" Willy asked.

Jenna shrugged. "No idea."

Over his shoulder Mack said, "My dirty laundry."

"What! You made me carry your dirty laundry?" Jenna fumed. "That's ridiculous! Why would you bring that on a mission?"

Charlie came up next to her. "He's messing with you, Ms. Collins."

"Oh." Of course. Stupid. Her cheeks got even hotter. Mack loved to get a rise out of her and keep her perpetually off balance. He knew how much she hated that.

"Can I carry your pack?" Charlie asked.

She should have said no, but her arm was getting tired already. The thing weighed a ton. "Thanks." She handed it to Charlie and smiled. He sure was cute. Not make her heart explode handsome like Mack, but pretty darned cute.

As if sensing her thoughts, Mack waited for her to catch up. "You coming?"

She shot him her best withering look. "You bet your fat ass."

"Hey!"

Someone whistled from a helicopter that was doppled green and gray with camouflage paint. A man with a long dark braid leaned out the pilot door. "About time. If you all are finished with the hen party, I'd like to lift off. We've got a family to rescue."

Jenna was shocked. Were all SEALs buff and handsome?

"That's Ty Whitehorse," Mack said to her. "The gang's all here."

CHAPTER FIVE

Tavon opened the copilot door and hoisted himself inside the cockpit next to Ty. Good thing Tavon sat up front. Jenna had the distinct impression that he disliked her. Maybe more than dislike. A flicker of hatred flashed in the man's eyes when he spoke to her. What in the world had Mack told him?

Mack opened the larger doors to the main cabin and climbed in. Willy went in, plopped down across from Mack, and dropped his pack into the seat next to him. Jenna peeked through the opening and paused. From floor to ceiling, everything was the color of gun metal. There was another large door straight across from her. Dear God, she hoped that the doors would be closed for the flight. Flying was stressful enough without worrying that she might fall out.

The cabin was bigger than the helicopter she'd flown in before, but it wasn't spacious. There were three seats crammed in behind the pilot and copilot in the cockpit. Ty and Tavon had placed their packs in those seats. Back in the main cabin area, two rows of seats faced one another with four seats to a row. A walking aisle ran between. With big men and all their gear, it would be a little tight.

Where should she sit? Every molecule in her being ached to sit next to Mack, to let her leg brush against his and take comfort in his strength, and confidence. But she was determined to obey his rules. She wouldn't touch him because she'd promised him that she wouldn't.

"You go first," she said to Charlie.

He jumped in, put his pack in the seat next to Mack, and sat on the other side of it. Good. That problem was solved. Jenna sat down at the end of Willy's row, as far away from Mack as possible. It was physically impossible to touch him now.

Mack's gaze flicked to her for a mere few seconds, but she felt the warmth on her face before he looked away.

"Hey, Ty! How are you, man?" Mack stood up and offered his hand to the pilot.

"Can't complain. I'm still working and flying, even if it's mostly a taxi service for politicians and their shit." Ty grinned.

"I'm grateful Senator Tonell convinced the Ecuadorian Air Force to let us borrow the Knighthawk."

"It's not as stealthy as a Black Hawk, but it's fairly quiet," Charlie said.

Mack eyed the controls. "Everything looks new. Is it armed?"

Ty shook his head. "I wish. I think they just bought it and were focusing primarily on search and rescue."

"If we blow it up, we buy it," Tavon said.

Mack gave Willy a pointed look. "We'd better not blow it up. This is a snatch and grab. Our mission is to get the hostages and bug the hell out."

"I see we have a new member to the team. Hello, miss. My name is Ty. I will be your captain. For your flying pleasure, I will play some tunes. Please sit back and enjoy the trip."

Willy stepped in front of her and pulled the giant door closed. "Just keep us in the air this time. Nothing like what happened in Kosovo."

"Hi, Ty. I'm Jenna. Very nice to—" She was so happy to see that the doors would be closed in flight and that she wouldn't be sucked out to plummet to her death that it took her a moment to hear what Willy had said. "Wait! What happened in Kosovo?"

"You don't want to know. And we can't tell you," Charlie said.

Mack shook his head.

"Great," Jenna groaned. She hoped Ty Whitehorse knew what he was doing.

Sitting back, Mack put his headgear on. Trying to mimic him, Jenna grabbed hers and stuck it on her head. It didn't fit well with the baseball cap, so she yanked the cap off, shook out her hair and tried again. Ow, her hair was twisted up in the set. Trying not to yelp, she untwisted it and shoved the thing on her head again. There, that was better. No, it was still uncomfortable. She took it off pushed her hair back and tried again. She glanced up to see all eyes on her.

Mack shook his head. His deep voice came through her headphones. "You ready?"

Thumbs went up. Jenna quickly followed suit.

"Let's rock and roll."

Ty Whitehorse pressed buttons and flipped switches. The helo blades started rotating. Music twanged through the headphones. The guys played music on the way to war?

Mack glared. "Whoa. Hold up. What in the hell is this?"

"It's country music," Willy said. "Since you're working out there in the boonies, kicking shit and rescuing lost barnyard animals, we figured you'd be into it."

Charlie covered his mouth and coughed.

"Well, crap, boys. I'm working for a P.I. Do I look like a shit-kicker to you?"

Tavon's deep laughter drowned out the others.

At the moment, Mack looked like sex-on-a-stick to her. He caught her eye, and she realized she gave him one of those "hot looks" she'd promised to quit doing, at least during the mission. She turned toward the window and focused on taking calming, cooling breaths.

"Take us up, Ty, before I beat some sense into Willy," Mack growled.

"Doubt it'll work. But I'll hold him down for you." Charlie cracked his knuckles.

Mack whipped his finger through the air and the helo lifted.

The men around her seemed charged up. They were happy and joking like they were going off on a grand adventure instead of into battle. This is what they loved to do. They were just like her father. She gritted her teeth. Who loves going to war?

Snow covered peaks appeared outside her window. If she didn't know better, she'd forget they were on the equator.

"Are we flying over those mountains?" She hoped the scratchy microphone obscured the tremor in her voice. She really didn't like to fly. It wasn't something she advertised, since she was a travel agent, after all.

"Some, yes," Ty replied.

"That's no mountain. It's a volcano." Tavon pointed at a snow loaded peak. "Let's hope it's not too active today. I'm in no mood for lava shit."

She looked at Willy. "That's Cotopaxi?"

"Yep. One of the world's most active volcanos. Oh man, I'd love to see that baby blow," Willy said.

"Great." Her fear of flying raised its ugly head.

"We're not flying over it, Jenna. It's too far south. We're heading northeast," Charlie said.

"Oh. Good." Tavon was messing with her? What was this, pick on Jenna day?

As the helicopter sped toward the jungles of Colombia, Mack's guys put on their vests and ammo-heavy belts. They had helmets, gloves, and knee pads that matched their camouflage fatigues. Each one of them had packs loaded with survival kit supplies, knives, ammunition, hand guns, grenades, and rifles. It was warm in the helicopter. Jenna could only imagine how hot the men were under all that gear.

Studying the satellite images, they discussed the best places to set up camp to launch their attack.

"The call from Jacob came from here." Mack pointed to a spot on the map. "I say we land in this ravine." He pointed to another spot on the map and listed the GPS coordinates. "We'll hike in. Agreed?"

Charlie nodded. "All's clear on the satellite. We should be good."

"Agreed." Willy turned to Jenna. "The ravine will be a natural sound buffer. The guerrilla bastards won't hear us land."

"Hear that, Ty? Do you have the coordinates?"

"Roger that," Ty said.

Jenna got up and sat closer so she could see the map. "The hiking is going to be tough. Thick brush, dense trees. I've taken expeditions through this sort of terrain before. Not fun. We had blisters on our feet for weeks." Her new hiking boots, purchased yesterday, weren't broken in. Already, the stiff leather rubbed her ankles.

"You up for the challenge?" Charlie asked her.

"Jenna won't have to worry about blisters," Mack growled. "She's staying behind."

"What? No way, Mack. I'm going with you." Her voice exploded through the headsets.

Tavon turned around from the front seat. His dark eyes flashed. "You're a liability, boss. We can't let you go."

"Exactly. Don't give me that look, babe. You'll stay near the helicopter where it's safe. We may need to bug out fast if everything goes south. Got it?" Mack said.

"As much as I hate to leave a beautiful chick behind, they're right. We want you safe." Willy winked.

Charlie shrugged and nodded. They all agreed. She was to be left behind.

"But—!" All eyes were on her now. "Fine." She bit off the words.

Crossing her arms, she leaned back and stewed. Her boss had told her to go to Colombia and bring the Harmonds back, not stay inside a hot helicopter. But she didn't have to listen to Mack, did she? Let the SEALs go off on their own, and she'd go with the backup team she'd already arranged. With one team or the other, she'd rescue Jacob and his family.

Discreetly, she pulled out her cell phone and sent a text message to Roberto, complete with the GPS coordinates. "We'll be landing here in a ravine. Meet me. Bring your men."

"Did you guys get the photos and satellite recordings I sent you?" Mack's voice was loud and clear through the internal communication system.

Jenna's head shot up. He was watching her.

Ty gave him a thumbs up. The Handlys nodded.

"Any questions?"

"Just one. Can I try out my Willy Special on those guerrilla bastards?" Willy wiggled his eyebrows.

"After the hostages are freed, I don't see any reason why you can't light up the CRAF's world. Do you, Jenna?" Mack's gaze was intense.

Repocketing her cell phone, she hoped he wouldn't question her about the text she'd just sent. "Um. Okay?" She still had no idea what a Willy Special was.

"Thanks!" Willy rubbed his hands together.

"So, Jenna. You're a travel agent, huh?" Charlie leaned over, his shoulder bumping hers. "I'd like to take a trip. How much would it cost me?"

"Nothing. I'll send you to the moon right now." Willy shook his fist.

"Like you could, puny man." Charlie leaned closer, his gaze on her lips. All the testosterone in this helicopter made her head spin. "I'm serious, Jenna. Ballpark figure."

"It depends on where you want to go. The Harmonds were on a year-long vacation, until…you know." She frowned. "I usually make all the arrangements, every stop, every adventure, for the entire trip."

"Around the world? That's got to be a few pesos," Willy said.

Charlie blinked. "Yeah. I might have to save my pennies for one of your trips, Jenna."

"What do you want, Charles? She's flying us to an EXtreme, dangerous get a way in the unique jungles of Colombia." Willy sat back and crossed his arms. He had a tattoo of a red dagger on his bicep. "My brother can be ungrateful."

"Corporate will be grateful to get the Harmonds back. I'll see what I can do."

The smile Charlie gave her melted her heart. "Thanks, Jenna. I've always wanted to take my mom to Costa Rica. Do you think you could arrange that?"

"Wait! Oh, no." Willy shook his finger. "He's not getting brownie points with Mom again. He's already got her in the palm of his hand. If Charles gets to take mom to Costa Rica, I get to take her somewhere too."

"Whatever. You know she loves me more." Charlie crossed his arms, revealing a black bird tat on his bicep. Jenna wondered what it meant.

"I'm sure we can arrange something that your mother will love," Jenna said.

"You guys ready to discuss business?" Mack asked. He had on his scowling face.

"Sorry. Yes, of course," Jenna said.

"Good."

They all leaned forward and discussed the plan—land the helo, find the hostages, strike fast, and bug out. The men talked quickly and over each other. They discussed strategy, weaponry, and how best to pull off a jungle surprise attack. She pulled her notepad out of her backpack and started writing as quickly as she could.

Mack's eyes were on her again. She could almost feel his heat. "What're you doing?"

"Taking notes."

"Is there going to be a quiz?" Willy patted her leg. "'Cuz I want to cheat off the hot, smart girl."

"What else is new?" Charlie razzed. "He'd still be in third grade if not for the smart girls."

Mack's nostrils flared. "Done yet?"

Willy shifted uncomfortably in his seat. "Yeah, sorry, Mack. Jungle warfare, surprise attack, got it. I was listening." To Jenna he whispered, "Can I look at your notes?"

She ripped out the page and handed it to him.

When they started arguing over which ammo and gun would be best for the situation, she zoned out. On her cell phone, she Googled "Colombian hostage rescues." She read about a military operation in 2008 that had succeeded in freeing fifteen hostages without a single shot being fired. The rescuers had gone undercover to trick militant guerrillas into thinking that they were part of their network.

On her notepad, Jenna wrote: "Rescue without gunfire. Would it work?"

Maybe if they used her men on the ground as the undercover contacts, no one would get hurt. She chewed on her pencil.

Feeling Mack's gaze on her, she dug through her backpack to look at the transcriptions again.

She'd transcribed everything she'd heard on the phone during the attack on the Harmonds. She had translated the Spanish words into English and double-checked them with a Spanish interpreter in case she missed subtle nuances. She had high hopes she'd find clues as to what CRAF planned to do with the Harmonds. Disappointingly, the interpreter hadn't turned up anything of value. The guerrillas mostly barked commands for the Harmonds to "do as they were told" without following up with the usual made-for-television version of—"And no one will get hurt." The worst of it came at the end— "Shut that boy up before I put a bullet in his head!" a gruff voice commanded before the line went dead.

Jacob. Was he okay?

If she let herself, she could still hear the gunshots and screaming. She squeezed her eyes tight. *Focus on the notes*. There might still be a clue she'd missed. Something other than the sight of a beaten and shot Andrew being dragged to an unmarked car.

The same worries kept running through Jenna's mind. If this was kidnapping for ransom, why hadn't CRAF called in their demands? And would they keep the rest of the family alive if Andrew dies? Or had died. She had a horrible feeling she'd witnessed his brutal execution on the satellite feeds. Billionaire Andrew Harmond, the man who gave her fits by ignoring her plans and instructions, and reminded her so much of her own father, had better still be alive.

His family needed him. And so did she.

***

It felt good to be planning a covert mission again. Mack lived for these moments—taking an impossible situation, planning for all possible scenarios, and making it work. He was good at it. He'd never lost a hostage. Men, yes, hostages no.

The dead men haunted him and made him better at his job. He'd be damned if he'd lose another brave soul, another hero. He hadn't lied to Jenna. These guys in the Knighthawk were the best of the best. The Handly brothers were screwballs and crazy, but shit, they knew their business.

Ty Whitehorse was an Apache warrior. Mack had no doubts he would've been fighting alongside Geronimo in the Apache Wars had he lived in the late 1800s. The man was a great pilot and an ace tracker. He was also the only corpsman on the helo. Ty had been trained by an actual Apache medicine woman and had taken pre-med in college. He'd be perfect for this mission. Andrew Harmond needed medical treatment. Mack had seen that satellite video and agreed with Jenna—Andrew had more than one bullet in him.

The Handly brothers and Ty Whitehorse all had Navy medals. They were heroes who would die for him, as he would for them. But there'd be no dying on this mission. Not on his watch.

Tavon...Mack looked at the back side of the humongous head with the deepest respect...Tavon was the meanest SOB you'd never want to meet in a dark alley. He could rip a guy apart with his bare hands and not make a sound doing it. He was also the best friend Mack ever had. Tavon was also the main reason that he went out with the admiral's daughter in the first place. Neither Tavon nor Jenna knew that little secret. He'd carry that sucker to his grave.

Befriending Tavon Sting had been a challenge in itself.

Mack had met Tavon during BUD/S, the most grueling underwater demolition training in the world, bar none. In those days, Mack hadn't gotten too attached to the other trainees, because, hell, they'd been dropping like flies with their wings ripped off.

He had basically ignored the black monster because he thought Tavon would fail the underwater portion of the training. No one could be that solid and float. Mack was smart enough to steer clear of a man big enough to swallow him whole.

Then one day during an especially intense underwater exercise, Mack made a decision that slung his own ass in trouble. After a grueling exercise, he was bent at the waist trying to suck air to fill his depleted body with oxygen, when he realized Tavon was up. Damn, the big dude would never survive this test. He fully expected Tavon Sting to ring the brass bell and head home.

It took four strong men to bind Tavon's arms and legs and dump him in the deep end of the pool. As Mack had expected, the giant sunk like a rock. He was supposed to snake his body up to the top for air, propel himself through the water to one side of the pool, do a flip-turn and swim to the other side while bound. The exercise took a tremendous amount of strength and coordination. It also helped to not be a giant boulder. Tavon didn't have a rat's chance in hell.

It was painful to watch. After several long seconds Tavon finally made it to the top. He sucked in a huge breath, coughing and sputtering and immediately sank again. He fought and somehow made it to the top, but he wasn't moving forward and the clock was ticking. Soon he'd be out of time.

"Come on, man." Strangely, Mack wanted Tavon to make it.

Tavon sputtered, his black head bobbing just above the surface like some messed up cork being yanked down by an anchor.

"On your back!" Mack encouraged. "Catch your breath and move!"

Like a freaking horror show Tavon wiggled through the water getting nowhere.

"That's it! Five feet to the wall!" Mack yelled. The other trainees' eyes were on him. Why did he care so much? Tavon hadn't made friends in the group and Mack wasn't his buddy.

By a miracle, Tavon hit the wall. When he flipped he must've gotten water up his nose because he struggled and coughed like a drowning man. No one moved.

"Get going! Time's running out." Tavon kept going, hacking and roaring as he went. Mack followed along the edge of the pool. "Two minutes!"

"He's going to ring out," someone said behind Mack. "Ten bucks says he doesn't make it to the top this time."

More guys gathered around. "I bet twenty," someone else said.

Tavon thrashed underwater. Mack saw the fear in his big dark eyes. Raw panic had set in. He'd pass out in the next few seconds, meaning an automatic dismissal. No one could help him or risk being thrown out as well.

"Dammit! He's not coming up." Mack didn't wait a second longer. He dove in. It was no easy feat to bring the monster up to the surface, especially with him thrashing and fighting the whole way. Something hard and heavy—had to be Tavon's elbow, though it felt like a sledgehammer—clipped Mack under the jaw, making him see stars. Tavon suddenly went limp. He'd passed out.

Mack worked like a sonofabitch to drag the big man toward the surface. For a second he wondered if he'd have to be rescued too. Finally, he made it to the top and other strong arms pulled Tavon all the way out. They rolled him on his side and the big man puked a kiddie-pool worth of water. Mack took a long minute to catch his own breath before climbing onto the deck.

When he got to his feet, something ginormous clocked him. Blinking through the stars, Tavon's big face snarled down at him. "Thanks a lot, asshole! You got me disqualified."

"Riley!" the commander called. "Get your ass over here and give me twenty. After that you get to eat your lunch. In the surf."

He'd saved the dude's life and now he was going to pay for it.

"You will have the opportunity to repeat the exercise," the commander promised Tavon. "Not your fault that Riley chose to be a hero."

Sitting in the cold Pacific Ocean, his teeth chattered as he ate his nasty lasagna MRE. Why'd he bother to save Tavon? Stupid. Next time, he'd let the boulder sink. He spit sand out of his mouth and a healthy portion of slimy cold lasagna. A dark shadow blocked out the sun pimpling his wet skin from the cold.

"Why'd you do it?" Tavon snarled.

Mack shrugged and took another bite of his crappy lunch. "Apparently, I'm an asshole."

Tavon plunked down next to him, splashing ocean water on his MRE. "I was drowning."

"No shit."

"Can you teach me so I pass next time?"

"If you don't hit me again. You've got a killer right cross." He rubbed his sore jaw.

Tavon laughed. It was the kind of sound that could pull together the slashed up parts in a man's gut and make a guy feel...not so shitty. It was then that Mack knew he'd made the right choice. He'd never let the boulder sink and maybe, just maybe, they'd both get out of BUD/S alive. They'd become best friends. They had each other's backs. Mack eventually told Tavon the story of how the admiral's daughter had ripped his world apart with her petite hands. He'd left out a few key parts the man didn't need to know. Like how damned sexy Jenna was and some of the awe-inspiring things they'd discovered together in the bedroom. Most importantly, he hadn't told him the real reason he'd met Jenna in the first place. No one needed to know that little detail. Especially not Tavon, or Jenna.

Tavon listened silently and didn't judge. Well, he hadn't judged Mack.

Now, on the helicopter, it was obvious by the missile glares he shot at Jenna that Tavon judged her. A lot. Would Tavon hate her so much if he knew that she'd saved his career? What would he say if he knew Mack had seduced Jenna just to get Big T's ass out of the brig? Funny how that plan had backfired. Sure, Tavon was freed, but Mack was sentenced to a life of wanting a woman he couldn't have.

Sitting this close to her and not touching was painful. Maybe he'd boot Charlie out of his seat to be next to her. Damn, he wanted to touch her. All over. Why had he ordered her to keep her hands to herself? Those pretty fingers were busily scribbling in her notepad. What in the hell was the woman doing? He'd have to burn those notes so they didn't fall into enemy hands. And now who was she texting? What was she being so sneaky about?

"Earth to Mack," Willy said.

Mack looked up to see the guys all staring at him. "What?"

"We're landing in twenty minutes. Are we sure of the final coordinates?" Ty asked.

"As sure as we're going to be. We haven't gotten any more calls from the kid. But the signal hasn't moved."

"That's a good thing, right? We told Jacob to hide the phone so that we could track him." Jenna's eyes were wide, scared.

He grimaced. "Jacob might not have the phone anymore. Guerrillas constantly move their captives through the mountains and jungle to make it harder for us to find them. Jacob may have been forced to leave the phone behind."

"But...you're saying we could arrive too late. They might already have moved him."

"That's pretty likely."

She growled her frustration. "This is insane!"

"If we find an empty camp we won't be too far behind them. Ty is the best tracker I know. We'll find them."

"In time?"

He raised his hand. "What do you want me to say, Jenna? If anyone can do this, we can. Willy, Charlie, you're with me."

Mack moved to the windows. The Handly brothers followed suit. Tavon's eyes were scanning from the front too.

"What are you doing?" Jenna asked.

"Nothing, Jenna. Just stay where you are," Mack said.

"Mack! Don't keep me out of the loop. What are you looking for?"

"Snipers. Missile launchers. Bad guys from either or both sides," he said through clenched teeth.

"Oh." Jenna sunk back into her seat.

He'd frightened her, but maybe she needed to be scared. This was no tea party. This was war.

CHAPTER SIX

Before they touched down, Jenna peeked out the window. Her heart sunk. The thick canopy of trees hid the ground from view. Finding the Harmonds without GPS would be impossible. With it? It might still be. She hoped Charlie was as good a recon Black Pirate as Mack said he was or this mission was doomed.

"There's the ravine," Ty said. "I'm going to land in that grassy spot."

"Copy that," Mack said.

When the helicopter came to rest, Willy jumped out first, his automatic rifle leading the way. Charlie followed close behind with his weapon ready and so did Mack. Tavon went out the front. Jenna's heart pounded as she waited.

"All clear," Charlie reported.

She scrambled out after them, her eyes scanning the jungle. It was incredibly silent. No bird sounds, no insects, nothing. Weird. The last time she was in the Colombian jungle, the nature sounds were near-deafening.

"Mack! Something's not right." She grabbed his arm.

"Hold up." He lifted his hand, causing the whole team to freeze in their tracks.

Gunfire rang out from the jungle. Ty, the closest to the trees, would have been a dead man if he'd kept walking.

Mack smashed her to the ground, his body heavy on hers. "Get down! Stay still." He shot over her toward the trees. A man screamed in agony.

Tavon was close by. "Oh two hundred! Three hostiles."

Mack followed his lead, and they both opened fire. The three men fell where they stood.

"Oh nine hundred, behind the rock." Willy lobbed a couple grenades. The explosion shook the ground beneath Jenna. "No more rock. Hostiles are toast."

"Big group of hostiles. Eleven hundred," Ty yelled.

Gunfight erupted. Jenna put her hands over her head and ducked down under Mack as low as she could. Her face pressed into the dirt.

"More coming our way," Charlie added.

"Shit! Pull back." Mack started to rise. "Jenna, stick with me!"

Charlie army-crawled next to them. "Can't pull back. They're coming from behind. We're boxed in."

"Who are they? CRAF or cartel?" Tavon asked.

"Pickup trucks, not too organized. Locals, maybe," Charlie said.

"Shit, Charlie. Friend or foe?" Tavon roared.

"Guess we'll know when they start shooting," Willy answered.

She could feel the deep breath Mack exhaled. "Spread out, take 'em down. Eleven hundred first."

Rapid fire exploded Jenna's world. Her ears screamed, her body trembled, and her limbs were impossibly weak, useless. The voice of terror screeched in her brain—*Get up, run!* But she wouldn't. She'd stay here with Mack. Waiting for the burning bullets. Waiting for the end. At least she'd be with him as she died face down in the dirt.

"They're shooting at each other." Tavon's voice reached her through the chaos.

"We've got friends!" Willy sang out.

Jenna lifted up to see that men rushed from behind, their weapons blazing. Bullets zoomed over her head toward the enemy hiding in the bushes. So much for hoping for a hostage rescue without gunfire.

"Stay down!" Mack hissed.

Out of her peripheral vision, Jenna caught snatches of the new guys. They were in trouble. They didn't have the body protection or weaponry that Mack's team did. Without cover they were horribly exposed, but they kept coming, shooting as they ran. One by one, the men were cut down, sliced to bits. Screams of agony shot through her like a hot poker. She bit back the urge to scream with them.

"Willy! The Special. Use it." Mack ordered.

"It's not ready. But I've got something. It's risky this close."

"Do it!" To Jenna, Mack said softly, "Open your mouth, babe. And hang on."

Open my mouth —?

The explosion that came would have sent her flying if Mack wasn't pinning her down. It felt like her heart hit her chest bone and her eyeballs shook in their sockets. Smoke choked out the air, making them all cough. She struggled to drag in a clean breath. Mack rolled off her, but continued to shield her from the enemy.

"You all right?" His lips said, but she couldn't hear his voice.

"I'm deaf."

"It'll pass. Your eardrums would've blown out if you hadn't opened your mouth to stabilize the pressure."

She frowned, only catching Mack's every other word.

"All clear," Charlie's lips said. He followed the statement with his thumb up.

"Whoo-ya, got those suckers," Willy said, or something along those lines.

Their smiles told her that the eleven o'clock enemy had gone the way of the rock that Willy had blown up—all disintegrated.

"We're safe?" She asked, barely hearing her own voice.

"Yes, babe." Mack stood and pulled her to her feet. Ignoring the no touching rule, he wrapped his arms around her and hugged her tight. From that moment on, she'd like the smell of gunpowder and dirt. It would remind her of safety and life.

The ringing in her ears started to ease back slowly. She picked up bits and snatches of conversation.

Tavon's deep voice came through more clearly than the others. "Who were those guys? Locals just happened to come by out here in the middle of nowhere?"

Jenna didn't answer. She had a very bad feeling that she knew the answer to his questions.

Still holding her, Mack gave orders over her shoulder. "Willy, Charlie. Look for the hostages."

"No one survived the blast, Mack," Willy said.

"Maybe the hostages are hidden close by. Go."

Jenna's gaze flowed toward the place where CRAF had been shooting at them. A crater was left behind scarring the earth black. There were no trees. No bodies. Oh, God, if the Harmonds had been tied up to one of those trees…

"Ty, help the survivors," Mack said.

"On it." Ty grabbed his medical supplies and ran toward the group that had been fighting with them. He checked pulses, searching for the living amongst the dead. "Got one!"

Mack gave her a gentle squeeze. Streaks of sweat ran down his dirty cheeks. "Stay here."

Part of her agreed with him. She did not want to go over there. But she had to know.

"I'm coming," she said softly.

"Of course you are." He held out his hand and she gladly took it. She'd need his comfort now, more than ever.

Tavon checked bodies, shaking his head as he moved on to the next body, and the next.

Ty knelt down and pressed his cravat to the wounded man's neck. Blood seeped out of the bullet hole, turning the tan cloth sanguine. The poor man had been shot at least three times. The top of his head was missing. His pale lips moved silently. But the face, that strangely pale face, was so familiar.

Oh, God, she knew.

"I can't...I'm sorry..." She broke from Mack's grip and stumbled backwards.

Before she could stop herself, she ran. Fast. Hard. Her heavy boots pounded the dirt. She dove inside the helicopter and fast-crawled toward the back. Cradling her stomach, she willed herself not to throw up.

"It's okay." Mack was there. Pulling his gloves off with his teeth, he caressed her cheek. "Breathe, nice and easy. That was brutal out there, but you're safe. Look at me, Jenna."

She couldn't take her eyes off her new boots. The soles were blood-stained. "Roberto...is he...did he die?"

"Roberto?"

"The man Ty is working on. Will he make it?"

Mack's silence was answer enough.

"What about the others? Some of them had to survive. Please, Mack. Tell me the truth."

"Shit." He dragged the word out slowly. "Those guys were your backup team."

Her head shot up. "Yes."

He slammed his fist into the seat next to him. "You sent them a text, didn't you? That's what you were typing. I can't believe it. You sat in this helicopter and told them exactly where we'd land. Holy shit, Jenna, what were you thinking?"

He was mad at *her*? "Good thing I was thinking! We might be dead now if my men hadn't showed up. They saved us."

"Saved us? Don't you get it?" His voice came through her plugged up ears nice and clear. "Your men gave our coordinates to CRAF guerrillas! That text got us ambushed. We could have been killed!"

Her heart pounded in her throat. "You don't know that! My guys tried to save us."

Tension tightened the cords in his neck. His face was inches from hers. "One of your saviors was a guerrilla spy."

"Impossible! They work for me."

"*Worked*, Jenna, they're all dead now." He punched the seat again and crawled out of the helicopter.

***

Mack stomped through the brush. Dammit! The woman almost killed him. For real this time. She could've killed them all. He was angry, and his body still vibrated with adrenalin, but a deep sense of relief rushed through his veins too. His girl was safe. Thinking that he'd lose her out there? That scared the living shit out of him.

He walked slowly toward the guys. Hopefully, they extracted human intel out of "Jenna's men" before they all expired. Shit, he still couldn't wrap his brain around the fact that she'd brought in another team. They went over this! They agreed. Wasn't he running this show?

No, dumb shit. What in the hell were you thinking?

Jenna was never going to fully give up control. The mission was doomed if she didn't trust him to get the job done. Doomed? Hell, none of them would get out alive if she didn't stop giving the enemy their GPS coordinates.

His cell buzzed silently in his pocket. Knowing who was calling, he ignored it. He was in no mood to placate an angry admiral. The Collins father-daughter duo was driving him insane. The text buzzed. He glanced at it.

Where the hell is she? Call me!

Mack's lips twitched. "Trust me, Admiral, you don't want to know."

A boot up the ass was coming for disobeying direct orders. Jenna was not in the United States, nor was she safe or sound. When Admiral Collins found out his little girl was in the middle of a gunfight, he'd murder Mack. Torture first, then murder.

Stand in line, admiral. Your little girl might get the job done for you.

He dropped the cell phone into his breast pocket and jogged toward his men. The guys finished clearing the area.

Charlie checked in first. "No survivors, Mack. It was a guerrilla meet and greet. They didn't bring the hostages with them."

"That's a good thing. The blast was fierce. If there were hostages, they'd be dead," Willy added.

Charlie holstered his gun. "How's Jenna? She looked like she lost her best friend."

Mack flinched. His gaze settled on the dead bodies around them. "She knew these guys. They worked for EXtreme Adventures."

"No shit? Our girl's having one helluva week." Willy snagged a rifle and ammo from one of Jenna's men. "Guess it's okay to borrow since we all play for the same team."

Shielding his eyes, Ty stared at the helo. "Are you sure she's okay, Mack?"

"She'll be fine." He hoped it was the truth. No horror quite compared to watching men die on your command. He'd been there, done that more times than he'd like to remember, and yet, he never forgot their faces. Or the way they died. Jenna wouldn't forget, either. She'd push the gory sights and sounds deep down and kick them under the mental rug, but the scene would play out in her nightmares like a screwed up show on a perpetual loop. The terror, self-doubts, and grief lingered like a mind-rotting infection. He wouldn't wish that shit on an enemy. Jenna didn't deserve it either.

"Any intel from the last guy? Roberto. Did he have a clue about where the hostages are being held?" Mack asked.

"He didn't know anything more than we do. The shithead working for CRAF guerrillas was named Franco. He's dead too. Too bad Roberto decided to exact punishment before we could question him," Tavon said.

"Great." Mack swiped the sweat off his face. "Worse than square one. CRAF knows we're here. Surprise gone."

"Yeah, but they might think we're all dead." Tavon grinned. "Won't that be a helluva surprise?"

"Right! Willy hit them fast and hard." Ty smacked Willy's helmet.

"Yes, I did." Willy smiled, wiggling his helmet back into place. "Poor bastards didn't have a chance to shit their pants."

"Or alert homebase. The chief guerrilla probably thinks we're all dead. If CRAF comes looking for their fallen comrades, we've got 'em. If they don't come, we can track 'em from here. Win-win." Ty smiled.

"Good. Unpack the helo and let's get a move on it while the trail is fresh," Mack ordered.

"What about Jenna? We can't make her stay with the helicopter now. CRAF might come back." Charlie's face was screwed up with concern. What in the hell had gotten into him?

"Yeah, I'm not leaving her." Willy stood shoulder to shoulder with his brother. They both crossed their arms in a show of strength. The Handly brothers were serious.

Mack grimaced. Thing One and Thing Two picked this moment to go white knights on him? They could save it. He'd already made the decision. "She's coming with us."

The admiral was going to shit bricks.

Mack wasn't happy about it, either. The no touching rule would have to be rescinded. The new plan was to have Jenna stick to him like skin. He'd be her body armor and protect her with his life. And she'd have to do what he told her to do, whether she liked it or not.

What could go wrong with that plan?

CHAPTER SEVEN

In a matter of minutes, the guys had emptied the Knighthawk. There was a mini-argument about whether or not to throw the camouflage netting over the helo. Would CRAF guerrillas believe they'd gotten the netting up before they were ambushed and killed? Ty argued that it didn't matter. What was important was to keep their means of escape hidden from aircraft. In the end, camouflage netting covered everything they'd leave behind.

Jenna sat on a boulder, hiding out beneath the thick trees. Part of her wished she could disappear forever. Her gaze drifted back to the bloody scene behind them. Her stomach clenched. No. *Stop thinking about the bodies! Make a plan. Get it together!*

Closing her fists, she pressed them into her thighs. The light pain focused her. She repeated the mantra from her self-help CDs. *You are the boss of your life. You control the outcome.* In a moment like this, she realized the tapes were crap, but she could handle this. She'd have to.

The air was thick with hot moisture. Sweat ran down her back from the muggy heat. Reaching into her pack for a water bottle, her fingers grazed a foreign object. She pulled out a plastic baggie. Inside was a peanut butter and jelly sandwich. The sandwich had been cut into four squares, just the way she liked it. Mack made her a sandwich on the jet?

As if knowing that she was thinking about him, he strode over. Sweat glistened on his skin. "You found my surprise?"

"I did. Thank you." It touched her, but she treaded lightly around Mack. Was he still mad at her? She didn't want to think that she'd given away their location and gotten all those men killed. Questions and doubts poured acid in her empty stomach.

Mack stood over her. "You eat. I'll put on your make-up."

She stopped mid-chew. "Excuse me?"

He lifted a small shiny box and smiled. "Your war paint. We all need to be as camouflaged as possible. Your face stands out in a crowd, babe. It'll be a beacon in the jungle. Relax. It won't hurt."

She took another bite. No one had ever put make-up on her before. Not even her mother. And did he just compliment her?

He dipped his finger in the camouflage paint. "I'll darken the light spots on your skin and lighten the dark to make you look less like a human, more like a tree, or shadow. Lift your hat." She did. "Move your hair. Good. Your forehead will be dark green."

His fingers felt so good on her skin. She finished chewing as fast as she could and held still.

"Shadows pool around the eyes. I'll paint your eye sockets light colors. Get it? The coloring is the opposite of what faces usually look like. Close your eyes."

Taking a soft breath, she let Mack touch her wherever he wanted.

"Now your cheeks." His voice was softer now too. She kept her eyes closed and focused on his touch, his voice, the heat coming off him. "Your cheeks, nose and brow are all dark green. Wait, okay. There you are. You'll blend in now."

Surprisingly, he touched her lips with his finger. It was almost a kiss. She opened her eyes.

"Gorgeous," he said quietly.

So was he. She couldn't take her eyes off him. "I wish I had a mirror."

"Here." He turned the silver face paint canister around and she could see her distorted image in it.

"Gorgeous? I'd say I look perfect for Halloween."

"I've got another surprise. Hold out your hand." When she did, he put a little present in her palm.

"Oh, Mack. A Snickers bar?" Her favorite candy bar of all time was melting and a little misshapen from being jammed down in one of his pockets, but she ripped it open and savored the first bite. "Oh…this is…mmmm."

He chuckled. "Later, we'll break out the MREs."

"You're not hungry?" she said with a full mouth. She licked each of her fingers.

"Babe, I'm starved." His gaze traveled down to her breasts and back up again. So that's what he was hungry for. "Nothing I can do about it right now."

"Can I have a bite?" Willy asked.

She choked. "Pardon? Oh, the candy bar." She lifted her empty hands. "Sorry. It's gone."

Willy laughed. "Dang, Jenna. That was two seconds."

"Woman likes her chocolate." Mack winked, sending heat between her legs. "Charlie, any new intel? Movement on the LST?"

And just like that, the sweet moment was gone.

"Not a lot of movement. I've intercepted a few signals that don't amount to much yet." To Jenna, he explained, "I'm scanning cells, radios, all electronic signals. The directional microphone is up and running to pick up communication. If they fart, I'll hear it."

"Before we go, someone should scope the trail from above," Mack said.

"On it." Ty grabbed a pair of high-powered binoculars and headed up the ridge.

"I'll send the satellite data to your phone," Charlie called after him.

Ty waved and disappeared.

Charlie shrugged. "Dude doesn't say much, but he's the best tracker I've ever seen. I'll have the satellite feed up in two and send the video to him. Ty will compare the video to what he sees out there and we'll have a plan in no time."

"Good. Everybody ready to roll once Ty gives the signal?" Mack asked.

Tavon nodded. "We'll be ready."

"Hey, Jenna. Come here," Willy called.

She had the distinct impression the guys were trying to make her feel better. Did they think she'd snap? Break? Her insides were still quivering from the guerrilla attack, but she wasn't fragile. She'd prove to them she wouldn't get in the way or slow them down.

She walked to a tarp that had been spread on the ground. Across it were a mind-boggling amount of guns and ammunition. "Wow, looks like we've got an arsenal."

Willy rubbed his hands together, as excited as a kid on Christmas morning. "Here we've got our grenades, grenade launchers, sniper rifles, combat shotguns, handguns, stun guns, knives of various shapes and sizes, and the most important thing of all is—"

"This!" Charlie produced a black tablet.

"An iPad?" Jenna asked.

"I was going to say my one-of-a-kind Willy's Special. The best explosives around," Willy said.

Charlie punched Willy in the arm. "Nah, that's old school. Not nearly as impressive as my iPad. Wait until you see what this baby can do."

"What's going on here?" Mack's voice came from behind, sending flames licking up her spine.

"Charlie is trying to make Jenna believe his sissy computer has more boom than my Willy's Special."

"Yep. In the right hands. Well, my hands, to be exact." Charlie casually draped his arm over Jenna's shoulders.

"Why don't you take those hands off Jenna and show us what you mean?" Mack hadn't raised his voice, but she heard the possessive rumble in it.

Charlie raised his arms as if he was being arrested. "Sure thing. I need to send Ty the current satellite pics first, and then it will take only a few minutes to demonstrate my genius."

Willy snorted. "Gonna take a lifetime, bro."

Mack stepped closer to Jenna so that his shoulder bumped hers. She looked into his impossibly deep blue eyes. They had that edge to them that made her insides go mushy. Lord. Had she given him a hot look?

"How are you holding up?" His gaze traveled to her lips and back up to her eyes.

Her lips parted of their own accord. Wait, he got to touch her and look at her that way? That wasn't fair after he made her promise to keep her eyes and hands to herself.

She leaned slightly, very gently bumping his shoulder back. "I'm okay. I just—" She blinked away the vision of Roberto's pale lips and the blood... "I want this to be over. Let's find the Harmonds and go home before anyone else gets hurt."

Charlie rummaged around inside a black bag. He pulled out three rifles. "Gather around kiddies, the mind-blowing iPad show is about to begin."

"Whatever, genius," Willy said.

"A start-up company in Texas needed a weapons specialist with extensive computer software and hardware experience. So brilliant genius did his work, people were amazed, miracles performed, yada-yada, and I created this." Charlie waved the tablet.

"You created the iPad?" Mack asked.

Willy snorted. "Sort of like Gore creating the Internet."

"No, no." Charlie's eyes sparkled. "I created the smart weapon. With this baby, I can turn an ignorant, half-blind, weak-ass slob who can barely aim a rifle—let's just call him Willy—into an elite, long-range marksmen." He flexed his biceps. "Who's the man now?"

Everyone stared at him.

His face fell. "You guys don't get it?"

"Sorry, Charlie. Maybe if you slowed down a bit for us mere mortals," Jenna said.

"You, Jenna, are a goddess. But for the others I'll speak slowly and use sign language. You're looking at the world's first integrated system—hardware, digital optics, and tracking technology designed to guide a firearm to hit a long-range target. Precision aiming skills not required. The iPad tells you where to point and you shoot."

Jenna scrunched her nose. "You can shoot with the iPad?"

"Once you download the interactive tracking mobile app and use the rifles I brought with me." He tossed one to each of the three men.

Mack, Willy, and Tavon all studied their rifles while Charlie rocked on his heels with anticipation. Jenna peeked over Mack's shoulder. "What's different about these rifles from say the ones you can buy at Wal-Mart?"

"These rifles have a network tracking scope with a digital display interface. The laser tags moving objects. Sort of like painting them. It's really cool. A guided trigger releases only when there is a high percentage shot. If everything lines up, the shooter fires as well as Mack does."

"It sounds like a video game," Willy said.

"It is! The scope on the rifle connects by Wi-Fi to the iOS app on the iPad. You could use your iPhone too if you download the app. You watch the scene like a live video and line up the target accurately. How would you like to be my beautiful assistant, Jenna?"

"Mack?"

"You sure this is safe?" Mack growled at Charlie.

"They've been tested. The smart weapon goes on sale this summer at your local retailer."

"Freakin-A. Just the kind of thing I want to see in the hands of street thugs." Tavon growled. "Cops barely have a chance as it is."

Mack gave his rifle to Jenna. "It's okay, babe. We might need you out there to cover us. Or if things fall apart, you should know how to protect yourself."

She gulped. It had been a long time since she held a gun. "What do I need to do?"

"First hold the weapon properly." Charlie tried to step behind her, but Mack beat him to it.

Mack pulled her against him. "Relax, babe. I'll show you how."

With her back pressed into his chest, her body melted. She was able to block out the ugly visions running amok through her brain and concentrate on his strength, his warm breath in her ear. How did he do that? He calmed her nerves just by touching her. The air got hotter and sweat ran between her breasts.

"Good. Now open your legs a little. Bend your knees."

Oh Lord. His soft voice sent delicious tingles up her spine. When his knees pressed into the back of hers, she closed her eyes.

"See that tree over there?" he asked.

Her eyes flew open. Focus. She had a loaded weapon in her hands. "Yes."

"Aim at it. Don't think about the rifle, pretend that it is just an extension of your arm. I'm going to step back now. Hold steady. Take a deep breath and let it out halfway, and then hold it. Pull the trigger."

She did as she was told. Nothing happened. She lowered the rifle and looked at Mack. "Something's wrong with this thing."

"See? She aimed too low. The guided trigger kept her from shooting. This way she saved her ammo and didn't shoot wildly. Keeps the shooter from hitting her own foot," Charlie said.

"Or one of us," Willy said.

"Thank God for the safety feature. I'm a bigger target than the rest of you little boys," Tavon said, coming up behind them. "Hey, Mack when you're done playing around, can I have a little help? I'm having issues with my face." Tavon was partially war-painted. The white stinger was lime-green.

"Dude, we all have issues with your face," Willy laughed.

"Careful or he'll rearrange yours," Charlie warned.

"What's the problem?" Mack asked. He released Jenna, leaving her feeling cold and slightly unstable on her feet.

"I can't get this crap to go on right over the beard. Will you shave it off?"

Mack eyed the big man. "You sure? Doesn't your wife love the beard?"

"She does, man. A whole helluva lot." Tavon's huge shoulders sagged.

"I've always wondered. Which came first, the white stinger, or the name Sting?" Willy asked.

"Mrs. Sting. She always comes first. And frequently." Tavon hitched one eyebrow. He handed Mack the largest, scariest knife Jenna had ever seen. "Do it, Mack. Before I change my mind."

Tavon sat on the boulder. He tipped his face up so that Mack could reach him. Jenna shivered. How could anyone sit still while that blade scraped over his throat? It showed a tremendous amount of trust.

"Let me turn the volume up on the tablet, Jenna. You listen to the commands and do what it says," Charlie instructed. "Normally, a sniper like Mack has a spotter like Tavon to give him wind speed directions. Mack would then adjust the scope dope on his rifle for the distance. The dope is all the data that can cause a bullet to stray off target—wind speed, temperature, elevation of terrain, humidity."

"Okay...I get it, sort of." Jenna felt the weight of the rifle in her hands. "The iPad is my spotter?"

"Exactly! Paint the target and let the iPad tell you what to do next."

She got back into her shooting stance and aimed again. A woman's voice, much gruffer than the one on her car's navigation system, told her to lift the rifle higher. A little beep went off and she assumed she'd locked onto the target. Letting out her breath, she closed one eye, aimed and was rocked backwards when the rifle fired. There wasn't a loud boom since the sound suppressor was on, but she felt how powerful the weapon was. Just like old times.

Charlie rushed over and took the rifle out of her hands. "You hit it! You're a natural."

A natural. That's what Dad had called her when he first taught her to shoot. At nine years old, she had been so desperate to impress the old man that his words had rained down on her like diamonds.

"Try again!" Her dad had encouraged and she did. Her young self had hit every target she aimed at. She had reveled in his smile and soaked up his adoration. After that, she'd practiced day after day, imagining that she'd finally found something to make her daddy love her enough to stay home.

Reality smacked hard the day she had won the Target Shooting Nationals for her age group. With the shiny trophy under her arm, she'd walked home to her dark house. Mom had passed out drunk, and Dad was in the middle of the Indian Ocean. That trophy had gone in the back of her closet. She'd never picked up a gun again.

Until today.

"What happens if the target is moving? Toward me, say. What do I do then?" She asked Charlie.

"Same thing. Paint the target to lock on, listen to the instructions, and shoot the bastard. Aim for the center mass, his mid-section—not his heart, not his head—his belly. You'll have a better chance of hitting the target."

"Just aim at a spot ahead of the moving target. When he gets to that spot, you pull the trigger." Willy aimed and shot at an imaginary target.

She didn't want to shoot anyone, but she'd be prepared. She'd cover them and do what was necessary. If it came down to Mack's life being in the balance?

She'd pull that trigger until the guerrillas ripped the rifle from her cold, dead hands.

"Wicked shooting, Jenna." Charlie took the rifle and iPad from her. "I'm going to pack everything up."

She glanced at Mack, but he was still shaving Tavon.

Willy tugged on her cap. "Charlie and I have a bet going, but we need intel. What happened between you and Mack? I heard you dumped his ass."

Jenna froze.

"Careful," Tavon said to Mack. "That's my pretty face you've got under the knife."

Using his bandanna, Mack wiped a streak of red off Tavon's jawline. "You must have jerked."

"Like hell I did," Tavon grumbled.

"So? Is it true?" Charlie was back, standing close. She was sandwiched between handsome Handly bookends.

"Drop it, Willy," Mack warned.

Jenna lifted her chin. "It was a mutual parting of ways."

The muscles bunched in Mack's broad back. "Right. Mutual."

"Shit, Mack!" Tavon slapped his hand over his cheek, staunching another nick. "Talk or shave. Don't do both."

"I totally get it, Jenna. You don't need to spell it out. Mack didn't fulfill your..." Willy wiggled his eyebrows. "...needs."

"I'm going to beat you, Willy." The warning was clear. She did not need to see the anger sparking from Mack's blue eyes to know he wanted to shut down this conversation. Immediately. He was angry? What about her anger, her hurt? She had loved him, more than she'd loved any person in her life, but it hadn't been enough to make him stay.

"Later. After you've moved that blade off my jugular," Tavon said.

Willy's mischievous face with the deep dimples and the white toothed smile was much easier to focus on than the intense heat coming from Mack.

"You're right. It was about needs. I needed him and so did the Navy. Mack made his choice," she said softly.

Willy's grin slipped. "You're an all or nothing gal, huh?"

"Yep. All or nothing." Sadly, she wanted all of Mack, but was left with nothing.

"Huh. Whatever happened to the girls who just wanna have fun? They seem harder to find these days." Willy's eyebrows crinkled as if he was trying to figure out women.

Jenna liked to have fun, but she was ready to have a life.

Mack gently slapped Tavon's cheek. "You're done."

"Finally." Tavon jumped up. "I'm lucky to have survived that shave."

Jenna was suddenly nervous that Mack's undivided attention was on her. She lifted her shoulders and met his gaze.

CHAPTER EIGHT

Mack watched her, remembering a different story. In his version, Jenna was the one who'd made choices long ago that didn't include loving a Navy SEAL. Two years earlier, Mack was looking for a way to get to the admiral when he'd happened to meet the man's daughter.

Mack had been walking through the 32nd Street Navy Exchange in San Diego (NEX) when a beautiful woman breezed in through the main entrance, short-circuiting his brain. Her blonde hair had been long enough to touch the waist of her short skirt, and her tanned legs had seemed to go on for miles.

"Hey, Billy. Have you seen my dad?" His trained ears zoomed in on her voice, soft and sweet, as she chatted up the cashier.

The young cashier had sharp predator's eyes that took in the woman's soft curves. He laughed too loudly, leaned in too closely. "You're in luck. No admiral here."

"Pshew." She smiled. "I've been avoiding him all day."

Mack cocked his eyebrow. That sexy sweetheart was Admiral Collin's daughter? This could be good for him. Really good. Mack had been trying to figure out a way to get Tavon out of the brig for breaking a guy's face during a bar fight. The admiral had the power to release Tavon. And lookie there, his ticket to the admiral just walked through the door. On sexy legs.

Silently, he moved through the NEX, pretending to be shopping as he stalked his target. The woman had some of the biggest most expressive brown eyes he'd ever seen. And her smile defined gorgeous. This had escalated from a good plan to his lucky day.

"Gone on any cool trips lately?" The cashier was still trying his moves on the admiral's daughter.

"Costa Rica and Bali. Last month I sailed on a pirate ship in the Indian Ocean." She tossed her hair back and Mack felt the movement all the way into his gut.

He roamed closer, picking up objects he didn't need. A bottle of perfume—ugh too sweet. A purse—yeah, really not his style and didn't match his camouflage. A gold bracelet—no one to give it to. He kept selecting items at random as if he meant to buy them. As if he gave a damn about anything other than the long-legged blonde in the short skirt with the sparkly brown eyes and easy laughter.

"You've got a great job. Hey, I'm going on a break. Can I buy you a soda?" The hound-dog cashier was all but salivating. Mack had the sudden desire to make the guy disappear.

"No, thank you, Billy. I'm more of a..." As if sensing his gaze on her, she turned and warmed Mack with a smile. "...double-chocolate mocha girl."

Striding forward, he held up a Starbucks card. "Can I buy you a double-chocolate frappe?"

She cocked her head. "With extra chocolate sprinkles?"

"Is there any other way to drink a frappe?" Hell, he didn't know. He was more of a black coffee guy. Sweetened drinks weren't his thing.

"Tempting, but I don't get involved with Navy guys."

He couldn't stop staring at her full lips. "I don't, either. We've got a lot in common already."

She laughed, a hearty sound that stirred him up faster than any girly giggle. "Maybe we do." Her gaze took a lazy stroll down him and back up. The straight pearly whites she flashed made him think she saw something she liked. "Forget the coffee. There's a mom and pop ice cream shop on Coronado. I'll buy you a double-fudge sundae."

He let out a low whistle. "Damn, how'd you know? That's exactly what I'd like to eat." And other things. All kinds of other hot, sweet things. He warmed up to this idea really fast.

The hound-dog cashier glared at him as he walked out of the NEX with his arm draped over Jenna's shoulders. Mack shrugged at the guy. He couldn't believe his luck either.

Outside she give him the once over in the afternoon sunlight. She had the cutest freckles on her nose and the most serious dark brown eyes. "What's your name, Lieutenant Commander?"

"Mack." It was rare when a woman recognized his rank.

"I'm Jenna. Nice to meet you." She held out her hand and wiggled her fingers. "What kind of a car am I driving?"

Bold, he'd give her that, but she wasn't getting his keys. "It's not a car." He pointed toward the Harley Davidson. "You okay on the back of a motorcycle?"

Her eyes widened. "No. Would you be?"

She had him there. He'd never ridden on the back of any bike. He didn't trust other motorcyclists. "We'll take your car."

The hottest grin he'd ever seen spread across her pretty face. "I'll drive the Harley."

"Hell, no."

She placed a hand on his chest, her big eyes capturing his. "Please? It won't be the first time. You can trust me."

He pulled her hand from his fast-beating heart and locked his fingers with hers. It surprised him how well her hand fit in his.

"Trust you, huh?" She was small but exuded power and control. For no decipherable reason, he did trust her.

"We'll go as fast as you want. I'll be gentle with your…" Her gaze dipped lower. "…machine. It's going to be a great ride."

"You don't have to be too gentle."

Heat flashed between them. He handed her a helmet and strapped on his. "All right, Jenna, you're driving. But one little swerve, babe, and I take control."

"I don't swerve." Rising up on her toes, she kissed his cheek. "And you won't be sorry."

He wrapped his arms around her tiny waist and hung on. She was right. He wasn't sorry. She loved speed, he got that, but she was also careful and drove with confidence. A heady mix, this one. Intriguing.

She bought him the best ice cream he'd had in his life and they sat in a booth at the back of a small shop. Damn. He never knew that a girl licking cold ice cream off a spoon could be so hot.

He scooped the last drips of chocolate syrup out of his bowl. "Why don't you get involved with Navy guys?"

She sat back and crossed her arms. "They only want one thing."

He reached forward and wiped chocolate off the corner of her mouth. "One thing, huh? I can think of, oh, fifty things I want." Many of them involved her lips.

"Only fifty?" Her pink tongue dabbed at the place he'd just touched as if trying to taste him. "I'm talking about the one Big Thing—the admiral. My father."

He sputtered and choked.

"You okay?"

"Yep. Swallowed wrong." He took a sip of water.

"Navy guys want favors. Better training, a bump up the ranks—one wanted to get into the SEALs. Can you believe that? They think dating me is a one shot ticket straight to my dad. Morons. As if I can be used that easily."

He choked on the water again.

She pounded his back. "You really need work on that swallowing thing."

"I know. Go. On."

"The funny thing is that my dad and I butt heads all the time. I rarely talk to him and never about my personal life. He's domineering, and I don't like to take orders. Mostly I avoid him as much as I can, except for Christmas and Thanksgiving, if he's in town. That's about it."

There went Mack's plan to get to the admiral.

She eyed him. "Are you going to eat that cherry?"

He handed it to her and she popped it in her mouth. Heat rushed to his groin. "No Navy guys. Ever?"

She toyed with the stem. "I don't date any military men, you know, seriously. They all leave eventually, and there's that chance they'll never be back." She glanced up quickly. "Sorry. But it's the reality, right? Who needs that heartbreak?"

He nodded. "No need for apologies. You say it like it is. I like that about you."

"You do?"

"Hell, yeah. I don't date seriously, either. Leaving is a bitch. Waiting, not knowing, keeping the home fires burning? I wouldn't ask that of anyone I love. I've always thought this job is harder on the families than it is on the sailors."

Her mouth fell open.

"You okay?"

"It is hard. You have no idea... I'm a Navy brat, but I'll never be a Navy wife."

Deep emotion flashed behind her chocolate brown eyes. He'd seen haunted faces like hers on battle-weary men and a time or two in his own mirror. What haunted Jenna Collins? It was just another thing about her that would keep him awake at night.

"I understand."

"No one really does. My mother drank herself to death out of loneliness because of the Navy." She lifted her chin. "I'll never be my mother."

He reached out and took her hand in his. Gently, he rubbed her knuckles with the pad of his thumb. "I'm sorry, Jenna. That must have been very hard."

She shrugged. "Sorry. I don't usually tell people that."

He took her hand in his and locked their fingers together. "Go on. I'm a great listener."

"You don't want to hear this."

He leaned forward. "Yes I do. Please. Tell me."

She studied his face. After a long moment she began, "Mom only drank when Dad was on duty. When he was home, she threw out the bottles and cleaned herself up, becoming the perfect bride. When he left...God, Mack, it was horrible. She missed him so much. At night, I had to cover my head to block out her wails. She was a mess. I took care of everything—the food, the bills, picking her up off the floor and walking her to bed, putting make-up on my bruises, hiding the truth from the neighbors and the Navy. Everything."

He ground his molars. "She hurt you?"

"Sometimes. But she never remembered touching me like that, so I hid the truth, even from her. I never told anyone. It wasn't good form for an admiral's wife to be a lush."

"How old were you?"

"My earliest memory of being scared? At six, I cooked mac-and-cheese on the stove and begged my mom to eat it. I was sure she was going to starve. Jeesh, it's a wonder I didn't set the house on fire."

"Or burn yourself! Dammit! Where was the admiral in all this? It's bad enough your mother was drinking heavily with a child in the house, but what about your father? Who leaves a six year-old to take care of her sick mother?"

"He didn't know. He was out at sea protecting America from bad guys."

"Shit. That's why I'll never be married. I love what I do, and while I'm serving the country, it's best to keep things simple." He tucked a strand of her hair behind her ear. "Where does that leave us?"

She gave him a slow heat-packed smile. "Hungry. I know a great Mexican restaurant in downtown San Diego. It's way off the beaten path, but really, really good."

"You treated for the ice cream."

"I figure it's fair since you're letting me drive the Harley." She held out her hand and wiggled her fingers for the keys. "I like all that power between my legs."

Power throbbed between his legs too. He dropped the keys in her palm. The plan to seduce the admiral's daughter had taken a one-eighty, but walking away was a big hell, no.

He'd made a big mistake that day. He should've walked and saved himself the heartache.

***

She didn't like the pain on Mack's face. He was remembering things they should both forget. It was time to redirect the conversation. "Charlie. How will we find the Harmonds? It seems impossible without Jacob's cell phone."

"Impossible? Nah," Charlie grinned. "You have me! And the most high-tech communications system in the world. If we get close to the guerrillas, I'll hear them."

"We get close enough and I'll blow them sky high." Willy high fived his brother.

"First, we figure out how to sneak in and extricate the hostages without any of us getting shot or blown up. And that takes time, skill, and intelligence. We let Mack plan this thing so we do it right," Tavon said.

"Keep monitoring the LST and comm units. I want to find those bastards with their pants down," Mack said to Charlie.

Jenna sighed. "I wish I knew this area better. I'll contact my trackers. These are local guys who lead expeditions through these jungles. They might know where we should start looking."

"What is your problem, lady? Don't you think you've screwed up this mission enough?" Tavon glowered like an evil Jolly Green Giant.

"Excuse me?"

"Leave her alone," Mack warned.

"We should leave her *behind*," Tavon growled.

"Of all the pig-headed..." Her blood boiled. Had Tavon forgotten she was in charge of his paycheck? "How about your wife? How does she feel about you leaving her behind?"

He was fast for a big man. Before she could blink, he stood over her, his barrel chest rising and falling before her eyes.

"Listen lady..."

"Knock it off, you two." Mack stepped into the fight.

They were like three green peas in a pod. Jenna was one steaming pea. "Believe me, boys. She's not happy. No woman wants her husband to leave her and risk dying on foreign soil."

Tavon's black eyes were predatory. In those depths, she saw more than anger. She saw truth. She also saw that he wanted to kill her for speaking it.

"Yeah, okay, I believe you. Shit, I have no idea what a woman wants," Willy replied, working to defuse the tension he'd caused.

"He's right about that. Willy's horrible with women, and yet they keep falling into his bed. No one knows why. It's a great mystery." Charlie shrugged.

"Oh, we all know why. The Handly men are hung like bulls."

"You said it, brother." Charlie slapped Willy on the back.

"Would you two shut up?" Mack snarled.

Something buzzed. Mack pulled his cell phone out of his pocket, read it, and dropped it back in again. "Stand down, Tavon. She's not mad at you. It's me. Go ahead, Jenna. Tell them why fighting for the country, eliminating threats, and rescuing hostages makes me an asshole."

A stream of sweat rolled down his painted cheek, and his eyes...Her insides twisted at the sadness she saw there. She couldn't get lost in that emotion. Not now.

"No, Mack. That makes you a hero. All of you are heroes. And I am so proud of what you do for the country. I am." She looked at the faces surrounding her. "But I don't need a hero in my life. I need a man who loves me with everything he's got and doesn't let go."

Mack leaned closer. The world narrowed down until it was just this man standing before her. His jaw tightened in anger, and his lips... She couldn't take her eyes off his lips. "I didn't let go. You did."

She had to. How does anyone hold onto the wind?

Charlie nudged his brother. "Let's check the satellite again. Looks like you've done enough damage here."

"I'm coming." The brothers quickly moved away.

Mack's cell buzzed again.

"Why don't you get that?" she asked.

Tavon stepped back. "Go ahead, man. Take it."

"It's not important. I'll answer it later," Mack mumbled. "What's taking Ty so long?"

Another buzz. It had to be a text. And if he wasn't going to answer it in front of her...

"Seems important." She studied his face. Tavon was all but forgotten. "Is your girlfriend calling?"

"No. Just drop it."

Narrowing her eyes, she said through clenched teeth, "The father of an ex-girlfriend calling?"

Mack tipped his head skywards and air seeped through his lips. "Yes."

"Damn you, Mack!" She shoved him as hard as she could. He didn't budge. "You're working for him, aren't you?"

"Jenna—" He reached for her arms. He wanted to hold her now?

She blocked his hands. "Don't touch me. I should have guessed the admiral would behind all this. Just like old times, right? Nothing ever changes. I thought you came back for me. I hoped we could...and after the jet...but no...stupid, stupid me!"

"Come back for you? You ended things, babe. You didn't write, didn't return my calls. A Navy SEAL wasn't part of your grand plan, remember? I was outside your freaking realm of control. You cut me out of your life. Simple as that."

Simple as that? She laughed. There was nothing simple about what she went through. Well, it was sort of a laugh, more like a croak, or a cry. The way her lip quivered it was definitely a cry. "I'm a control freak? What about you? Lieutenant Commander Mack Riley is always in command."

His nose was almost touching hers. Waves of anger rolled off him. "That's where you're wrong. I lost control the moment I laid eyes on you."

Mack slammed the knife into the tree trunk behind her. "I'm going after Ty. Bring an extra scope and follow me, Tavon."

She was still shaking as he disappeared over the ridge.

CHAPTER NINE

Slumping to the ground, Jenna pulled her knees to her chest and covered her face with her hands. How had her life gotten so screwed up?

Giving her heart and soul to a SEAL had been a mistake. Given the chance, she'd do it again for the rest of her life. He touched her as no one ever had, made her laugh, think, and turned her on in a hundred different ways. Mack was the perfect man she could never have. But that hadn't stopped her from wanting him.

Mack was strength. With him she'd let go of the death grip she had on being in control and could simply be herself. She'd never known that sort of peace with anyone. She'd didn't trust anyone like she did Mack. On their third date, she let him choose a restaurant. In the booth at the back of a smoky steakhouse he'd said, "Damn, woman, you take my breath away."

"Is that so?" He'd been doing a good job of stealing hers too. Smiling, she ran her finger along the rim on her glass, collecting salt. Across the top of his hand she drew a heart with the crystals. "I can think of other ways to take your breath away."

"But you don't get involved with guys in the Navy."

"I sleep with them. Sometimes."

Heat poured over her, through her. She needed Mack Riley more than she needed to take her next choppy breath.

"Now we're talking." He reached under the table and touched her bare knee. From there he moved his hand slowly, slowly up her inner thigh, while never taking his gaze off her face. "I have a question for you, but don't take too long thinking about it..."

Oh, God.

His hand touched the edge of her panties. He slowed even more, the anticipation building. Her cheeks were on fire, her lips parted. "Jenna, do you want me..."

She gasped when he found her sweet spot.

"To make hot, passionate, dirty..." With one finger he pressed against her nub. She gripped the table cloth with both hands, tipped her head back and shut her eyes. "Nu-uh, open your eyes, baby."

She did. Every inch of her body responded to him, begging for more.

"What's the answer?" He made tiny circles against her nub. "Do you want me to make love to you. All..." She was breathing heavily now. Wetness soaked through the cotton fabric. "night..." She panted, coming undone. He pressed a harder and a tiny squeal escaped her lips. "Long?"

"Yes, yes. Please, Mack."

He threw the money on the table and got her out of there before they both exploded.

Once at her place, he lifted her into his arms and made love to her like no one had ever been loved before. Sweet Lord, he'd been magnificent in bed. And on the couch. On the balcony. In the shower. Before she'd known what happened, she'd given Mack her heart. Madly. It had been a mistake to love a SEAL, but she couldn't have stopped herself any more than she could've stopped the ocean, which carried all Navy men away.

The rays of sun filtering through the trees stopped hitting her skin. Jenna uncovered her hands to see Tavon glaring down on her. His stance was more than a little intimidating. His blood streaks and patchy face paint made him seem diabolical.

She mentally eye-rolled. Did he think he scared her? Men assumed that they could push her around. More times than not, they realized they were sadly mistaken. She was an admiral's daughter, for heaven's sakes. She'd risen to the highest ranks possible without actually being a founder at EXtreme Adventures. Who did this giant green man think he was?

"Do you have something to say to me?" Jenna asked.

He shook his head.

Tipping her chin up, she forced herself to look into his angry dark eyes. "Then why are you glowering over me? And why are we still here? We should be out tracking the guerrillas. What's taking so long?"

"Sorry, *boss*." He didn't need to add air quotes. The way he spit out the word got his point across. "We're not going anywhere until Mack has figured out the routes in and the exits. He's our navigator. He'll use the intel from Ty and Charlie to make it as safe as possible for us. Until then, we monitor movement, traffic, and sit tight."

"Sit tight?" That was one of her pet peeves. Along with, "just be patient" and "let a man handle this."

She longed to pinch someone's head off. Too bad she couldn't get her hands around Tavon's big head.

"We don't go in half-cocked. Intelligence reports indicate that CRAF typically surround their captives with several layers of armed guards. There's a chance any attempt to rescue the captives will cause the guards to shoot them outright." He put an imaginary gun to his head and pulled the trigger. "Boom. The Harmonds are dead."

She tried not to flinch. "That's why we should bring in more men. Trackers and fighters. Let's build up our army."

Tavon towered over her. "Don't you get it, lady? CRAF supporters could be anywhere. Peasants, rebels looking for a cause, they all could be part of the guerrilla network. They have families and grannies, and hell, who knows what to tip them off? Have you stopped to think about why the Harmonds were taken captive so easily? You had men posted throughout the area and yet none of them got there in time. Why?"

Jenna swallowed hard. "You think one of my guys took the Harmonds?"

"I know it. Franco was the mole. Roberto gave up the name with his last dying breath."

She pressed her hand to her stomach. "Franco was one of my men."

"The truth stinks, doesn't it? What do you think of your army now?"

The truth burned. She'd given the orders. Requiring minute-by-minute tracking of Andrew, she was the one to broadcast the family's location to men who were supposedly protecting the Harmonds. Franco was a guerrilla spy... Oh, no. Was she to blame for the kidnapping and the death of her men? Swallowing bile, she focused on maintaining her composure. Tavon was trying to get to her. She wouldn't let him see he had.

"We'll find some more good men. I'll text EXtreme Adventures to find out who we can trust."

Tavon leaned closer. She could smell his woodsy deodorant. "You call in one of *your* men and you might as well announce to the guerrillas that we're coming. Just like you did when you gave them our landing coordinates. Do you want to kill all of us?"

"No. Of course not!"

"Then stay out of it! Let us do the job we were hired to do." If he could shoot bullets with those dark eyes, Jenna would be dead already.

Was he trying to push her buttons? If so, he'd lit them all up.

She glared right back. "Hate all women, Mr. Sting, or just me?"

When he grinned, he looked like another person entirely, but just as intimidating. "I love women, Ms. Collins. Except for bossy, blowhard man-eaters."

Ignoring the comment, she swung her arm toward the jungle. "My family is out there. My responsibility. I'll do whatever it takes to save them. Understand?"

He whispered in her ear. "Mack is my family. My responsibility. I've got his back and will do whatever it takes to protect him. You feeling me?"

The threat lifted the hair on the back of her neck.

She wiggled her finger so that he'd dip his big head toward her. She whispered in his ear, "Twenty thousand bonus of my own money for you. Just keep Mack alive."

He pulled back until they were face to face. The angry light in his eyes dimmed back. Blinking a few times, he said, "What did you say?"

Lifting her lips in the best grin she could muster, she doubted she looked a fraction as intimidating as he did. "You heard me."

"Hell." He dragged the word out long and hard. "You want him back."

"Of course I do." Good Lord. What did he think? That she'd staged this elaborate hostage situation to get Mack killed? "I love him, Tavon. Always have, always will. Do your job and protect him. Keep him safe."

He rubbed his hand over his bald head. "I don't want your money."

"Fine. Give it to charity. Do we have a deal?" She stretched out her hand.

He rocked that big head from side to side and kept his hands to himself. "I'll bring my brother out alive. I always do. But you've got to understand one thing—I destroy Mack's enemies. With a gun, grenade, stick, my bare hands, it doesn't matter. Dead is dead. Consider yourself warned."

Tavon Sting grabbed a scope and followed after Mack.

Jenna let out a deep breath. She felt *that*, all right.

***

As Mack crept up the hill, he focused on his surroundings. He listened for enemy noise, smelling, tasting the air for guerrillas. All he heard was the sound of the jungle. Nothing was out of place except for him and his team. Silently, he stepped over the thick vegetation. His boots climbed the hill, but his mind was still back at the helo landing. With Jenna.

Seeing his girl shoot had done all kinds of things to him. First, he'd forgotten that Jenna wasn't his girl. When would he get that through his thick skull? Hard to do when she'd looked amazingly hot with a rifle in her hands and had felt so good in his arms. As she'd leaned into him, nearly melting in his arms, he'd smelled her warm skin. He had the crazy desire to drag her behind the helo and have another round of sex therapy.

Then the admiral called and everything went south—the tenuous trust that had been building between them, the cease fire, letting the past stay in the past. All of it slipped away. He couldn't let it get to him. He had a mission to accomplish and lives to save.

Mack sprinted the last hundred feet up the hill.

Even though Ty was in plain sight, it took Mack's trained eyes a few seconds to spot him. Ty was a perfect chameleon on the ridge. Flat on his belly with his binoculars up to his eyes, the man's BUD/S blended in with the grass and dappled light filtering in through the trees.

Scoping out the area for hidden dangers, Mack flattened himself next to Ty and brought the binoculars up to his eyes.

"Whatcha got?" Mack asked.

"Matching the coordinates from the kid's cell phone, CRAF should be there." Ty pointed to a thick patch of trees.

Mack's binoculars followed the line from Ty's finger. "And?"

"And nothing. No movement, cars, people, nothing."

"Shit. They've moved the captives already. We're screwed."

"Maybe not. I saw..." Ty paused for a second. "...there."

Mack trained his sights in the new direction that Ty was pointing.

A thin line of white rose up through the trees. Smoke!

"Damn. That's close!" Mack said. Too close. If those were CRAF guerrillas down there, they were almost on top of them. He tapped his comm line. "Charlie, I'm sending you new coordinates. Figure out what we've got. Send Tavon after us and tell Willy to protect Jenna. We're going in."

"Copy that," Charlie said.

"Protect Jenna!" Mack said one more time.

They moved quietly and efficiently through the trees. Tavon caught up with them at the bottom of the hill. He and his men were chameleon killing machines. Mack's heart pounded hard and sure. His breath was nice and even. This is what he was trained for. The vest, belts, ammo, and weapons weren't heavy. They kept him balanced, stable, and grounded. His boots didn't make a sound. It would be difficult for the enemy to see them, and surprise was on their side.

Motioning with his fingers, he instructed Tavon to watch the flank while he and Ty advanced. The smell of cooking meat rose up in the air. They were close. Slowly, slowly, he moved a mirror to peek around the tree.

There! Two men sat by a fire cooking what looked suspiciously like a squirrel.

Mack raised two fingers. With his peripheral vision, he watched Ty. He hadn't spotted any others. Slowly, he turned toward Tavon. The big man shook his head. No others. He checked his cell.

Charlie's text said. "See only two. Could be others. Canopy thick."

Were these two men CRAF guerrillas? Mack had no idea. Was it a setup? Mack didn't know that either. There was a high probability CRAF knew they were alive and coming for them. If so, they were about to be ambushed one more time. He might never see Jenna again.

His heart oozed sadness. Damn, he loved his girl. There it was—the blinding truth that becomes so clear on the battlefield. She'd almost killed him, and given the chance she might finish the job. But the truth, like death, was impossible to dodge forever.

He loved the admiral's sexy daughter. There was not one damned thing he could do about it.

Spinning his finger through the air, he gave the signal. "All in!"

Taking a big breath, he lifted his rifle and rushed out from cover.

CHAPTER TEN

Mack pointed his rifle between the older man's eyes. He didn't need Charlie's smart weapon. At this range, he wouldn't miss. Ty aimed at the other man, who could have been the first guy's son. Tavon guarded their six.

"Don't move," Mack said quietly.

The man startled and of course moved. Shit. Mack held his position and did not take the guy's head off his shoulders. The man's eyes went wide, and he looked like he messed himself.

"CRAF?" Mack said.

The two shook their heads.

"You're not CRAF guerrillas?"

Violent head shaking that could have meant they weren't CRAF or that they weren't talking. Who knew?

"Ty, talk to them. Do they understand me or not?" Mack had not lowered his weapon.

In Spanish, Ty asked them again.

"No!" The older guy said followed by a few of the dirty Spanish words Mack knew. He spit his disgust in the fire.

"Could be an act," Tavon whispered in his ear.

Mack nodded. "Ask them where the CRAF guerrillas are. The truth and no one gets shot."

Spanish words flew and Mack waited, scanning the jungle, knowing they could be sitting ducks.

"They say the guerrillas were on the move this morning."

"No shit, they were on the move to take us out at the helo," Mack said.

Ty shook his head. "No, he's talking about a different bunch."

"Freakin' rabbits are multiplying. How many CRAF groups are we dealing with?" Tavon asked.

"Apparently, they spilt up when they heard we were coming. The son here saw them in the jungle and hid until they passed by. CRAF guerrillas were armed with rifles and AK-47s. They dragged a group of blindfolded people with them. Captives," Ty interpreted.

"Do these guys know where the guerrillas were headed?"

"East. That's all they know. They steer clear of them because the guerrillas steal their goats and money and sometimes mess with their women. They say they hate the bastards and the drug cartels too. They hope the U.S. sends them all to hell."

"Do you believe them?" Mack asked.

Ty studied their faces and postures for a long moment. "Yeah. I do."

Mack lowered his rifle. "Okay. Gracias. Enjoy your squirrel. It looks almost as good as an MRE."

They retreated back the way they came.

"The son said that the guerrillas never sit still for long. Move, move, move. Keeps the captives disoriented and makes it harder to track them."

"Can you track them?" Mack asked.

Ty grinned. "Do bears shit in the woods?"

"How would I know? I'm no park ranger, and I don't like bears."

Ty smiled. "They do. It's big, stinky crap. I came on a fresh pile once in Montana. It was still steaming."

"Nice. Thank you for sharing that beautiful story. Let's get the others and follow the CRAF's trail before this shit stops steaming."

"One good thing, we know the captives are still alive." Tavon crossed his huge arms. "Or at least they were this morning."

"Yeah. Can't wait to tell Jenna." Mack smiled. That oozing ball of sadness had melted in the heat of the moment.

"You poor sonofabitch," Tavon said. "You're in it deep."

Ty laughed. "Yep, over his head."

Mack ignored them. "Let's go."

They were back on the ridge about to head over the other side.

"She's got you, brother." Tavon closed his big hand as if he was squeezing the life out of a small woodland creature. "Nothing more to do but kiss your balls good-bye."

"Shut up."

Ty laughed again. "Wow, Mack. It's nice to see you like this."

"He's such a goner." Tavon expression was full of disgust.

"Whatever, lunatics." Mack started jogging. "Come on. The heat must be getting to you."

Tavon jogged beside him. For a big man, he was remarkably quiet on his feet. Ty came up on the other side. Silent, Apache wind. "And Ty, you should hear what she says about him."

Mack slowed.

"Don't play with the man," Ty said.

Mack stopped. Crossing his arms he said. "He doesn't have Jenna-intel. He's just messing with me."

"Oh, I'm messing with you all right. Ready for this? Our boss said she'd pay me a twenty-thousand dollar bonus—from her own bank account—if I watch over Macky boy. She wants me to keep him alive."

"How much did she offer to keep me alive?" Ty asked.

"Not one damn penny, my friend. She only cares about our C.O."

Mack scratched at the sweat running under his helmet. What did it mean?

"I'll watch your back, bro. But you'd better protect those balls." Tavon held up his closed fist. "Seems Jenna wants them back."

Both men were still grinning at his expense by the time they made it back to camp.

Jenna crawled out from behind a boulder and rushed to him. Her hat flew off and her long blonde hair swirled freely around her war-painted face. Before he could stop her, she threw her arms around his neck. Holding on tight, she kissed his cheek. Hell, why'd he want to stop her again? Her lips were green from his face paint. Some of hers had smeared on him. So what?

"I was so worried. Thank God you're back." The emotion filling her eyes was real. Just as real as the swelling going on in his heart.

"What about me?" Ty asked.

Jenna rubbed his arm. "Yes, thank God Ty's back too."

Ty smiled, his white teeth looking exceptionally bright under the camouflaged paint.

"And...you too, Tavon." She waved her fingers at him.

Tavon rolled his eyes and walked away.

"Oh, Mack. When you went over the ridge after those guys..." She swallowed hard. "All I could think about was the way we left things. I know you work for my dad. It's your job. I get it. I shouldn't have assumed things would be different than they are. I'm sorry I reacted the way I did."

"Me too, babe. Your dad did contact me because he wanted me to look out for you and keep you safe." He spread his arms. "I'm doing quite a bang-up job, aren't I?"

She didn't answer.

"But I didn't have to agree to the job. You convinced me to do the right thing, so I'm here. Let's try to leave the past behind us for now and rescue your clients. Are we good?"

"Yeah. We're good." She chewed her lip as if she wanted to say more. He waited, but she kept those words behind her pretty green lips.

"All right. Pack up. We roll out in five minutes," Mack said. "CRAF is on the move and we're going after them."

***

Ty and Charlie led the way. Jenna fell in behind Mack and Willy. Tavon took up the rear. The sun's light slanting through the trees told her it was getting late. Jenna was nervous about going deeper into the jungle, away from the helicopter and the last remnants of sunlight. CRAF could be anywhere.

"What happens when the sun sets?" she whispered.

"We've got night vision goggles," Mack told her. "And our helmets have infrared chemlights on them. The naked eye can't see them, but we can see each other with our NODs."

"NODs?"

"Night Optical Devices. Since you don't have any, you'd better stick close to me." He pulled a glove off his hand and tucked it into his pocket. Then he offered his bare skin to her and she gratefully took it.

It was amazing how a little thing like holding his hand could make all the difference in the world. His skin was warm and safe. Just like Mack. Her fingers laced with his, fitting perfectly. She'd forgotten how much she missed that.

"Here." Ty stopped walking. "This is where they camped."

Looking closer, Jenna saw a few burned twigs by Ty's feet. How had he seen those?

Mack whispered in her ear, "Hide behind that tree. Don't come out until I say so." He planted a light kiss on her cheek and spun his finger through the air in some kind of signal. The guys all fanned out. Their weapons were raised as they searched the area.

It was getting dark now, and Jenna couldn't see well. Every now and then she'd hear a twig snap. She gripped the tree. After what seemed an eternity, Mack nearly scared the soul out of her.

"They're gone, Jenna. I found this." He handed her a silver object.

She realized before she opened it that it was the driver's cell phone. "Jacob left it behind. Does that mean—?" Her voice came out pitchy and raw.

She was so damned tired of this. So scared. She could think of only one reason why Jacob had left the phone behind. If those CRAF bastards hurt him and Anna, she'd hunt them down and kill them herself.

"It just means Jacob couldn't bring it. Maybe he hid it and couldn't get to it before they moved him. It doesn't matter now. Ty doesn't need the cell's signal. He's picked up their trail already. Come on, babe. We've got to hurry."

Darkness fell fast in the jungle. Jenna couldn't see a thing. She clutched Mack's hand and tried her hardest not to slow him down. It wasn't working. At least five times she walked up the back side of him, or got tangled in his boots.

"Sorry." Her voice choked with exertion.

He gave her hand a squeeze. To Tavon he said, "You guys go ahead."

"Your head's stuck up your butt if you think I'll leave you behind," Tavon growled.

"My head is where it should be. Go on. Jenna and I will be right behind you."

Tavon gave Jenna a fierce look. He'd be happy to leave her in the jungle for all the trouble she was causing.

"Get going! We'll follow you."

Two seconds later, Mack and Jenna were alone. It would have been sexy and romantic if she wasn't so scared. And exhausted. She felt like she was going to hyperventilate from the fast-paced hike and the worry.

"Let's stop for a second so you can catch your breath," Mack said.

"I'm fine." She tugged on his arm. "Let's hurry before we lose the guys."

"We won't lose them. I can still see the infrared chemlights on their helmets and I'm in constant radio contact with them." He pulled on the wire to his ear-piece. "But you should rest a bit."

Why? Because she was hungry, thirsty, her feet were killing her, and she was about to have a panic attack because she had no idea where the Harmonds were?

He ran his thumb along her neck, slowly, deliciously. Heat flushed her skin.

"Your heart is racing, babe."

Really? With bad guys close by and a hot SEAL even closer?

"I'm fine." At least she would be once she had Jacob's little hand in hers. Until then, her fears, aches, and pains didn't matter.

"We've been running for the last seven miles through mountainous jungle terrain. In the dark! You're not trained for this, Jenna. I'm just looking out for you."

"I'm not the one to worry about. Let's go." She tugged his hand again.

Mack chuckled softly. "Always so damned stubborn."

"I am not."

"You do things your way, or not at all."

That pushed a button. "That's not true."

"Name one thing."

She spun to face him and wished she could see his eyes under those goggles. "One thing I did that I didn't want to do? Is that what you are asking?"

He lifted his goggles and his eyes burned into hers. "That's what I'm asking."

She didn't have to pause. The answer had formed in her brain before he lifted his goggles. No, before that. It started eighteen months ago on a miserable day she wished they could do over. She moved closer. Her lips brushed his.

"I left you, Mack. I didn't want to. I had to. It was the worst mistake of my life."

He stared at her, his mouth open.

A whistle broke the spell. She could have believed it was the trill of an exotic jungle bird except that Mack pressed his finger to the earpiece and listened.

"Ty found their campsite. Let's go."

***

Mack wouldn't let himself think about her words. Why did she leave him if she didn't want to? What kind of fresh hell was this? No. He had to put it aside. Later there'd be time to straighten out past mistakes. Hell, he was of half a mind to start some new ones. Maybe—he glanced at Jenna running beside him—he already was.

Tapping his comm line he whispered. "Location?"

There was no response.

"Dammit." He tapped it again. "Location?"

Static came through his earpiece, followed by Tavon's soft voice. "Sector A. Eleven hundred, five hundred yards. Six hostiles. Fully armed."

"Sector A. Oh nine hundred. Seven hostiles. AK-47s," Ty said.

"Sector B. Oh one hundred. Four hostiles. Armed. One RPG launcher," Willy said.

"Sector B. Oh three hundred. Three hostiles. AK-47's," Charlie reported. "No captives in sight."

Mack softly let out a deep breath. "Shit. Fall back. Maintain visual."

"Copy that," they said in unison.

"What did they say?" Jenna asked.

"That we've got our work cut out for us."

Mack needed to set up an overwatch to spy on the hostiles and figure out where the captives were hidden. This was not going to be an easy snatch and grab. It was exponentially worse now that he had Jenna pressing against him. He needed to get her out of harm's way. He'd been serious when he told her that he couldn't focus with her sweet little body close by. His thoughts ran to how best to protect her. Keep her safe.

"Mack, found a natural berm. Good for overwatch," Ty said.

"Copy that. Be right there." When he faced her, her heat pulsed in his goggles. He cupped her jaw. "Follow me close. I'll find you a place to rest out of harm's way."

She tipped her chin up. "I want to stay with you. I left you once, Mack. I'm not doing it again."

She was tiny, but the look on her face was ferocious. Her words did some serious twisting in his gut but he didn't have time to dwell on them. "When this is over, we'll sort us out. But until then, you have to listen to me. It's my job to keep you safe." He placed a gentle kiss on her lips. "Please, let me do my job."

She nodded.

Could Jenna turn over total control? Doubtful, but at least she was trying. Taking his hand she stuck close, trying to imitate the slow, stalking way he moved. He had to hand it to her. She was a fast learner.

They reached the berm. It was a fifteen foot high hill made by some ancient rockslide. The guys were already flat against it, peeking over the top, their rifles resting on the peak and pointing over the other side. The slope was gradual enough that the team didn't have to dig their feet in to keep from sliding down. It was perfect.

"Wait here." Mack pointed to the spot where Jenna stood at the base of the hill. "I'm going to climb up and check things out."

"Be careful."

"I will."

Before he had a chance to move, she grabbed him by the vest pockets and pulled him to her. And then she let him have it.

Sweet mother of God. He didn't have a chance to catch his breath before her lips smashed into his. That kiss must have singed the hair under his helmet. Wrapping his arms around her, he held on, matching her hunger, her need with his own. He didn't want to let go.

"Eh-hmm," someone above him said.

Yeah, right. CRAF, war, captives—he reminded himself where he was. Reluctantly, he released Jenna. "I'll be back. Don't move."

***

How could she move? That kissed had stolen the strength right out of her legs. She sat down in the dirt and pulled her knees up to her chest.

Jenna was no Pollyanna idealist. She knew her relationship with Mack teetered on a thin sheet of ice. At any moment, they could fall through and she'd lose the love of her life forever. Again. Would he leave her once the hostage rescue was over? She really didn't know. His lips wanted her. Other parts obviously did too. But his heart, and most assuredly his mind, were still eighteen months behind, locked inside the fort he'd built when she hurt him. He wasn't ready to let her in.

Jenna was a woman with plans. Many plans. Rescuing the Harmonds was top of the list, and right next to it was to grab hold of her sexy, hard SEAL and never let him go. Life was ridiculously cold and lonely without Mack. She'd lost everything that was important to her when she walked away and she was determined not to be a loser anymore.

Looking up the slope, she watched him and the rest of the team. The men were lying prone on the slope using their scopes and binoculars to spy on CRAF. What was going on down there? Could they see Jacob? Anna? Andrew and Marcella? Jenna couldn't stay behind. Her family was out there and she needed to be part of the plan to rescue them.

She climbed the hill.

CHAPTER ELEVEN

"**W**hat's going on?" The soft voice came up behind Mack.

Jenna! What in the hell?

Sliding backwards on his belly, he grabbed her hand and pulled her down with him until they were far below the peak.

"Hey, ouch, what are you doing?" She whispered far too loudly.

He put his finger to his lip and jammed his finger toward to the bottom of the berm. They slid to the bottom.

When her feet were firmly back where they were supposed to be, Jenna let out a breath. "I have to see, Mack. Please. I'll stay down and out of the way. I'll do anything you say."

Right. Sure, she would.

He rolled his shoulders, easing the tension. Why fight it? She'd only do her thing in spite of what he wanted. Her strength and stubbornness were some of the many things he loved about her. He paused. No tense correction there. He did love her past, present, future. Maybe one day she'd feel the same way.

"All right. I'll let you use my NODs, but there's no talking. No sound until we are back here at the bottom of the berm. Got it?"

The berm would block most of the sounds they made, but he couldn't risk Jenna crying out if she saw something horrendous happening to the kids. Jenna gave him a thumbs up signal. She understood, but would she do what he said? Only if it suited her. That's the way Jenna was built—she did things her way. Pulling the baseball cap off her head, he swapped it for his helmet with the night vision scope. It was huge on her. He pushed the helmet on as best as he could and adjusted the snaps under her chin.

As she climbed the hill, he shook his head. He could control a team of elite fighting men but this stubborn sweet thing was uncontrollable. Shit, how he loved her. He climbed up beside her. She was as flat as she could make herself. When she was ready, he pointed to where she should look.

CRAF guerrillas were down there sitting around a campfire, smoking cigarettes and playing with their rifles. A couple of idiots stumbled around drunk already. *Good. All the better to snatch and grab hostages from, you assholes.* He hoped they would all be passed out, but knew the team wouldn't get that lucky. A couple of guards leaned against the wall of a shack, wary and alert as if they sensed the team's presence. Most people had a sixth sense that could "feel" eyes on them. These guards knew they were being watched.

He'd bet a thousand bucks the hostages were inside the shack.

Mack jabbed Charlie in the shoulder and made a signal toward the shack. Charlie used his infrared equipment and held up two fingers. Two people inside. Where were the others? Charlie scanned the area, slowly, checking for body heat signatures. No other shacks. No other captives.

Dammit! CRAF guerrillas had split the Harmonds up. The snatch and grab had suddenly become significantly harder.

Jenna scanned the camp with his scope. He sensed her tense up, heard her short intake of breath. When he wrapped his arm around her back, she scooted closer until she was tucked under his armpit. Jenna was a warm and sweet smelling comfort in the midst of a scary night. She continued to watch the scene below them, unaware that he watched her.

***

Oh, God. The guerrillas had a small army of men down there! Through the night vision goggles, Jenna saw that each one of those creeps was armed with military-style weapons. And what was that thing over there? A grenade launcher? How would her five guys fight all that? Guilt swamped her. If anyone on her team was injured...it would be her fault. Her guys could all be killed.

Why'd she call Mack? She should have let someone else handle this, the whole U.S. military, guys she didn't know and love. But if she waited for the government to act, would there be anyone to rescue? The Harmonds might not survive.

"Mack and I will slip in and take out the two guards." Tavon's voice was so low she barely heard him. And what did he mean take them out? The image of Mack and Tavon slitting men's throats and dragging them into the bushes popped into mind. Sweat rolled down her back.

"We'll keep going until the guerrillas realize we're not there to party. Then it's balls all in."

"I call the RPG launcher." Willy's voice had the charged up enthusiasm of a teenager calling shotgun. "And any unfortunate bastard who happens to be standing within ten feet of it. I'm going to light up Colombia like the Fourth of July. Hooya."

"I've got those three." Ty pointed. "They look like my cousin's tribe. I hate those guys."

Jenna listened with one ear as she scanned the camp. She was getting used to the strange green-light flatness of scene through the scope. Where were the Harmonds? No Jacob. No Anna. Only scary looking armed men. CRAF were either hiding the kids and their parents, or they were all dead. A little sound of anguish squeaked out before she could stop it.

Mack pulled her in closer, nearly covering her body with his. With her nose pressed into his vest she breathed in the smell of him. The leaves he'd stuck into the netting of his ghillie suit had a musty-jungle fragrance. She caught a hint of his sports deodorant too and remembered how much she loved that smell. Under all that was something better. It was a fragrance that had no better description than simply—Mack. The smell of his skin comforted her like a blanket of protection, wrapped in sex and love.

"You okay?" he whispered, so softly his lips brushed her ear. A tingle curled up her neck and into her scalp.

She nodded, taking another deep inhale. Unfastening the helmet, she handed it back to him. Jenna didn't want to look at the CRAF army with their big guns and rocket launchers anymore. Everything seemed hopeless. Without saying a word, she maneuvered herself back down the berm.

Mack was quick to follow her down. "Jenna?"

She paced. "It's impossible, isn't it?"

"We've had worse odds."

She flung her arm toward the CRAF's camp. "How? Didn't you see all those men? There's no way. Those are killers out there! Lots of them."

He took hold of her arms and looked into her eyes. It was dark, but she could still see the intensity in his baby blues. "It's what we do, Jenna. I told you. My guys are the best. We have a plan and it will work."

"What about the kids? I didn't see Jacob or Anna. Do you think—?" She swallowed hard.

"There are two individuals inside the shack. I don't know which two. It looks like they split the Harmonds up."

"Why would they do that?'

"To increase their chances of success."

"That means…" It felt like the blood drained out of her face. She reached for his hand, her fingers linked with his. "There's another army of CRAFs guarding the other two hostages somewhere else?"

"Yes." He adjusted the baseball hat on her head. "So the plan is, we strike fast and hard. We attack this camp and rescue the hostages in the shack before the assholes have a chance to notify the other group that we are coming. Then we rinse and repeat on the second CRAF group and bug out."

No part of his plan sounded easy. Would either one of them survive this night?

"What do you want me to do? Should I cover you with the iPad?"

He chuckled softly. "You have no idea how funny that sounds. No, babe. *You* need to take cover. No matter what happens down there, you stay out of harm's way. Got it? Charlie will stay behind to monitor the radio, CRAF, and relay intel we need. You stick near him. Even if the plan doesn't succeed, you steer clear of the firefight. I need to know that you are safe."He leaned closer and kissed the tip of her nose.

"I'm sorry I got you involved with this, Mack."

"Hey, I'm not. I'm glad you called me."

She brought his hand to her chest and pressed it against her pounding heart. "I missed you so much."

"Me too, Jenna." The soft reply turned her to mush.

"Promise you'll come back to me."

His teeth shone in the dark. "Always, babe." He pressed a gentle kiss to her lips and climbed back up the hill.

Jenna was not good at relying on other people's plans. And this plan, the one where her man sneaks into a hostile's camp and gets himself killed, made her sick. Literally. Mack had barely left her side before she vomited in the bushes. She had to get a hold of herself or she'd be no help to Mack, the team, or the Harmonds.

"Three, two, one, execute," Mack ordered.

She sucked in a deep breath as the men slipped over the edge and disappeared from her sight. Only Charlie remained to monitor the computer and radios. Jenna's limbs were so weak from fear that she wondered if she'd be able to climb the hill again.

But she had to. There was a rifle and an iPad next to Charlie. And she knew how to use them. Sort of.

Jenna wasn't about to hide in the trees while the others risked their lives. That wasn't the plan. If she could shoot a bad guy or two and help Mack, then dammit, she'd do it. The idea of killing flipped her stomach upside down.

She vomited once more, cursed herself, and started climbing.

"What's going on?" She whispered to Charlie.

He jerked in surprise. "Jenna? What are you doing here?"

"I'm helping. I'm going to use the iPad and rifle."

"Give me a minute and I'll set you up." He handed them over to her.

Charlie was distracted by something on the computer or maybe it was what he heard in his radio that bothered him. Even in the dark she could see his frown. Something wasn't right. Her heart seized. Where were the guys? It was all quiet down below. Without the scope, she couldn't make out any movements other than those of CRAF jackasses surrounding the campfire.

"Charlie? Where are they?"

He pulled his eyes away from the computer and pointed. There, there, there, and finally there. She squinted. No. She couldn't see them. Unless…yes, a movement, slow and deliberate, a partial shadow. If Charlie hadn't shown her where to look, she wouldn't have seen a figure that looked like Willy. Once she blinked, she lost him again. The guys moved slowly as if they were hunters stalking animals, as in her mind, they were. They each had made veg fans from tree branches that they'd zip-tied together. Slowly, one of the team members would rise up in the middle of the fan, eyes barely peeking over, catch a peek at the enemy, and slowly melt back down again. This was going to take forever.

"Uh-oh." Charlie pressed his earpiece down into his ear and listened intently.

Uh-oh? What did that mean?

"Charlie, what's going on?"

He held up a finger. Quiet. Listening, he hunched over the computer so closely that he looked like he was going to kiss it.

Come on! What's uh-oh? She wanted to shake him.

"Guys, I've got Spanish chatter," Charlie said into the mic. "Computer shows three Humvees. Close and moving fast."

More CRAF guerrillas? Were they bringing the other two Harmonds to the camp?

"Doesn't seem right, Mack. They're coming in hard," Charlie responded into the radio. "Not CRAF. Assume cartels."

How she wished she still had Mack's helmet so that she could see and hear what was going on. This was scary and maddening.

Charlie picked up something on his screen that made his eyes widened. He twisted his mic close to his mouth and shouted, "Bug out! Bug out! Cartel sonsofbitches with RPGs—!"

A high-pitched sound screamed through the night followed by an explosion. Charlie fell on top of her, smashing her face into the dirt. Another explosion rocked the ground beneath her. Her ears were still ringing, but she could have sworn she heard gunfire on the other side of the hill.

Charlie rolled off her. "Okay?"

Five years had been scared off her life. "Yeah. I'm okay."

"Guys, where are you?" Charlie yelled into the mic. "Report!"

Another explosion hit closer this time. Jenna covered her head. Shrapnel and rocks rained down like dirty chunks of hail.

Oh, God, Mack! She closed her eyes and prayed.

"Report!" Charlie repeated.

Gunshots blasted through the campsite below like a crazy video game.

"Report, dammit!"

"Keep your panties on, Charles!" A figure hurled himself over the peak and landed next to Jenna.

"Willy!" She kissed his cheek.

He flashed his pearly whites at her. "Damn, Jenna, I'll go back and come in again if you'll give me one on the mouth. I'll even do it ass first for a little tongue."

She socked him in the shoulder. "Where's Mack?"

"I don't know but Ty's right behind—" Ty Whitehorse flew over the peak of the hill and landed on Willy. "—ugh, I mean, on top of me. Get off, you crazy Indian!"

Ty rolled to the side. "Thanks for the cushy landing."

Another round of explosions rocked the area and Jenna cried out, "Mack!"

"Did you see Mack or Tavon?" Charlie asked.

"Not me. I was focusing on taking out that launcher," Willy said.

"The last I saw, they were stalking toward the shack," Ty said.

They all lifted up slowly and peeked over the edge. No one came up the hill. What happened to Mack and Tavon?

"Um, guys. You should check this out." Charlie pointed to the screen.

They eased back to look at the satellite images. Men were all over the campsite. Gunfire blazed and body after body fell. It was a war. Dear God, where was Mack?

"The shack is gone." Charlie pointed to the satellite image. "Nothing left of it."

CHAPTER TWELVE

Jenna couldn't breathe. Her body was numb, and it felt like she'd been kicked in the head. Mack! She needed Mack. He had to climb up and over that hill and wrap his muscular arms around her or she was going to die. Here and now. Die. A high-pitched sound screeched through the night. Another RPG?

"Jeez, relax, Jenna."

"Breathe," Ty whispered.

The high-pitched squeak continued in her ears.

"You've got to get her to quiet down. I can't hear the chatter," Charlie said.

The guys were all talking to her at once. She had no idea she made the horrible whining until Ty got in her face and put his gloved hand over her mouth. "Look at me. Focus on my voice. Breathe."

She did. His gloves smelled like metal and gunpowder.

"If I move my hand will you stop screaming?" Ty spoke softly as if she were a scared pony about to bolt.

She nodded.

"Good, girl."

"I've got them!" Charlie's voice rang triumphantly. Mack!

Jenna scrambled over to Charlie. "Where? Why doesn't he come in? Get him to come in right now!"

"They've got the hostages. Hang on. What do you need, Mack?" Charlie listened for a long hard beat. "Yeah, okay. Ty, come here."

Ty scrambled over to Charlie's radio.

"I've got Mack on the line. They pulled the hostages out of the shack in time. A minute later and he and Tavon would have been flattened. He needs you to talk to the hostages."

Jenna frowned. "Why Ty?"

Charlie handed the headset over to Ty and answered her question. "Because we rescued the wrong hostages."

"Mack doesn't have the Harmonds?"

"No. He's got two cartel big-wigs. CRAF kidnapped them for some sort of leverage in the Coke War. Apparently, the cartel wants them back."

Jenna's jaw dropped. The guys could have been killed and the Harmonds weren't even down there? Where the Harmonds still alive? "Where's my family?"

"That's what Mack is trying to find out. He and Tavon have the two men sequestered behind a thick grove of trees in the jungle."

Ty spoke Spanish into the mic, speaking quietly. He calmed the hostages down, just as he had calmed her. Ty had a gentle way with people.

Jenna was fluent and wished she could hear what the men were saying on the other end, but more than that, she desperately wanted to hear Mack's voice through the radio. "Can you turn it up a little, Charlie?"

He did.

Mack said, "Ask them if they saw the Harmonds."

Ty did and the hostages responded that they had earlier that morning. There were two men, a woman, a young girl and a boy.

Two men? Was one of them Andrew?

"Ask them which way they went," Mack said.

Ty did and there was some discussion between the two men. "North" was the final answer.

"Ask them if anyone was injured —." Gunfire cut off Mack's words.

"Oh crap, CRAF spotted them." Charlie was behind her. "Mack, get out of there!"

A barrage of gunfire exploded out of the earpiece. Ty yanked it away from his head.

"Tavon! Holy Shit!" Mack yelled. "Tavon's down. Hostages down. I returned fire. Got six of them."

"Mack!" Jenna yelled.

Charlie grabbed the radio from Ty's fingers. "Mack. Take cover. That was just the beginning. Butt-load of firepower coming your way."

"Where are they?" Willy stared at the satellite image. "I'm going in!"

"Right behind you!" Ty said and the two of them dove over the peak.

Jenna stared at Charlie. He looked as stunned as she felt. An expression that her dad used frequently exploded out her lips. "Whisky Tango Foxtrot!"

Too many things were going through her mind. Was Mack okay? Would he be able to protect himself? Would the guys get him out of there before CRAF caught up to him? She swore right then and there that she'd kiss Willy hard if he rescued Mack. And she'd kiss Ty too. But Mack, Lord, she'd show him how glad she was to see him when she got the chance.

What about Tavon? He'd been shot. Was he going to make it? He was her least favorite of the group, but Mack cared for him and that was enough for her. She prayed that Big T. was going to live to glare at her another day.

And...the Harmonds. She prayed for them too. They were still out there somewhere, lost in the jungle. Wow, how naïve she had been to think that she and a group of SEALs could walk right in and take them out. It was an impossible task to rescue hostages in the midst of the Coke War. CRAF and the cartels were blood-thirsty savages hell-bent on slaughtering each other. Fine and dandy. After they shot at her guys and scared her to death? She wanted the U.S. to wipe them off the face of the earth. But not until Mack, the Harmonds, and her boys were all strapped in their helicopter seats and heading for Quito.

"What's happening?"

A fierce round of gunfire over the radio stole the words from her as fiery bullets ripped the jungle to pieces.

Charlie studied the LST. "Oh two hundred. Two hostiles. Yes! Got 'em."

Jenna leaned over Charlie's shoulder. She watched several bright blobs on the screen converging toward one. Mack?

"Oh four hundred! Three!" Charlie instructed. Boom, boom, boom. "That's it, Mack!"

Suddenly, there were three less blobs on the screen. Mack had put their lights out.

"Charlie! Look!" Seven men were fanning out, coming in closer, and surrounding Mack. Four in the front three behind.

Jenna wanted to grab that LST and scream at Mack, "Run, sweetheart, run!"

But Mack didn't run. Not from anything. Especially if Tavon was down and needed protecting. With her heart in her throat, all she could do was watch and pray for a miracle.

"Careful, Mack, you're surrounded," Charlie warned.

The gunfire that followed was loud and terrifying. World War III erupted down there. Covering her ears, she silently screamed. She had to do something! The iPad. Grabbing the rifle next to Charlie, she powered up the iPad, hit the button for Target Guided Shooting and did as the robot's voice commanded.

Paint the target with the laser. Which one? Through the scope, she picked out the guy who was closest to her and mentally crossed her fingers. Oh, God. Deep breath in, partially out, hold it, pull the trigger.

Boom. The rifle jerked back in her hands. The figure fell face forward into the ground. He never got back up.

Charlie swiveled around to face her. "Dang! That was you?"

She nodded as horror washed over her. Did she kill a person?

"You got one! All right, Jenna. Get back up here and try again."

She swallowed hard. Could she do it again? Her hands shook, and her thoughts spun down a dark ugly hole. She'd killed a man. Did he have kids at home? A little girl who would miss her daddy?

"Behind you, Mack! Watch your six." Charlie yelled into the headset. "Oh three hundred, three guys."

Jenna didn't wait to hear more. She painted another target, took a deep quivering breath, let it halfway out, and—

Boom!

She didn't pull the trigger. An explosion went off in CRAF camp that resembled the end of the world. The earth shook. She was knocked backward halfway down the hill. The flash was so bright that Jenna could still see it through her closed eyelids. She scrambled to find purchase and scoot herself back up to Charlie.

"What happened?" She asked Charlie, but he didn't hear her. Gunshots stole her words. Jabbing Charlie in the arm, she lifted her hands in the universal "What in the hell was that?" hand signal.

Charlie grinned. When he spoke she read his lips. "Willy's Special."

She leaned over and looked at his LST. There were only four hot bodies out there now. Did they have their arms around each other?

Turning her face toward Charlie, she mouthed, "My boys?"

Nodding, he pointed to the four fiery blobs lighting up the screen. They were on their way back. "All clear. Enemy obliterated."

She didn't bother wiping at the tears streaming down her face. Her green make-up was bound to be smeared all over the place. Her boys were okay. Thank God. Jenna crawled over the peak of the hill and slid on her butt to the bottom. She surprised the guys and they all stopped walking.

She ran for Willy first.

"Jenna! What are you—?" he started to say.

She didn't give him a chance to finish. Grabbing his green-painted face, she kissed him with a resounding smack.

"Whoa," he muttered.

Tavon held his arm at the elbow. Gently, she placed her lips on his cheek. "I promised Mack I wouldn't kiss him."

"Shit. Did not expect that." Tavon laughed. "Hey, my arm feels better."

"I didn't promise that I wouldn't kiss you guys." Tugging on Ty's braid, she brought his face toward her and planted a sweet kiss on his lips.

"Well, now, isn't that a nice welcome—?" Ty started to say.

He was cut off when Mack growled, "Jenna! What in the hell—?"

"Sorry, Mack. I'm breaking my promise." She leapt into his arms. Wrapped around him like an amorous spider monkey she sealed her lips to his. She hadn't given Willy her tongue as he'd asked for. Nope, she'd saved that treat for Mack. She plunged in. All her fears, relief, and love poured into him. After a long, delicious, minute she pulled away. He was breathless. She didn't care if she ever breathed again.

"Holy shit," he whispered.

"Sincerely. Makes a guy want to go out there and shoot off another Willy's Special." Willy winked. "I'll do it, if I get a kiss like Mack's."

Ty and Tavon both slugged him.

Mack carried Jenna toward a grove of trees. "We'll be back in a few minutes. Jenna and I have some unfinished—"

Her lips stole his words. It didn't matter. The guys all knew what he meant.

**

They barely made it to the trees. Not because Jenna was heavy but because he couldn't wait anymore. He had to kiss her away from the guys, away from the battle. Just the two of them here and now. Pressing her back against a tree, he buried his face in her neck. She smelled sweet and felt so good. He wanted her so bad.

"Mack, I thought...Oh, God, if anything ever happened to you..." She trembled in his arms.

Pressing his forehead to her's, he gazed into her eyes. Damn, was she crying? "I'm here."

"I wouldn't survive it, Mack. I swear." The moon's light filtered through the trees just enough that he could see the sadness and want in her face.

His hands dove into her hair. It was on his tongue to say that he'd never leave her, but promises made during war were not always kept. And he wouldn't lie to her.

"I'm here," he repeated. It was the best he could do.

Gently, he placed his lips to hers. His heart pounded harder than it had back at the guerrilla's camp. Soon they were both working to catch their breath. He wanted her a thousand different ways. Even though he would have given his left nut to be able to lie down on a bed of leaves and make love to Jenna all night long, he didn't have that luxury.

"We'd better catch up with the guys," he said.

She took a deep breath, straightened her shoulders, and nodded.

He bent down and picked up the cap that had fallen off her head. Lifting her hair off her shoulders, he let the soft strands fall through his fingers before he pulled it back into a loose knot. Placing her cap back on her head, he looked deeply into her eyes. "You are so damned beautiful."

She caught his hand and pressed it to her cheek. "I thought I'd lost you."

He didn't know if she meant out there at the CRAF's campsite or eighteen months ago. It didn't matter. The crack in her voice did funny things to him. Heat punched deep inside and melted his heart like an old piece of chocolate.

"You didn't." While adjusting his H-gear—the chest-harness that carried his magazines and other shit—the truth pounded through his mind. Call it the eternal truth. "You can't. I'm not going anywhere."

"You mean it? After this is over, we can start again?"

He would be a damned fool to put his heart in her hands. Jenna Collins was a flight risk, a destroyer, a Mack killer. Leaving him eighteen months ago was a real whammy, worse than any of the surprise attacks his instructors pulled in BUD/S training. He never wanted to go through that again. But when she looked at him like that with heat and need, he had to take the risk.

"What do you think we've been doing?" he asked.

Lieutenant Commander Mack Riley had been called many things. In the dark, thick jungles of Colombia he added damned fool to the list. But he was happy. For this two seconds, anyway. He'd deal with tomorrow if they survived the night.

He opened his hand for her to take. She placed a warm kiss on the tip of his thumb and laced her fingers with his as they walked back to the team.

***

The guys were ready to move by the time Mack helped Jenna up the hill.

"That was fast." Willy's eyes twinkled with mischief.

"Careful, William. He's going to kick your ass," Charlie warned.

"Really, really fast," Willy teased. "Super-speed. Like I barely blinked and you were done. Like a teenager, Mack. Maybe you and I better have a talk about how to please a woman."

"Shut up!" Mack growled.

Jenna ignored the comments and the half-chuckles as she passed the Handly brothers. Those boys were hot, no question about it, but they couldn't hold a candle to Mack. She still felt the flames licking her insides from her brush with his fire. She wanted more. When this was all over, she'd love Mack for all she was worth. And never stop.

She went straight to Tavon. "How's your arm? Can someone shine a flashlight over here so I can see the injury?"

Charlie gave her his flashlight.

"Ty took care of it." Tavon turned his massive arm toward her. It was all bandaged up and still bleeding. Obviously much more than a flesh wound.

She winced. "It looks like it hurts." She flashed the light all over his large frame. "Your arm. Is that the only place you were shot?"

"Nah. I took three to the chest. Those bastards just knocked the wind out of me. I'd be sharing a beer with my Maker right about now if not for the body armor."

It was strange and horrible to talk about death so easily like it was an everyday occurrence.

"Your arm's still bleeding! Are you going to be able to use it?" Mack was getting a good look at Tavon's wound for the first time.

Tavon tried to lift the arm but it didn't move. "Damn, guess I'm going to have to be a lefty."

Mack cursed. "Have you ever shot with your left hand?"

"A few times." Tavon's face was grim in the light.

"Did you hit what you were aiming at those times?" Willy asked.

Tavon shook his head. "Not exactly."

The guys all cursed.

"This night is turning to shit." Mack swiped at his forehead. "It was risky before. I'm not sure how we are going to handle this without Tavon in top shape."

"I can help." All eyes were on her. "Ask Charlie."

Charlie looked up from his LST. "Yep. She took out one of the insurgents. I can hook her up with the smart weapon. She'll be almost as good as Tavon."

"No," Mack said. "Absolutely, not."

"You need me." The memory of shooting a stranger rolled through her. Had she really killed a man? That CRAF guy must not have worn body armor, or her shot had been exceedingly lucky. She could still see him falling face forward into the ground. The hair on the back of her neck lifted.

"It's too risky." Mack put his hand on her neck and the hair instantly settled down.

"I want to do this," she said softly. "We're running out of time. Let me do it."

Mack's cell buzzed. "Dammit. The man is persistent. It must be a family trait." His eyes cut toward her. "I'll be right back. You guys research the trail." He pulled out his cell and stepped away into the darkness.

"So? Am I in, or not?" Jenna asked the guys.

CHAPTER THIRTEEN

"**W**here in holy hell have you been?" Admiral Collins' voice roared through the phone.

Mack winced. "Colombia, sir. My team is in the process of tracking and rescuing hostages as you ordered."

"Don't chap my balls, son. I ordered you to keep my daughter safe at home. Where is she?"

Mack tapped his forehead. *Think. Come up with something good.*

"Lieutenant Commander! Answer the question."

"Yes, sir. She's with me."

Admiral Collins sucked in a sharp breath. "In war-zone-freaking Colombia?"

"That is correct. Sir."

Admiral Collins could rip a man's head off better than best of them. Mack waited patiently for his punishment. Instead of a brutally long tongue-lashing, there was a split moment of silence. Dropped call? Could he be that lucky?

"I will deal with you later. For now, listen." The voice coming through the phone was sharp and serious. "You need to get out of there. All of you. Now!"

"But sir, we're closing in on the hostages—"

"At this point, I don't give a rat's bunghole about the hostages. You get in that helo and fly. Hear me?"

How could he not? The admiral was shredding holes in his eardrums.

"Jenna won't want to leave without the Harmonds."

"Make her! At gunpoint if you have to."

The admiral was lucky that Mack wasn't standing toe-to-toe with him. "I will never point a weapon at Jenna. You hear me? Give me a damned reason to convince her to leave without her clients, and I'll consider shutting down the mission!"

Admiral Collins sucked in a breath. "All right. You don't have the clearance, but I say you've got the need to know. The President is taking offensive actions to stop the Coke War. An all-out bringin' in the rain air strike is ready to launch. By tomorrow, the guerrillas and cartels will be in hell."

All the blood drained from Mack's limbs. "Hold on. I'm sending you our coordinates."

"No need, son. I know where you are. I've been monitoring you by way of Jenna's cell phone. If you tell her I put a tracking device in there, I'll bloody your damned nose."

The SOB was devious. "Are we in the pathway of the air strike, or not?"

"Would I have told you I was tracking Jenna if you weren't?"

He squeezed his eyes tight. "How much time do we have?"

"Three hours. Max. Don't tempt your luck. Get your asses out of there. Immediately."

"Copy that." The world had just gotten a whole lot scarier. Jenna shouldn't be here. He jogged back to the team.

Jenna followed the shooting instructions on the iPad, trying to be the next spotter on the team. She'd never fill Tavon's massive shoes.

"Hey." Mack massaged her shoulders, kneading away the stress and ache.

"That feels so good." She melted under his hands.

He longed to put his hands all over her, nip her neck, plant kisses down her spine, nibble the tickle spots above her hip bones, fill his hands with her soft breasts, and make her moan. She'd arch her back and tempt him by pressing that sweet ass of hers against his erection. He could take her here and now, and make love to her for a month straight.

But there would be no month straight.

All he had was about sixty seconds, and even those were slipping away fast. This relationship, or whatever was happening between them, didn't stand a chance. Hell, it was doomed from the beginning. He was a SEAL who took orders and acted on them. Jenna didn't take orders, not from him, not from her dad, and she'd never forgive him for what he was about to do.

Leaving the little boy and his family behind in the kill zone of an air strike? Yeah, Jenna would be rabid. His heart sunk. She'd likely pound her fists against his chest, call him a murderer, and tell him to go to hell. He wouldn't blame her. But what could he do? He had to protect her. He had no choice.

She leaned into him, putting her head on his chest. "What did the old man have to say? No, let me guess. He wants me to come home immediately, right?"

He wrapped his arms around her, memorizing the feel of her in his arms for the last time.

"Mack?" She looked up at him. "What did he say?"

He let out a deep breath. "This time, we are going to listen to the old man. We're going home. Now."

"What?" She spun around to face him, breaking out of his arms. Anger sparked in her eyes. "Are you crazy? We're not leaving now."

"What's going on?" Tavon came up behind them. His arm was in a make shift sling.

"Get the guys. We need to bug out," Mack ordered.

She put her hand out and stopped the big man. "Don't do it, Tavon. We're not leaving until we have the Harmonds. Whatever the great admiral threatened you with, forget about it. You work for me, remember?"

Mack shook his head. "Babe, how would I forget? You remind me every five minutes."

"Good. Rescuing the family is more important than your career or whatever Daddy dearest is waving in your face." She started to walk away. "Don't answer his calls anymore, and let's get moving—"

"Stop." He grabbed her arm. "We've got to get back to the helo."

The guys gathered around.

"Why? I haven't heard any chatter. What's happening?" Charlie wondered.

"Armegeddon," Mack said. "The president is bringing the rain."

"No shit," Willy said softly. "An air strike here?"

Mack nodded, his gaze on Jenna. "Right on top of us."

"When?" Ty asked.

"Three hours, tops."

Willy slapped his thigh. "This is FUBAR. Can't they wait for us to rescue the Harmonds before they drop shit on us?"

"No, and we aren't waiting around here to become collateral damage," Mack said.

Jenna lifted her chin. "Then we'd better hurry and find the Harmonds."

"We don't have enough time," Mack growled.

"I say we try. Give it an hour and a half to look for the Harmonds before we, um, bug it. Please, Mack, we've got to try."

"Bug out," Willy corrected, bumping her shoulder. "And I like your style. I agree with the boss. I'd like to blow up a few more assholes before we get out of dodge."

"I'm in." Charlie grinned. "I'll monitor the channels. We'll know when the birds are in flight. That should give us enough time to get back to the helo before the ordnance hits the deck."

Ty scratched his chin. "It won't take me long to get the Knighthawk up. I say let's give it a go."

Tavon grimaced. "I'm not much help. But when have we ever turned tail?"

Mack's gaze went from face to face. "You guys serious? You want to do this?"

Tavon elbowed him with his good arm. "Stop thinking with your heart, bro."

Mack shook his head. "You guys are seriously insane. All right. Ninety minutes to find the Harmonds, and that's it. At ninety minutes and one second, we'll be running for the helo."

Instead of poking him in the chest with her long slender fingers, Jenna reached up and kissed his cheek. "Thanks, Mack."

"Thank me later if we get out of this mess. Let's rock and roll. HUMINT said to go north. We'd better run."

***

The guys ran, fast and silent. It was still dark and Jenna knew she wouldn't be able to see them if they got too far ahead.

"HUMINT?" Jenna gripped Mack's bicep.

"Human intel. The cartel hostages—before they were shot to death in the gunfight that got Tavon—said CRAF took the Harmonds north. I wish I had gotten more information. Would be nice to know if the Harmonds are still alive before we go deeper into the war zone."

She swallowed hard. "Yes. That would be nice."

They passed the campsite. The guys went straight through, but Mack took her on the outside edge of the battlefield, trying to shield her from the worst of it. What she saw, she'd never get out of her brain. The movies didn't do war justice. Bodies were strewn all over the place. The smell, the blood, the horror was almost more than she could bear. Mack led her by the shack where the captives had been held. The thing was completely leveled. God, he'd been in there!

Mack couldn't have known that the next dead man they came to was the one she'd shot. Even though it had been dark and far away, she knew the man by the way he was lying. She couldn't stop replaying the image of painting him in her scope, pulling the trigger, and watching him fall forward. Dead. Would she ever get that out of her head? Her teeth clattered. Her stomach flopped so badly she worried she'd be sick again. She gripped Mack's hand and closed her eyes. Wishing the scene away didn't make it so.

"Come on, babe. I've got you." Mack pulled her quickly through the destruction and back into the jungle.

As she held onto Mack, she steadied her breathing and told herself she was not a monster. The dead guerrillas were not good people. They had kidnapped an innocent family and were trying to kill her men. She'd done the right thing, the only thing, for Mack and the guys. She'd do it again if she had to. Let the devil deal with the evil bastards. She and the team were on the side of right and good. And later, once they were all safe, she'd go back to the therapist for a while and get her mind straightened out. She had a bad feeling she'd be shooting that guy over and over in her nightmares. But today, she'd box up and bury the dead in her mind. She had to keep fighting. It was the first time she understood what her dad did to survive.

Charlie was to the left of them, monitoring the radio and LST as he went. How could he do all that and keep an eye out for bad guys? She was barely able to fast-walk in the semi-dark without tripping and crashing into Mack. Willy was off to the right moving quickly, scanning the area, rifle up. Tavon was bringing up the rear, protecting their flank, silent and strong ready to shoot with his left hand.

"Where's Ty?" she asked quietly.

"He's up ahead searching for their trail." The words had just left his mouth when Mack pressed his ear piece to his ear. "Good. Ty reported in. He's got them. Can you run faster?"

Her feet were screaming expletives, her big toes and ankles sporting painful blisters, and her back ached. She was exhausted from lack of sleep and stress. But tonight she was learning she was stronger than she ever knew. With Mack close enough to touch, she could do almost anything. Why hadn't she understood *that* eighteen months ago? No. She couldn't think about her mistakes. For now, she was alive, and the Harmonds were still out there.

"Of course." She ran faster.

***

As they moved, Mack ground his molars. The admiral would have done him a favor if he'd been forthcoming up front. If Mack had known missiles would be heading this way, he'd have done things differently. For one, he would have tied Jenna to a bed in California to keep her from getting on the jet. Damned admiral. The man had a way of pulling strings without the team knowing about it.

Mack thought about the first date he'd had with Jenna. In those days, he'd been under the mistaken impression he was calling the shots—the man in control. The plan had been to seduce the girl in order to manipulate the admiral to save Tavon. How hard could it be?

On the second date Mack, knew he was in big trouble. The admiral's daughter was unlike any woman he'd ever met. He liked that. Maybe too much. In a tiny hole-in-the-wall that looked as if it should be straddling the Mexican border, he sunk his teeth into one of the best fish tacos in the universe and gazed into her eyes. "Holy shit."

"Good, right?" Jenna flashed him one of her pretty smiles.

"Friggin' delicious." He wiped the juice dripping off his fingers. "How'd you find these places?"

"Being a travel agent for EXtreme Adventures has its perks." She dipped her chip into the salsa. "I get to try out great restaurants and hotels, but I'm always on the lookout for gems that tourist companies miss. I want my clients to have the best trips of their lives. Unique food, excitement, the whole enchilada of adventures. It's more than a job to me." Her eyes sparkled when she talked about her work. There was nothing sexier than a woman who exuded confidence and passion.

"You travel a lot?"

"Corporate sends us on expeditions once a year to learn about different travel zones our clients might be interested in seeing. On my next trip, I'm going back to South America—Peru, Colombia, and Brazil. You ever been there?"

"South America? Um, I can neither confirm nor deny that."

"Ah, I get it. You're a Navy SEAL. Let me guess. Team Six, or the real name—DEVGRU."

He leaned closer. "I can neither confirm..." He rubbed her chin with his thumb. "...nor deny."

"I see." She tipped her head down and planted a quick kiss on his thumb. Sparks shot up his arm. "Well, if you ever find yourself in the small village of Salta, in northwest Argentina, I recommend Armando's Cafe. You'll think you have gone to heaven."

Wait, was she serious? His internal SEAL sense tingled. "Armando's? Is that what you said?"

"Uh-huh. Do you want me to write it down?"

"No, I think I could remember that. What's so special about that cafe? What we've got here is damned good."

She dipped a chip in salsa and fed it to him. "This food is good, but it's too...American. I like authentic foods that taste like the culture they came from. Home grown to the natives, exotic to me."

"Like guinea pig smoked in banana leaves?"

She blinked. "That's Armando's specialty. How'd you know?"

He didn't answer. It was no coincidence Jenna had been in that village. He didn't believe in coincidences when it came to top secret missions. What the hell was going on?

She studied him as if she could almost see the puzzle he turned over and over in his head. "You can't confirm or deny?"

"Exactly. We aren't having this conversation."

"Should I change the subject?"

"Nope. Tell me what you liked about Salta," he probed.

Her eyes flashed with excitement. "Everything! The people, the colonial architecture, the canyons, exploring the Cabra Corral dam area searching for ancient rock paintings, all of it. I could have stayed for months. Every day would've been a new adventure, but there was some sort of political shake up in Argentina and corporate pulled me out. I didn't get to say good-bye to Armando's little boy. He was the cutest little five year old ever. All boy. Dirty, loud, and sweet. I gave him a cheap plastic dump truck and you'd think I bought him the real thing. Gosh, he loved that truck."

Mack sat straighter. "A red plastic dump truck?"

She cocked her head. "Yes. How did you know?"

"Hell." He shook his head. He'd been played.

Months earlier, he and his team had been sent to Salta to eradicate a Nazi. Or rather a Nazi-copycat. The rat bastard was two generations too late for the real Holocaust, but idolizing the monsters of old, he'd thought he'd become the next Mengele of Argentina. People disappeared from the fields, hookers didn't show up to work, and wives didn't come home from the market. Bodies found in shallow graves had been tortured. The problem? No one was sure who the monster was. No one outside of

Argentina even cared, until an American exchange student turned up dead. The student's father was a U.S. Senator.

Mack and his guys had gone deep undercover, covertly digging up intel to identify the target. Once verified, Mack and his guys had made sure the Nazi stopped seeing the light of day. It had been a cut-and-dried take out mission. Or so he'd thought at the time.

Now he knew otherwise. While in Salta taking out the trash, apparently he was also looking out for the admiral's daughter. His intel about the Nazi threat had been passed onto the admiral, who in turn had pressured EXtreme Adventures to get Jenna out of there in a hurry. Mack had no idea that he'd been used until now.

"Mack?" Jenna's brown eyes widened with surprise. "You knew the truck was red."

"I can't talk about it. Nor can I say that Armando's little boy has a blue plastic battle ship too, a USS Arizona to be exact. Although, I'm sure he likes the truck better because he couldn't stop talking about the pretty lady who made funny truck noises with her mouth. You're right, that kid was cute."

"You were there," she whispered, her lips tantalizingly close.

"I can't believe I missed you."

"I'm here now." She palmed his cheek, drawing him toward her.

"Yeah, thank God for second chances." Mack pressed his lips to hers.

Electricity shot through him in a heat punch straight to his groin. Jenna's lips were full, soft, moist…amazing. She continued to cup his jaw, holding his face close while they deepened the kiss. His tongue ran along the seam of her lips, and she opened up. He explored, tasted, taking all he wanted until her tongue pushed back, demanding her own exploration.

He ran his fingers through her long hair, and she moaned softly. The admiral's daughter was smoking hot.

The waiter slid the check tray on their table, interrupting the moment.

Jenna pulled back, gaze locked onto his. "We better go. This place fills up fast."

"Yeah, let's go." He was already imagining her naked in his arms. If that kiss had been an indicator, she'd be fantastic in his bed. Or hers, he didn't care where. It was the *when* that was important. *Now* was his preference. He reached into his pocket for his wallet, and she put a hand on his bicep to stop him.

"My treat, remember?" She placed the cash in the tray.

"Babe, this whole evening has been one helluva treat. Can I take you home?"

She toyed with the placemat. "That's not a good idea. I have that rule about Navy guys."

"I'm on board with that rule. Absolutely. No other Navy guys. They're assholes."

She laughed. "All except you."

"I can be an asshole. But not with you." He was dead serious. "We've got something, Jenna. I know you feel it. Let's see what happens."

She chewed her lip. "What are you doing tomorrow night?"

"Taking you to dinner."

She grinned. "Great. I know this fantastic vegan infusion café."

He held his hand up. "Meat, babe. I'm a man. Feed me meat. How about I take you on a surprise adventure of my own?"

"I like adventures." Pink tinted her cheeks. He could only guess what she was thinking.

He was having plenty of adventurous thoughts of his own. "It's a date, then."

As they left the restaurant, he put the keys in her hand. She'd drive them back to her car. He wanted to wrap around her and hang on while the roar of the engine vibrated between their legs. This memory of her hot body against his would have to last until he saw her again.

And again.

And every minute he could get away from base to be with her.

Falling in love with the admiral's daughter had snuck up on him like the exquisite burn of Scotch that starts in your mouth, sizzles down your gullet, and warms your heart. It had only taken a few dates to know he was a Jenna-addict. More than that?

He never wanted to recover.

CHAPTER FOURTEEN

Jenna started noticing the bark on the trees and flowers on bushes. It was getting lighter. A pit filled her stomach. Would they be able to sneak in and get the Harmonds once the sun was up? On the heels of that worry came an even greater one—how much time did they have left before the air strike?

They were moving slowly now. CRAF guerrillas must be close.

Mack gave her hand a yank and pulled her backward behind a small tree. He touched her lips with his hand, motioning her to be quiet. He tucked her in behind him, shielding her body with his, and lifted his rifle. Without moving, she had a tiny peep hole over his shoulder.

A man appeared about twenty feet in front of them. He had an AK-47 and what looked like a large knife tucked into his belt.

"Stop! Don't come any closer!" Jenna mentally commanded the man.

But he didn't stop. He kept coming straight for them. He was so close Jenna could see the little wiry hairs in his mustache. Had he seen them? The tree was too thin to block them completely from his view. Jenna held her breath and tried to become invisible. She knew Mack had the man in his scope, but if he shot now, would the rest of CRAF guerrillas come running?

The man yawned noisily, unzipped his pants, and relieved himself. Without glancing toward the tree she and Mack were hiding behind, he zipped up and went back the way he came.

It took several long seconds before Jenna breathed properly again. That was close. Mack lowered his rifle and reached behind to touch her. He pulled her into his back and gave her a reassuring squeeze. She leaned into him, taking an infusion of his warmth and comfort. She didn't want to move. Maybe ever again.

But Mack had other ideas. He pointed to a stand of thick trees off to the left of them. He wanted her to go there. Alone? Heck, no. She shook her head.

He pointed again with a quick jab of his finger.

Nope. She wasn't going anywhere without him.

He tipped his head skywards as if asking God, "Why do I have to be saddled with this crazy woman who never does what I want her to do?"

It was a typical Mack move. And it made her smile. Mack was still Mack, even out here in the middle of all this hell.

He took her hand and they quietly, and carefully made their way to the stand of trees.

"Do. Not. Move," he whispered in her ear. "We're going in."

She wiggled her finger so that he would turn his ear to her. "Harmonds?"

"They've got captives. That's all I know."

She wouldn't let go of his hand. It was as if she was physically incapable of loosening her fingers.

Lifting his night vision goggles, he moved closer until they were eye-to-eye. "Wait for me."

Her eyes welled. "Forever."

The look on his face took her breath away.

"Jenna..." He loaded that one word with such feeling she knew it was the start of a huge discussion, maybe the start of a whole new life. He struggled with how to say what he was feeling. Or even if he should.

Just then, Charlie popped up next to them. "The team's in place."

He nodded. "Keep an eye on her, Charlie."

"Roger that. But the lady is an ace." Charlie grinned. "She doesn't need me."

Mack frowned. Cupping her jaw in his hands, he pressed his lips to hers and whispered what sounded like, "My girl."

Mack slipped into the shadows before she had a chance to tell him that she loved him. Just like that, her man was gone.

"Good, the team is ready," Charlie whispered to her.

She bent over his LST. To her horror, the new CRAF camp was loaded with men. Her guys were outnumbered five to one. Bringing her rifle around, she pointed it toward the camp. Her iPad was on and ready. She looked through the scope. The only thing in their favor was that many of CRAF were still asleep. If they could sneak in quietly...

Boom!

She jumped as the loud sound rocked through the jungle. If her finger had been on the trigger, she would have accidentally pulled it. Her throat was so dry she couldn't swallow.

"Flashbang," Charlie said. "Here comes another."

Boom! Boom!

Even though he had warned her, she wasn't prepared for it. She jumped even higher and grabbed Charlie by his camelback. Her guys were making that noise? So much for sneaking in.

"Hooya! Look, Jenna, got 'em on the run," Charlie cheered.

Jenna couldn't take her eyes off the computer screen. Men were running like scared rats and being dropped one by one. The flashbang grenades had disoriented the guerrillas, and her team was taking full advantage of the situation.

Charlie pointed at the screen. "Look, six guys face down right there. Bastards are smart. They gave up without a fight."

"And there?" Jenna pointed to a bunch of figures near a tree.

"Yep, one of our guys is tying them up to that tree. If I had to guess, I'd say it's Ty. He's great with knots."

Gunfire popped off like a giant popcorn machine. Jenna studied each dot on the LST. Where was Mack? The Harmonds? She positioned herself again, looking through the scope, ready to take out the guerrillas one by one if she had to.

Another blast made her finger twitch.

"Damn. That wasn't one of our grenades," Charlie said.

"What? Is the team…is everyone okay?" Her heart shook.

"So far so good." A much louder grenade blast shook the ground beneath her feet. Charlie raised his closed fist. "Go get 'em Willy!"

Jenna couldn't believe it. Four more CRAF were lying face down in the dirt. They'd surrendered! Maybe this crazy plan was going to work after all.

Charlie leaned forward and turned a dial on his radio. "No, shit, no, no!"

The quick movement startled Jenna, and she gripped the pack on his back. He glanced at her over his shoulder. She didn't like the flash of fear that registered in his eyes before he shut it down it.

"Can you read me?" Charlie spoke to someone on the radio. "Request a delay in that order. SEALs on the ground. Please respond. SEALs on the ground. Shit! They've gone dark."

"What is it?" She was afraid to ask.

"Damned Air Force pulled up the clock and launched the B-2 Stealth Bombers. We're out of time."

The air strike had started? "No! We've still got an hour, don't we?"

Charlie didn't answer her. "Mack! Birds in flight. Do you read me? Birds in flight and coming in hot!"

"How much time do we have?" she asked.

"Forty-five minutes, if we're lucky."

"The Harmonds. Did the guys get them out?" She asked.

Charlie shook his head. "Not yet. We need to move out of here in the next thirty or we're all toast." More grenade sounds made it difficult to think straight. He shouted into his headset mic. "Willy, Ty, Tavon, come in. We've gotta roll!"

This wasn't happening! They'd come this far. She couldn't leave without the kids. Was there a way to stop the air strike?

She pounded her pockets for her cell phone and dialed Kat.

"Jenna!" Kat answered on the first ring. "Where are you?"

"Shh. I'm in Colombia," she whispered. "Where did you think I'd be?"

"Oh, no. That's not good. You're not supposed to be there. Your SEAL, um Lieutenant Riley, wanted to leave you behind. You know, to keep you safe."

Jenna rolled her eyes. Of course he did. "I can't talk about that now. You need to call Senator Tonell. Tell him that the Air Force is launching the strike too soon. Oh, and call my dad too. We need more time to get out of here."

"Wait, you're in the jungle! Jenna, the news said that the air strike has begun!"

"Well, stop it! Get Tonell to do something!"

Kat let out a low whistle. "I'll try, Jenna. Be careful."

She hung up. The senator would slow the strike. He had to. If not, her dad should be able to do something, right?

"Help," a voice called behind her.

She swung around. Did she hear that? Or was her mind playing tricks on—

"Please...Jenna." A little voice came again.

Jenna looked at Charlie, but he hadn't heard the mystery voice. He was too busy calling the team members, listening to the radio, and trying to get through to the Air Force.

Jenna rose, slowly, quietly. Putting her hands on her hips, she squinted trying to make out any figures in the dusky light. Was that a little hand waving behind that thick bush? Jacob? Oh, my God! Jacob was alive? He escaped from the CRAF?

"Did you see that?" she asked Charlie.

Charlie waved her off. He was listening intently to the radio.

Fine, he had his hands full. She'd go get Jacob herself.

Moving quickly toward the bushes, her boots got tangled in the vegetation as she went. Jacob was much farther than she originally thought. Soon she'd run half a football field distance away from Charlie. She turned her head from side to side. What was that sound? She stopped in her tracks. Her heart pounded.

"Jacob. Come out of there," she whispered.

A small whimper came from behind the bushes.

"It's okay. Remember we said we'd walk out together? Come take my hand."

"I can't," Jacob whined. "I'm…trapped."

Jenna narrowed her eyes. Something wasn't right. "Trapped? Are you stuck?"

He groaned.

Was he embarrassed that he'd gotten tangled up in the bushes?

Biting her lip, she wondered what to do. If she went to help him, she'd be worse than exposed, she'd be out of sight. The guys wouldn't know where she was.

She raised her hands and waved at Charlie. "Over here!" she mouthed, afraid to yell at him.

Charlie looked her way. She was sure of it.

Jacob cried out. He was hurt, scared, or both.

"Shhh. I'm coming," she said softly. With all the hair standing up on her neck, she remembered what Mack had taught her and stalked toward the bush. She stopped suddenly when the picture before her didn't add up. Jacob was on his knees with his hands tied behind his back. A cloth was shoved into his mouth. His eyes were wide with fear. A trap!

She pointed her rifle toward the bushes, slowly sweeping from side to side. "Stay down, Jacob. Come out you bastards," she ordered.

A man stepped forward with an AK-47 slung over his shoulder. Pulling Jacob's hair, he dragged the little boy out of the bushes. Jacob tripped and fell to his belly on the ground. He was face down, whimpering.

Jenna leveled the rifle at the man. "Don't touch him!"

The man pointed his weapon at her. "Drop it, *mujer*!"

Another woman might have been shaking in her blisters-making new boots. But seeing the terror in Jacob's eyes as he trembled in the dirt was enough to snap the final straw. Jenna was pissed. Without any hesitation she aimed at the man's belly and pulled the trigger. The man grunted and stumbled, his bullets wildly spraying the air. None of them hit her, but more men rushed out from behind the trees. She shot again, missing this time.

Someone tackled her, driving her straight into the ground. She was yanked to her feet and a thick arm around encircled her neck. Her rifle was ripped from her arm. A pistol pressed against her temple. "Come with us, *mujer*. Do not make a sound."

This couldn't be happening.

"Charlie! Help—!" she screamed until something hit her on the back of the head.

Everything went dark.

CHAPTER FIFTEEN

Mack lined up his shot and pulled the trigger. The insurgent was dead before he knew what hit him. Mack lined up another shot. And another. CRAF fell like flies. He scanned the area. One bastard was shimmying up a tree, pushing his rifle in front of him. What did he think? He'd get to take pot shots at his guys from the branches? Hell, no. Mack put the guerrilla in his cross hairs and pulled the trigger. One less monkey in a tree.

Bullets flew wildly around the area, but CRAF were not the best marksmen, especially when on the run. Sort of like shooting monkeys in a barrel. More like turds in a fishbowl.

"Mack, over here," Ty called.

"Go. I got this," Tavon let loose another round of hellfire on CRAF. It turned out he was not too bad as a lefty.

Mack slipped away and found Ty standing over an underground wood door. He lifted his eyebrow. "What have we here?"

"I don't think it's a wine cellar. Open it?" Ty asked.

Mack aimed at the door and held up his fingers. *Three. Two. One. Execute.*

Ty swung the door open and two dirty faces peered up at them from the depths.

"Are you the Harmonds?" Mack asked.

The nodded their heads.

Holy hell! They were alive! "Wow, I know someone who is going to be happy to see you." He was already anticipating the loving Jenna would spring on him when he brought the Harmonds out of this hellhole. He grinned. Yep, he'd play up this rescue for a whole lot of naked time with Jenna. A lifetime full.

Gunfire slowed down in the camp and things were quieting enough so that Charlie's call came through Mack's headset loud and clear. "Mack! Birds in flight. Do you read me? Birds in flight!"

"Are you shitting me?"

"B-2s, fully loaded. I couldn't stop them," Charlie said. "The streets are getting hot in Bogota. But intel says the leaders are hanging out here. Right where we're standing."

"Dammit! They can't wait another hour to blow them away?" Mack snarled. Then he realized that the scared people in the hole had no idea why he was raving. They hadn't heard the delightful news that they were all about to get blown sky high. "Sorry. We've got to be quick about this. Ty, jump in there and hoist them up. I'll pull from this side."

Marcella Harmond came out first. Mack removed her gag and cut the ropes on her arms.

"Thank you, oh my God. I never thought I'd see Americans again." She sucked in a deep breath. "Please, help my husband. He's injured."

"Nice and easy, Ty." Mack didn't really need to give instructions. Ty had a way with people and animals unlike anything Mack had ever seen. Carefully, they both lifted the injured man out of the hole and untied his hands.

Marcella cried hysterically, "The kids! Where are they?"

Mack swept the dark hole with his flashlight. It was empty. "When did you see them last?"

Andrew's voice was weak but he managed to say, "Not since we were yanked out of the car in Quito."

"Dammit to hell!" Mack exploded. "Charlie, the kids. Do you see them on the satellite?"

A grenade went off.

"Shut that crap up, Willy! I can't hear," Mack snarled. "Charlie! Do you read me? Where are the Harmond kids?"

"Ah, Mack, we've got a big problem," Charlie said.

"I know. Stealth Bombers are winging their way here and we are missing two kids."

"That's not all. Jenna's missing too."

He couldn't form the words, any words, to scream at Charlie.

"Sorry, Mack. They've got her. CRAF guerrillas took Jenna hostage."

Mack's world turned to shit.

***

Jenna woke up. Or at least she thought she was awake. Why couldn't she see? She wasn't dead. The excruciating pain slicing like a jagged blade through her head proved that point. Where was she? She tried to move and couldn't. Her arms were behind her back, and she was tied to a chair. Sweat dripped down her chest and landed on her bare legs. Damn it! They'd stripped her. She was in her tank top and panties. Bastards! Did they get a good long look at her? Touch her when she was unconscious? Fine. That was all they were going to get. If they tried to touch her again, Mack would pulverize them.

Part of the problem was not being able to see. Being blindfolded was never her idea of fun. Even in the bedroom, she liked to see what was going on, be in control. This wasn't control.

This was terror. Panicking, she screamed and gagged on the rag in her mouth. Coughing and choking, she had the irrational terror that she couldn't get enough air through the small opening they left for her nostrils. Was she going to suffocate?

No! Jenna, focus. Calm your pulse rate.

It took a few long seconds of thinking she was going to die before she realized she could breathe through her nose just fine. She forced herself to take more even breaths. Slowly in, slowly out. Her heart rate went down and she was able to think again.

She tried as hard as she could to see through the fabric wrapped around her eyes. Shadows? Light? No, it was pitch black in her world. She might as well have been blind.

She tried to fight, rock, and hop up and down. Struggling against the binding didn't work. Wiggling and thrashing only tightened the ropes that bound her wrists. The skin on her inner arms burned and the knife inside her head turned sharply. Her stomach rolled from the pain. Panic tried to race through her again.

No! I'm stronger than this. She'd been through many scary times and survived. This one was no different. Well, okay, it was very different, but the outcome would be the same. She'd win. All she had to do was think positive thoughts. Good thoughts.

Taking calming breaths, she focused her mind on Mack's beautiful eyes and the curve of his smile. God, he was so beautiful. He was also safe and strong. Could there be anything more comforting than falling asleep in his arms, her head resting on his rock-solid chest? And the way his angled face went soft after they'd made love…she inhaled softly. There was nothing more beautiful, more serene, than Mack's face resting in the afterglow.

Her heart slowed. Keeping Mack front and center in her mind was the key. She took a deep breath and started screaming.

"Heeeeeellllpppp!" She tried to yell through the rag, concentrating on not gagging as she did.

"Shh," someone whispered.

She turned her head and listened.

"Jacob?" Some noise seeped through the cloth in her mouth. Footsteps pounded close by, hard and heavy. Angry sounding, those were no little boy feet.

She yelled again.

"*¡Silencio!*" A man snarled in her ear.

The smell of sweat, dirt, and old booze hit her nose, and she gagged again.

"Please, let me go!" She begged, trying to make him understand. But the words were only a jumbled mess of syllables caught inside the rag.

A vicious slap to her cheek made her see stars in all that blackness. She pulled back, stunned and frightened. Would the bastard strike her again?

"Don't hurt her!" a little voice cried. "Jenna, it's me, Jacob."

She turned her head toward the sound of Jacob's voice and tried to call out to him. Incomprehensible noises got tangled up in the rag in her mouth.

The smelly creep slapped her again, so hard this time that her hair fell over her face. The old terror she used to feel as a little girl came roaring back. The smell of alcohol. The need to run, or hide from Mom. Get away! She couldn't breathe, couldn't think. But this bastard wasn't Mom, and if she didn't get a hold of herself, he might hurt the kids. Her panic eased back, and now she was really mad. Fighting mad. If she could get free, she'd bloody this guy's nose. Who hits a tied up blindfolded woman? Her face burned like fire, but she would not let him see her sweat. She flipped her hair back and sat up as straight as she could. Defiant, bold. Her new plan was to channel her inner SEAL and rise above this.

When Mack gets a hold of you, dude, you'll be wearing your balls around your neck.

The image made her smile. She heard the creep mumble something in Spanish and stomp away. A door closed.

Oh, God, Mack. Did he know she was taken captive? Was he still alive? He had to be. She wouldn't let herself think otherwise. She forced herself to pull away from the danger at hand and think good thoughts. Nice thoughts. Keep the terror at bay.

Just like she used to do when Mom hurt her.

As a little girl, she'd learned a coping device. Think good thoughts and take your mind to other places far away from the danger and the fear. Leave the bad place behind. This moment was similar and Jenna would survive it by focusing on what made her happy and whole. Mack.

When he came for her, they'd go back to California and start a beautiful life together. Baby Mackies were next on the list. How cute would his children be? She could only imagine his baby's beautiful blue eyes and dark hair. They might have her stubbornness, but that was okay. She could deal with it as long as she had Mack. She wanted that dream more than anything else, and she was going to have it.

If the guerrillas didn't torture her to death and the bombs didn't kill them all.

No, no, no. Stop it!

No negative thoughts. Number one on her plan was to survive. She'd keep Mack first in her mind and find a way to escape.

"Mmmrrrr," she mumbled. It wasn't a word, but she hoped Jacob would respond. She needed to know that he was okay.

"Jenna, don't move, okay? Don't scream. Don't do anything unless they tell you to. Please, Jenna." Jacob whispered somewhere to the left and behind her. "They don't like it if you disobey."

That didn't sound good. Had they hurt him? Oh, no. Anna! Where was she?

"Annnnnaaaaa!" Jenna screamed. "Annnnnaaaaa!"

"Shh, Jenna, please be quiet," Jacob whispered.

"Jenna?" A girl sniffled somewhere behind and to the right of her. "Is that you?"

Anna. Sweet Lord, thank you.

"Of course it is," Jacob said. "Who do you think it is?"

"I can't see her very well. It could be any lady in her underwear."

"It's Jenna. They brought her in while you were sleeping. She was all slumped over. I thought...I thought she was dead." Jacob said to Anna.

"You said she was going to rescue us," Anna hissed. "How's she supposed to do that if she'd tied up and bleeding?"

"I dunno."

"Heelllpmmmeee." Jenna rubbed her wrists back and forth trying to loosen her ropes.

"We can't help you since our hands are tied behind our backs," Anna said. "You're lucky they put you on a chair. Jacob and I are tied together on the dirty floor. There are rats down here, Jenna. Big fat ones with sharp teeth. And gross black bugs. I want to go home."

Jenna sighed. She did too.

"Did you see Mom and Dad?" Jacob asked.

Jenna shook her head and continued to struggle.

"Tell her to stop making noise and wiggling so much. They're going to hit her again. I can't stand to see that," Jacob whined.

Anna sniffled. "Whatever. She's not much help to us, is she?"

"Shut up! That's a horrible thing to say."

Anna didn't respond.

She had to get them out of there. She had no idea how long she'd been unconscious. The bombs could be dropping in any minute.

"Hellllppp!" she yelled again.

"Please, Jenna," Jacob begged. "Do as they say. No more yelling. No one can hear us, and they are just going to hurt you. Please, stop."

Jenna nodded, but only to calm Jacob down. She was going to yell her lungs out if she thought the team could hear her. She didn't care if the bastards slapped her around a little if she and the kids were rescued.

"Quiet!" Anna hissed.

"They're coming back. Pretend you're asleep," Jacob said.

Jenna heard a lot of scrambling behind her, followed by fake deep sleep breathing. Just as Jenna had learned to cope with her own mother, it seemed the kids had learned a lot about how to cope with their captors. Apparently, sleeping children were left alone.

Men stomped into the room. By the sound of the boots on the wood floor, at least three men had surrounded her. She started to tremble. Sweat drops landed in a constant drip on her thighs. Dear God, what were they going to do? The anticipation was just as bad as a slap across the face. But if they raped her in front of the kids...

"Heeelllllpppp!" she screamed.

The blindfold was ripped from her eyes. The scream died in her throat. The blinding light focused on her face surprised her. Another light, smaller and bright red blinking back at her. A camera.

"Tell them," a man said in a thick Spanish accent. "Tell the U.S. President to make the planes go back. No bombs on us. We got women and children here. CRAF good. The cartel very bad people. Drop bombs on them!"

Jenna took a second to comprehend the situation. They were asking her to tell the U.S. to drop the bombs on the cartel, not on them. The irony of the situation got to her. CRAF guerrillas were good? Is this why they kidnapped the Harmonds so that they could persuade the U.S. to help them fight the Coke War?

They shot Andrew Harmond and beat him up. She was stripped almost naked and had been slapped silly by these so-called good men. Who knew what they were going to do to her after she pleaded their case to the President. Rape, torture, death—these were not nice things. And at the moment, neither was she.

Jenna looked straight into the camera. She was ready to talk.

***

Mack's head was exploding. CRAF had surrendered pretty easily for a bunch of armed guerrillas. Their hands were tied together with duct tape, their weapons confiscated.

"Where are they?" Mack yelled for the tenth time.

"*¿Dónde estan los niños? ¿La mujer?*" Ty asked.

The men shook their heads and cowered. Not one of them would say where Jenna or the kids were. It was as if they didn't know.

Mack growled in frustration. "What's the Spanish translation for 'I'm going to boot your sorry asses to Siberia if you don't talk'?"

"Maybe they don't know. The leaders could be keeping the captives separate and don't tell the grunts where they have them hidden. It wouldn't be the first time. Remember Somalia?" Tavon said.

"We don't have time to beat the truth out of them, no matter how much we want to. Radio reports say the B-2s are less than thirty minutes out. The clock's ticking and bombs are on the way," Charlie reminded them.

"You need to find my children," Marcella Harmond called out from under a shade tree. "Please. Go get them."

Sure, lady, I'll get right on that. Mack's fists balled at his sides.

"This is my fault. Jenna warned me something like this could happen." Andrew Harmond hung his head. "I should have listened."

"Please be still, Mr. Harmond. I'm almost done." Ty cleaned the man's wounds and was bandaging a nasty bloody scrape on his arm.

Harmond had been shot twice at close range. The bullet to the leg had gone straight through without nicking the major artery. The other bullet had simply grazed his temple. The man was one lucky son-of-a-gun. Of course he'd been beat up pretty good too, but it was clear the man would live to make another billion bucks. Ty would see to it.

"Sorry. It's so hard to sit here." Andrew said to Ty. "Don't you see? I didn't listen to Jenna, I didn't think of the consequences, and now she and our children are out there in the hands of armed guerrillas."

Marcella wailed all over again.

"If they die—" Andrew began

"Shut the fuck up!" Mack growled.

Andrew blinked. "I beg your pardon—"

"You can't speak to my husband that way!" Marcella whined. Jeez, her voice got on Mack's last nerve.

"You too, lady. Close your trap, or I'll close it for you."

Her mouth promptly closed.

He stomped over to where they were sitting. "No one's dying on my watch. Do you hear me? No. One."

Everyone was silent.

Towering over the wounded man, Mack leaned in so that they were eye-to-eye. Andrew pulled back as if he was uncomfortable with the invasion of his personal space. Good. Mack didn't give a flying shit about what the man thought.

Mack leaned in again. "I understand you've been under a bit of stress, Andrew. I mean, hell, you were shot twice, and your face has been run through a cheese grater, but I will not listen to

160

your voice of doom. Jenna is out there! Do you hear me? I am more than ready to kill every guerrilla and drug dealer in this jungle to get her back. I might just kill the bastard who brought us all here in the first place too. Is it your fault we're in this mess? Hell, yes it is. You stay away from me. Got it?"

Andrew nodded.

"Good."

Mack spun around and saw the guys all staring at him. "What!"

"Nothing. It's just...whoa, Mack, are you okay?" Willy asked.

Tavon rolled his eyes. "Does he look okay? Come on, give the man a break."

Charlie was sitting on a stump, studying his cell phone. "Ah, Mack. I think you want to see this."

It was obvious that Charlie Handly was treading lightly where Mack was concerned. Jenna disappeared on his watch, and Mack was about to rip someone's head off. Charlie's blond head made for a perfect target.

"What?" Mack barked.

"Careful, brother. Charlie's not the enemy. Neither is Andrew." Tavon's large hands squeezed Mack's arm, not lightly. The pain helped to center him.

Waving his cell phone, Charlie said, "A transmission. It's close, real close. And it's a live feed."

Mack raced to Charlie's side. All the guys surrounded him.

"What is it?" Willy asked. "What are they recording?"

Ten seconds later they got their answer when the blindfold was ripped off Jenna's face.

A strip of long blonde hair hung over her face. Her beautiful brown eyes looked into the camera. They were wide with shock and fear. Her full lip was split and bleeding. The rosy outline of a handprint marred her soft cheek. She'd been stripped down to her white tank top and pink underwear. Fury bucked and rolled through Mack like a wild bull. He'd kill those sons of bitches!

He didn't know he was roaring, until Tavon punched him hard in the shoulder. He didn't feel any pain except in his heart. Jenna, sweet, Jenna.

Ty got in his face and performed some sort of Apache Jedi mind trick on him. "Be still, Mack. We've got to study this for ambient sound and visual clues. Her life depends on us."

"Ty's right. But if you can't watch, we understand." Willy's usually sparkling green eyes were full of sadness, grief. The dimples were gone. He didn't look like such a big goofy kid anymore. But he couldn't have felt as old as Mack did right now. Mack was dying.

Rubbing his shoulder, Mack gritted his molars as if they were CRAF bones, and stared at Jenna on the cell phone. He longed to touch her and get her the hell out of there. But all he could do was watch and plot his revenge.

"Tell them," a man off screen said in a thick Spanish accent. "Tell the U.S. President to make the planes go back. No bombs on us. We got women and children here. CRAF good. The cartel very bad people. Drop bombs on them!"

Jenna didn't speak for a second. Mack watched her swallow, and he found he was unable to do the same. His mouth was bone dry, his heart seizing in fear. Holy hell, this was the worst torture he'd ever endured. He wasn't sure he'd survive it. But he would survive to save Jenna.

"Tell them!" the bastard off screen demanded.

He was so going to rip that CRAF sucker's lungs out through his asshole. And take pleasure doing it.

"Shh," Charlie said to him.

Apparently, Mack had voiced his graphic desires out loud. He was losing his mind. Mack glared at Charlie, who was lucky he didn't have Mack's size eleven boot wedged in his colon.

Jenna sat up straight and tipped her chin up. She was proud, defiant. The fear in her eyes dimmed back. The strength that Mack had come to love shimmered right there on the surface.

"That's my girl," Mack whispered to her. "Don't let them get to you. Hang on."

There was no way she could have heard him, and it was impossible for her to be looking straight into Mack's eyes, but he sensed that she was.

"I'm here, babe. I'm coming for you."

CHAPTER SIXTEEN

Jenna licked her lip and tasted blood. She focused on the camera and visualized Mack standing in front of her, his deep blue eyes boring into her soul. She might never see the love of her life again. She had to make this good. Make him understand.

"Mack, are listening? God, I hope you can hear me. I love you, Mack Riley." Her voice quivered. She took a deep breath, fighting the tears, losing the battle. "Always have. You are my life, my soul, my every dream. I thank God I had a chance to touch you again. It'll never be enough. It's going to have to be. Get the guys out of here. Now! Go! Drop the bombs on these CRAF bastards and send them all straight to—!"

The blow to her cheek was so vicious that the chair flew backwards. She hit her head. All pain ended.

***

The live feed went dead.

Mack didn't roar. He didn't cuss. He didn't rip anyone a new one. He stood there motionless. Dead already.

"Brother, we're going to get through this." Tavon pounded his back. "We're going to get her out of there."

Mack couldn't hear anything except the slap to Jenna's beautiful face. It was as if he'd been clobbered upside his own head. Her chair flew backward. He burned with rage. Those bastards were going to pay. If she hit her head, she might be unconscious. She might bleed to death...His heart pounded so hard he couldn't see straight. For the first time in his life, he understood the terror Jenna felt when he went off to war. He just got her back. He couldn't lose her now.

"Yeah, well we'd better hurry. The radio report says the B-2s are in Colombian airspace," Willy said.

"I found her!" Charlie cheered. "Did you hear me, Mack? I know where they've got her!"

The only thing Mack could hear was Jenna's voice. "I love you, Mack Riley...Always have. You are my life, my soul, my every dream..."

"Where?" Ty asked. "Let me see the coordinates."

Charlie pointed to the LST screen and Ty memorized them. "Got it."

"Let's roll!" Willy jumped up and swung his rifle over his shoulder.

"No. Wait. What about the Harmonds?" Ty asked.

"Right. What do we do with them? We can't leave them here," Tavon said.

Ty stood up. "I'll take them with me to the helo, come back, and pick you guys up."

"Sounds good." Willy agreed. "That way we can bug out of this hellhole once we've got Jenna and the kids."

"Okay. I'll grab the Harmonds. See you all soon. Kick the bastard in the balls an extra time for me. No one hits our Jenna and lives to tell the tale." Ty lifted his fist. "Hooya!"

"Hooya!" The others repeated

Mack still hadn't moved. His gaze was fixed to the blank cell screen, willing her to come back on and say she was all right. If she wasn't all right—

"Hello!" Willy waved his hand by Mack's face. "Jeez, it's like he's in a trance."

Tavon shook his head. "He's heartbroken. I've seen this same shit before. Hell. Jenna was the problem then too. He barely lived through it."

"What are we going to do?" Charlie asked. "I screwed up. It's my fault they got her. I'd let him punch me in the face. Crap, I'd let him knock me unconscious if it would help. But I don't think it'll help."

"No. He needs to go save her. That's all. Sorry, brother, but I've gotta do this." Tavon hauled off and hit Mack again. Harder this time. The dislocated shoulder popped back into place.

Mack roared. "Tavon! So help me God, if you hit me one more time, I'll trade you to the cartels!"

"And he's back." Tavon grinned.

"What are we waiting for? Jenna needs us." Mack knocked Tavon under the chin with an upper-cut.

Tavon shook his big head. "I guess I deserved that."

"More than. But we're not even."

"We've got children to save too!" In a surprise attack, Willy knocked Tavon under the chin too and jumped back out of the way.

"Hey!" Tavon complained, wiggling his jaw.

"And U.S. missiles to dodge!" Charlie raised his fist. Tavon gave him such a murderous look that Charlie dropped his hand. "Um, yeah. Let's go."

They all took off at a run.

***

Jenna woke up. At least her eyes were open under the fabric. Blindfolded again. Oh, wow, she'd never been hit that hard in the face before. Her entire head ached—her eye sockets, her teeth, her nose—major pain. The back of her head hurt too. Was she bleeding? There was no way to tell without her sight or hands. She sniffed. The room smelled musty, with a faint hint of dirt and jungle. Something big rustled behind her. The kids?

"Jenna? Are you awake?" A tiny voice said.

"Jacob?"

"I'm here too, Jenna," Anna said. "Are you feeling okay? They hit you real hard. I'm sorry for what I said before. I don't want them to hurt you or us. I just want to get out of here."

She opened her mouth and wiggled her jaw around. It didn't seem broken. Hey! No rag in the mouth! That was an improvement, at least.

"Yeah, I'm okay. What's happening out there? How long have I been sleeping?" She acted as if she'd taken a nice long siesta instead of being knocked unconscious by guerrilla thugs. Again.

"You've been out about five minutes, maybe? They've been arguing a lot," Jacob whispered. "I don't know what they're saying, but they sound angry and maybe a little scared."

"Good. We want them scared. They know the good guys are coming to get us."

"When? I want to go home!" Anna cried.

"I know, sweetie, I do too. We just have to be patient."

"I'm tired and hungry, and I want my mom."

"Quiet. You want them to come in here and slap you too?" Jacob warned.

Anna whimpered.

"My team is coming. It won't be much longer now." Jenna's voice rang with more confidence than she owned.

She hoped the guys had been able to track the video feed to their location. If anyone could find her with that short transmission, Charlie could. But time was running out. How long before the bombs dropped? She had no idea but sensed it would be soon. She wanted to be saved and get the kids out, but she wanted Mack and the guys to be safe too. Lord, it was an impossible situation. She wouldn't fault the team if they left her behind. It's what she'd asked them to do. Ordered, really, and she was still the boss.

"Be safe, my love." Her tears soaked through the blindfold.

"What did you say, Jenna?" Jacob asked.

"Nothing." She sniffled. "Listen, are you kids still tied to one another?"

"Yes," Anna said. "Unfortunately. He's really, really stinky."

"You don't smell so great yourself."

"Hey! Stop it!" Anna said.

"You stop it!" Jacob grunted.

Were they shoving each other? It couldn't be too easy to be bound together all this time. "Guys. Guys!"

Just then, Jenna's cell phone went off. "Where's that coming from?"

The kids scrambled to search for it.

"In your pants. Up on the table. I can almost reach…" Anna struggled.

The phone kept ringing. Was it Mack? "Hurry!"

"There! I've got it—"

Crash.

The phone fell to the ground. Jenna could tell by the sound that it had slid away from them. The phone stopped ringing. Her heart sunk.

"Sorry, Jenna," Anna said. "It slipped out of my hands."

"Good going! What if it was Mom and Dad? Now none of us can reach it."

"I said I was sorry! I didn't mean to drop it. Really, Jenna."

"It's okay," Jenna sighed. "Good try."

The phone made a short beep.

"That sounded like a text! Can either of you read what it says?" she asked.

"I can. Almost. Sort of," Jacob said.

"Try real hard," Jenna encouraged.

"Okay. Something about..." He strained. "Tonell says, um, some words I can't read, sorry it's really far away, but at the end it for sure says 'remember the code. And then a bunch of words followed by... "No good. Take cover.'"

It wasn't Mack. It was a text message from Kat and she didn't need all the words to know that they were in deep trouble.

"What does it mean?" Anna asked.

She didn't answer the question. "Can you both wiggle in under a table or behind a piece of furniture?"

"Huh?" Jacob asked.

"Like that little table?" Anna asked, probably pointing. Jenna couldn't see anything through her blindfold.

"Why, Jenna? What's going on?" Jacob's voice was serious again. Worried.

You and me both, kid. "See if you both can fit under the table. Make sure your heads are covered." Jenna took a deep breath. "We're going to protect ourselves."

"What did the text mean 'take cover'? Does it have to do with the bad guys?" She could hear the terror quivering on the edge of Jacob's every word.

She didn't want to scare the kids, but they had to be prepared. "The U.S. Air Force is going to drop bombs on CRAF guerrillas—the bad guys."

"The Air Force is coming to rescue us? Isn't that great, Jacob? We're going home!" Anna cheered softly.

Jacob didn't say a word. Somehow he knew the truth—the Air Force wasn't coming to save them. No one was going home.

***

Mack was one with the tree he hid behind. Not moving, barely blinking, he made himself blend into the bark. The tree was far too skinny to cover him completely. The best he could hope for was concealment and visual camouflage. Since the sun had come up, it was getting harder to remain hidden. The other guys had their own tree shields and were all doing the same things he was—scanning the new CRAF camp, searching the perimeter, marking the rat bastards, and looking for the best shots. They were outnumbered at least four to one. Lousy odds.

But the guerrillas out there were bottom-dwellers. They hadn't gone through Hell Week in BUD/S training. They didn't have hard-won Trident pins pounded into their chests. They didn't risk their lives for their country, or justice, or freedom. The guerrillas were nothing more than yellow-bellied mongrels who kidnapped women and children for ransom. Who does that shit? Worse, they'd hurt the love of his life.

Mack wanted to rip their heads off.

"B-2s, ETA?" Willy asked in the headset.

"Fifteen minutes," Charlie replied.

"You guys cover me while I go in. Then get the hell out of here," Mack ordered.

"Hell no," Tavon growled.

Mack only moved his eyeballs toward Tavon. "Have Ty fly you all out of range until the air strike is over then come back and get me and Jenna. I'll rescue her and the kids. We'll go to ground if we can. It's our only chance."

"Double hell no," Willy said.

"Triple to the hell no," Charlie pitched in.

Mack's lip twitched. He knew that's what they'd say. SEALs don't leave team members behind. Ever. Even if their lieutenant commander orders them to. They were all going to stay put and see this thing to the fiery explosive end.

Charlie pointed toward a wooden cabin that was hotly guarded. He held up three fingers.

"Hostages?" Mack whispered into his headset.

Charlie nodded and pointed toward the ground. All three hostages were on the floor. Good, maybe they'd be safe and clear of errant gunshots. Or did Charlie mean they were passed out on the floor? Injured? He swallowed hard and forced his insides to stop quivering.

"Ready?" Mack asked.

Before the others could respond, a commotion broke out in the CRAF camp. Two men started arguing and a shoving match began. One of the men pointed to the sky and hollered like a crazy man. Had he seen the B-2s? Sweet Mother, were the bombers already here?

The man kept yelling and pointing at the sky. Suddenly, his terror got the best of him and he took off running from the group. The other guy didn't say a word. He pulled a pistol out of the back of his pants and shot the runner in the back. The runner cried out, pulled up short, and landed in the dirt. He lay there twitching and begging for mercy. The shooter's chest puffed up like a fighting cock's. He stood over the downed man and put a bullet in his head.

What in the hell was *that* about? The rest of the guerrillas stood stock-still, as if waiting for...what? Why didn't they move? React? Speak?

Then it hit Mack. The shooter was CRAF's leader—the big honcho himself. He obviously didn't want any of his men to leave. He knew the bombs were coming and yet he still demanded his men to stay put and fight it out with B-2 Stealth Bombers. He was a total psycho.

"Leader, oh twelve hundred," Mack whispered.

"Agreed," Tavon replied.

Mack's blood went hot. Was this the guy who'd slapped Jenna? If not, he was the one who'd ordered it done. Mack looked through his Leupold ten-power scope and put the honcho in his cross hairs. It would be a pleasure to end the world of this filth.

"Three, two, one, execute!" Mack ordered.

He pulled the trigger and for the first time in his life, nothing happened. What the hell? The three hundred Win Mag jammed? It was a first. Shit, this day was getting better and better. The crack of gunfire went off all around him. The team was moving in, taking their shots. Guerrilla rats scrambled.

Through his scope, Mack saw that the leader was on the move. Mack didn't hesitate. Pulling out his SIG SAUER P-226, he ran toward the fighting. He'd kill that honcho one way or the other and save the girl.

Or die trying.

CHAPTER SEVENTEEN

Gunfire shattered the jungle, coming close and closer to the shack where Jenna and the kids were being held. Guerrillas? Cartel fighters? Jenna listened with all her might. An explosion went off and CRAF guerrillas yelled. Another explosion. Rapid fire. It was chaos out there.

She smiled.

"Is it the Air Force?" Jacob whispered. It was clear the kid was terrified. "Are those the bombs?"

It wasn't the Air Force. It was Willy and his bag of tricks. "No. Those aren't the bombs. My friends are out there and coming to rescue us. They are Navy SEALs."

"No way! Really?" All the worry evaporated from his voice.

"Why would we be happy about stupid seals? I want the Air Force to fly us out of here. I want to go home!" Anna whined.

"Not sea mammals, dummy. Navy SEALs—the toughest, baddest dudes in the military."

Jenna couldn't fault that description. To her knowledge, they were also the sexiest, buffest, damnedest good looking men on the planet. And one of them in particular had her completely wrapped around his finger. And any other body part he wanted her to wrap around.

"That's right, Jacob. They're coming to get us out of here, but to be safe we still need to take cover."

"Because of the bombs? If the SEALs are here, won't the bombers turn around and go back?" Jacob asked. He was a smart kid.

"No. The air strike is still on." She had no idea how much time they had, but her gut said none.

Hurry, Mack!

***

CRAF knew they were coming. That was the only explanation for how quickly the guerrillas responded to the team's attack.

The guerrillas either had good intel or just suspected this was how it would go down. Mack guessed the latter. After all the crap those guerrillas had pulled, they had to know the U.S. military would come after them sooner or later. But there was no way in holy hell that they would ever have predicted how hard Mack and his guys were coming. This wasn't just war. This was personal. Those CRAF sons of bitches had taken a team member and beat the shit out of her on television.

They were going to pay hard.

"Go! Go!" Mack ordered and the team spread out, firing as they went.

Bullets flew at them right and left. The team kept moving.

CRAF bodies added up, but those who stayed alive kept firing rifles, handguns, semiautomatics of every shape and size. Mack could tell by the *snap, snap* that went off around his head, that there were a couple of submachine guns in the mix too. Those bad boys fired subsonic rounds that traveled faster than the speed of sound. It was as if someone was clapping sharply in his ears.

Mack aimed, fired, dropped a man, and repeated. Over and over. He didn't slow, didn't stop. Everything around him was a blur of bullets, screaming, and death. The guerrillas kept firing their shit at him, and he kept punishing them for it.

"Mack! Oh three hundred!" Tavon yelled.

He turned in time to see five guerrillas lock and loading behind a truck. Tavon took out one of them—that left hand of his was turning out to be pretty damned accurate—but the other four hostiles were still actively firing. They had AK-47s and a rocket-propelled grenade. Mack tried his long-range three hundred Win Mag again. This time it worked. He hit his target and the man holding the RPG was dead on his feet. A second after his body hit the ground one of his guerrilla buddies picked up the RPG and aimed it at them again. Son of a bitch! Mack took aim.

Willy lobbed special grenade magic from his bag of tricks. The truck exploded. Three guerrillas went airborne in a fiery blast, just like in the movies.

"Nice," Charlie said.

"Some of my good stuff. I'm saving the best shit for the end. You know, the grand finalé," Willy gloated.

Mack put a bullet between the last guy's eyes before he had a chance to launch his grenades. "Where's the head honcho?" During the truck blast he'd lost sight of the leader.

"Don't know, brother. I lost him too," Tavon said.

"I believe he's…." Charlie used his computer. "There. I've got him. He went inside the wood cabin. One figure standing inside the door, three curled up in the east corner on the floor. Scratch that. Two now standing. Close together. Looks like—" He gazed up and all Mack could see was the anguish on his face.

"What! Dammit, what do you see?"

"It looks like he's using Jenna as a human shield."

Mack was running before his mind registered that the soles of his boots were hitting the ground. Bullets were still flying at him. He zigged and zagged, shooting as he pounded through the dirt and brush.

"Wait, we...need to think...this through." Tavon was running behind him, shooting between words. "Don't go in alone."

Explosions were firing off too. His guys would have to handle CRAF back there without him. There was no time to plan. No time to think. Jenna needed him. Now.

***

Someone opened the door to the cabin and stepped inside. From the sound of his shoes on the floor, he moved quickly and was agitated.

"Not him," Anna whimpered. "Please. No. He's the bad one."

"Stay away from us!" Jacob demanded.

What was going on? Jenna wished for the hundredth time that she wasn't blindfolded.

"Who's there?" she demanded.

Instead of an answer, someone grabbed her elbow and yanked her to her feet.

"Hey! Ow!" Jenna squealed.

"Let go of her!" The sound of a struggle behind her meant the Jacob made a movement toward the bad guys

"Jacob, no!" Anna squealed. "They all listen to him. Don't make him mad."

Were they hurting Jacob? She elbowed and kicked the man holding her, struggling with all her might to break free.

"Stop. I will kill you," a man snarled in English. He savagely pinched her arm.

She froze. The kids went silent.

"Listen, let them go," Jenna pleaded. "Please. They're just children."

Fingers gripped her chin, digging into her jaw. "Shut up, *mujer!*"

Was he the leader? What was he going to do with her? Oh, God. Anna said he was the bad one. How much worse could he be than the ones who had smacked her around?

Her heart pounded. She wished she could see the monster. She had half a mind to kick him in the shins, but knew she didn't dare, not with the kids to worry about. She held still, listening with all her might for auditory clues. Why was this guy here? What did he want?

"You come with me." The man started yanking her across the floor.

"No!" Anna and Jacob both yelled. "Don't go!"

She didn't want to leave the kids. She pushed back against him and dragged her feet. The man heaved, grunted, and called her every dirty Spanish word she'd ever heard, plus more. He seemed surprised that she was strong enough to make it difficult to move her. Really, creep? Is this the best you've got? She smiled. Yoga, swimming, kick boxing, and weight training kept her in shape. She was strong. This guy seemed to be flabby and was easily winded. She pulled her lips up in a snarl and elbowed him in the ribs.

It must have been the smile that infuriated him.

She didn't see the blow coming. The leader of the CRAF guerrillas punched her in the stomach, knocking the air out of her lungs. She doubled over trying to breathe, but nothing happened. Fear set in. Only one other time she'd gotten the wind knocked out of her.

When she was seven she swung on the monkey bars in the small backyard on the base. Pretending to be a great gymnast, her hand slipped off and she landed flat on her back with air exploding from her lips. She couldn't breathe and thought she'd die right there. If she died, who'd take care of her mother? Who'd pray for Daddy to come home safe from the battlefield? Who would find her dead body?

Her burning lungs felt like they did when she was seven years old, only this time a maniac was yanking her by the hair while she tried to breathe. And two kids screamed behind her. They could die if she didn't protect them.

The man laughed. A horrible, scary laugh that sent shivers up her spine as he dragged her toward the door.

"See, *mujer*? Better to do as I say." His voice blew into her ear, causing an involuntary shudder to crawl up her sweaty back. "Have you learned your lesson yet?"

Jenna had a bad feeling the lesson wasn't over. She might not live through the rest of it. She gulped air trying to move oxygen in and out of her lungs.

The door opened.

Air rushed across on her damp body and tugged at the tank top and panties that were sticking to her skin. Shock made her suck in a big breath and got her lungs working right again. The musky smell of the jungle came in with the blast of air. She caught another odor—metallic and thick—that threatened to flip her stomach. Blood. Outside, the screaming and the unmistakable sound of gunfire and grenades didn't end.

The creep came to a jerky halt. Moving behind her, he snaked his arm around her neck. "Stay back! Or she dies."

The cold pressure against her temple could only be one thing—once again she had a gun to her head.

Jenna didn't have to be told what was going on. She knew who had come through the door.

"Mack."

CHAPTER EIGHTEEN

It was Mack's worse nightmare—Jenna, blindfolded and nearly naked, trembling in the arms of a killer holding a gun to her head. In the back of his mind he kept thinking about those bombs. If they dropped right now, this second, would the honcho's trigger finger twitch? Would he watch Jenna die? The kids were crying in the corner.

"Hi, babe. Just sit tight, don't move. This thing is almost over." He focused through the scope of the Sig 226 that he pointed at the assailant's head.

"I knew you'd come for me," she said softly.

His heart twisted into a knot. "Of course I did. You okay?"

"Yes, but I'm ready to leave this rat hole." Jenny flinched as the assailant threaded his fingers through her hair and yanked her head backward.

Mack's finger twitched on the trigger. "Release her. Now!"

The man shook his head. "I have a better idea. You leave."

Mack cocked his gun. "I'm not screwing around with you. Let her go!" Dammit! He was seeing red and tilting dangerously into the out of control zone. He had to calm down. Jenna's life depended on him handling this situation right. If his heart rate rose any higher, it would affect his shooting accuracy. In close quarters like this, he couldn't afford to miss.

"And if I don't?" Honcho grinned. "She is your woman, no? You don't like the way I touch her?" The honcho ran his left hand up Jenna's side and cupped her breast.

"Get your hands off me, creep!"

The bastard was messing with Mack's head, trying to unnerve him and make him do something stupid. Or maybe he was buying time while his guerrilla backup surrounded the cabin. Whatever the case, Mack couldn't fall into the trap.

"You heard her. Let her go now, and I won't make you eat your own balls."

"Go to hell, American pig!" Honcho snarled.

You first, you slimy piece of shit. Mack took a deep breath and forced his heart rate back down. Focus. Relax. "Listen, man. You are completely surrounded. It's over. Drop the gun."

"Leave. Or I put a bullet in her brain. And then I will shoot the young ones!" The man motioned toward the kids huddling in the corner.

"No! Do as he says!" Anna cried out.

"Be quiet, Anna," Jacob whispered.

Mack couldn't be distracted by the kids or the terrified whimper that came from Jenna's lips. "I'm going to say it again. Drop. Your. Weapon."

Honcho yanked Jenna even closer. "Shoot me, and you kill your *mujer*."

Mack took a long look at Jenna. His strong, brave girl was so fragile, so completely out of control, in the hands of a madman. But worse than that. She was in his hands too, wasn't she? He didn't have a clean shot and couldn't pull the trigger. How would he live with himself if he shot his beloved Jenna? He'd never survive it. Well, he'd only survive a second. Then he'd turn his weapon on himself. This trip to South America had taught him many things. Not the least of those was that he was still madly in love with the admiral's daughter. He'd learned the hard way. There was no living without her. He wasn't going to try.

Mack lowered his weapon.

"Kick your gun to me and get over there. Face to the wall!" Honcho ordered.

***

Wait. What was going on? It sounded like…no. "Mack! Don't surrender!"

"It's okay, babe."

"No, it's not. Don't you dare give up your weapon. He'll kill you."

"There are worse things than to be dead. I can't risk hurting you." Mack's voice was soft. She could hear his sadness and anguish. Something clattered to the floor. His gun!

"Against the wall!" the creep ordered.

"Please, don't hurt him." Her insides shattered. The man she loved with all her heart was about to be murdered. She whimpered. The guy would surely turn the gun on her next. They'd both be dead in a matter of minutes.

And then she heard it, a soft click. It didn't surprise her that the creep didn't know what was coming. Her senses were becoming more and more acute. Her hearing especially was getting better every minute that she was blindfolded. And if the creep didn't hear it…Hope flickered way down deep. It was a plan, a risky one, but one she was prepared to die for.

"Count to three, Mack," she ordered.

"Shut up!" the creep elbowed her in the spine. "On your knees, pig."

"Count, Mack. Please, just do it."

"One, two, three—" His voice was muffled. His face must have been against the wall.

"Execute!" she finished and slammed her head backward as hard as she could, head butting the creep in the nose. He roared in pain and she saw stars. He squeezed tighter, but she was still able to duck. A single shot rang out through the crack in the door. Something zipped past her cheek. She braced for the creep's bullet to lodge in her brain, but instead his weight pulled off and away from her. There was a sickening thump when the creep's skull hit the floor behind her.

"Bull's eye!"

She'd recognize that voice anywhere. "Charlie!"

Anna and Jacob both cheered and cried at the same time.

"Good shot, man." Tavon's voice. "Couldn't have done better myself with my right hand."

"Jenna." Mack's voice warmed her all the way to her toes as he untied her blindfold. "Jenna." He said again as if making sure he wasn't dreaming. "My God, Jenna."

She blinked in the light. Tavon and Charlie were cutting the ropes that bound the kids together.

"Hold still, guys. We'll have you out in a second," Tavon said.

Mack lovingly cupped her jaw. There were tears in his eyes. "I thought I'd lost you, babe."

"How can you? I'm yours." She wrapped her hands around his neck and pulled his lips to hers. Their tears ran together.

Willy peeked his head through the door. "Um, you guys ready to bug out? Ty's out here with the helo."

Mack eased back and wrapped his arm around Jenna. "You guys get the kids out of here first. Go!"

The kids were all too happy to run out of the cabin.

"Let's get you dressed." Mack grabbed her pants and helped her into them. She was suddenly very weak. She was more than grateful Mack was taking charge. "Okay, babe. Let's go."

Holding her hand they ran out of the shack. Most of the guerrillas were scrambling away from the helo like frightened animals. A few still shot at the team as they went and Mack fired back.

Jenna and Mack made it to the helicopter. A rope ladder swung in the wind.

"Climb, babe. I'll be right behind you."

She looked at him. He had to be kidding. There was no way that she could climb that thing. "I can't."

He kissed her on the cheek and whispered in her ear. "Hang on and just put one foot in front of the other. It's a lot like love." His lips quirked. "And do it before I get my ass blown off."

Okay. She sucked in a breath, held on and climbed.

At the top of the ladder, Willy and Tavon hauled her inside. Mack jumped in a split second later. He really was right behind her.

"Jenna!" Jacob cheered.

"Yay, she made it!" Anna sounded cheerful as well, especially now that she was holding her mother's hand.

"Thank God, you're okay," Marcella said.

The Harmonds were huddled together in four seats inside the helicopter with Andrew in the middle. Andrew's head was on Marcella's shoulder. They all looked like they'd been dragged through hell and spit out the other side.

"I'm fine. How are you, Andrew?" Jenna asked.

"I've had better days," he offered a weak smile. His usually tanned face was shockingly pale. His leg and arm were bandaged and he was obviously hurting. "But I'll be fine now that my family is all together again."

Jenna let out a big exhale. They'd done it. The Harmonds were safe.

"Get us out of here, Ty, before more CRAF guerrillas show up!" Mack yelled.

"Can't, Mack," Ty said. "B-2s are circling, missiles locked on us. They want to know the secret code or they will fire."

"What!" Mack scrambled up to the cockpit. "Why in the hell are they going to fire on us? Tell them who we are!"

"That's unacceptable. Tell them Andrew Harmond and his family are on board!" Andrew said.

"Tried that. They don't necessarily believe me about any of it," Ty said.

Everyone started yelling inside the helo at once.

"They can't do that!"

"Do something!"

"What's the code?"

"Damned Air Force!"

"Please. Stop them!" Marcella's cries rose above the others. "My family has been through enough already."

Jenna couldn't believe it. They'd all been through enough already. When was this nightmare going to end? They'd come this far and were about to be eliminated by the U.S. Air Force? Hadn't Senator Tonell talked to them? And what about her dad?

It was so loud in that helicopter it was hard to hear herself think. Jenna put her fingers between her lips and whistled. The sound piercing everyone's ears. "I may have something! Tell them that we're the SEAL team Senator Tonell spoke to them about. And um, maybe so did Admiral Collins."

Ty did.

A few seconds later the B-2 pilot said, "And...?"

"What do you mean, 'and'?" Ty asked.

"You could be partially right. But there's more. We need the code. I'll give you thirty seconds to give it to me," the bomber pilot said.

They looked at each other. Thirty seconds to figure out...what?

"They know we're not Air Force, right? How would we know what their secret codes are?" Willy complained.

"Jenna, if you've got a plan, this would be a real good time to share it," Mack growled.

She pinched the bridge of her nose. The Air Force needed confirmation that the helicopter was loaded with Americans and not hijacked by CRAF guerrillas. Or cartels. Or both. Kat and Tonell could have devised a code to prove that they were who they said they were. But what? Wait…the text! Kat had said…wait, what did the text message say?

"Jacob, what did the text message say on my cell?"

He shrugged. "I couldn't read it all."

"Remember the code. That's what it said," Anna pitched in.

Jenna pounded her pockets. "My cell phone. Where is it?"

"It was in your pants. I dropped it, remember?" Anna said.

"And then it slid across the floor," Jacob added.

They all looked down at the camp below.

"No. We don't have time for you to get it—" Tavon started to say, but Mack was already fast-roping out the door.

"Stall them!" Charlie said.

"We've got a situation here. Over." Ty's voice was strangely calm in the midst of this chaos. "We need more time."

"We have a mission to carry out," the pilot said. "CRAF and cartel insurgents are to be eliminated. Unless we have the code, we are to assume that your helo is carrying the enemy."

"I told you. We are Navy SEALs on a covert mission to rescue the Harmonds. We have them aboard. We might know the code, but it's on the ground. Five minutes. That's all we need!" Ty ordered.

"I'll give you three," the pilot barked.

Willy cursed. His face was hardened in anger.

Jenna stared at the cabin below and willed Mack to materialize outside the door. Nothing happened. A shot rang out down there followed by a hail of gunfire coming from beneath the canopy of trees. Someone was still shooting at the man she loved.

"Mack!" she screamed. "Get out of there!"

Tavon didn't hesitate. His injured arm didn't slow him down. He fast-roped out of the helicopter and his boots hardly touched the ground before he was shooting and running toward the cabin.

Willy and Charlie both started shooting out the open helicopter door. It was loud and crazy inside, with the kids screaming and the rifles blazing next to her, but Jenna couldn't pay attention to any of that.

She wouldn't take her eyes off the scene below. Where was Mack?

Come on, sweetheart, come on! Did he have to take cover inside the cabin? Was he shot? Oh God, was he okay? Too much time had passed since he had fast-roped out of the helicopter. The B-2 bombers must have been watching the scene unfold below as well. Surely, they knew that American SEALs were aboard the helicopter now, didn't they?

It didn't matter. Nothing mattered except getting Mack safely out of that gunfight down below and into her arms.

She blinked. Was that a helmet peeking out the door? Yes! Mack burst through the door keeping low, shooting and zigzagging as he went. Tavon followed close beside, him firing like a madman. Charlie and Willy hadn't let up the whole time. Their guns seemed to be in a constant state of shooting bullets. How much ammo did they have? Would they run out? She scrambled over to the cartons and hauled out several boxes of bullets.

"Here." She handed them to Willy and Charlie and took up her post by the window.

The enemy hadn't let up either. Gunfire seemed to be coming from everywhere.

An explosion rocked the helicopter. Grenades! They were launching grenades at the helicopter? Dear God!

"Get us out of here!" Andrew demanded.

"I'm not leaving without our men," Ty said.

Andrew probably said more, demanded more, screamed more, but Jenna didn't hear it. Explosions were going off down below. Frantically she searched the area, desperate to catch a glimpse of Mack. And then she saw him right as a grenade went off. Mack flew through the air, his arms swinging wildly.

"Mack!" She screamed.

"Oh, no, they didn't!" Willy chucked his own grenades at the enemy.

Smoke was everywhere. Jenna couldn't see and had no idea what was happening down below. The last image of her beloved flying through the air was burned into her brain. Was he dead? She started to sob.

Just then the loudest blast she'd ever heard exploded in the jungle. The helicopter rocked and then it was as if they were thrown in a blender. The helo started to spin wildly.

"What in the hell—?" Andrew began.

"Hang on!" Ty yelled.

Jenna watched in horror as Ty Whitehorse wrestled the controls. He reminded her of a bronco buster in a rodeo on a beast that was hell-bent on dumping him to the dirt. For the longest moment of her life, Ty fought to keep the helo up while it spun violently closer and closer to the ground, screeching and wailing as it went.

"We're crashing!" Jacob yelled.

Anna and Marcella screamed and held on tight to Andrew.

Charlie and Willy gave each other a deep meaningful look. Jenna couldn't quite read the expression. The brothers both shook their heads as if to say, so this is how it ends? After all the hell we've been through, this is it?

Everyone on the helicopter was going to die.

Jenna was afraid of dying, but she was terrified to the bone that the helicopter would crash on top of Mack and slice him to bits. She gritted her teeth, closed her eyes and prayed with all her might that Mack was out of the way. He had to be okay.

Finally, finally, Ty got the bird under control and brought it up again. It was the scariest ride of Jenna's life.

"Holy cow." Ty let out a huge exhale. "That was close."

"What in the hell happened?" Andrew asked.

"The Air Force, sir. Looks like they didn't want Willy to have all the fun. They dropped a bomb and took out the enemy." Charlie grinned.

They all looked out the open door and saw Mack and Tavon waving at them. Jenna's heart melted. He was alive! She swiped at the tears on her cheeks.

"I'm going to hover a little closer." Ty brought the helo closer to the ground.

Anna squealed. "No! I don't want to crash."

Ty gave her a sweet smile. "Don't worry, little lady. I haven't crashed a bird yet. And I don't intend to."

In no time at all Mack and Tavon climbed inside the helo. Jenna grabbed Mack by his vest and hauled him into her arms. She was bound and determined to hold her man for the entire flight home.

He wrapped one arm around her and with the other put a silver object in her hand. "Your phone."

She turned it on and read the text message.

Frowning she said, "It wasn't from Senator Tonell. It was a message from my father."

Mack rolled his finger through the air, prodding her on.

"Ty, please tell the bombers that Admiral Collins says, 'I love my pumpkin pie.'" She shook her head as a tear streaked whatever was left of her green face paint.

"Copy that," the pilot said. "You are free to go."

"Thank God!" Marcella said.

"Amen," Ty added.

"And may I say that was some extraordinary fighting. Some of the bravest I've ever seen. If you'd like to wait, we'll escort you back to Quito," the Air Force pilot said.

Ty turned his head to look at Jenna and Mack.

"No," Mack said. "Thanks anyway, but we've got injured parties and want to go home."

Everyone cheered. Ty relayed the message.

"Copy that," the pilot said. "Look for us in the Pilot's Bar in Quito. We owe you all a round of drinks."

"Hooya!" Willy said.

"Hooya!" Jacob imitated Willy and added his own air punch.

Tavon grinned. "Looks like we've got a Navy SEAL in the making."

"Okay, Ty, get us the hell out of here." Mack settled back into Jenna's arms.

"No, hold up. Hold up!" Willy scrambled to lean out the open door. He dropped a bag on the camp below and closed the door. "Okay, Ty, now go. And go fast. Really fast. Here comes the grand finalé!"

As they rose, bombers zipped past them, circled once and came again. Just as Willy's grand finalé erupted, more bombs dropped.

The team flew off in a blaze of brilliant explosions.

CHAPTER NINETEEN

"I love my pumpkin pie?" Mack rubbed her arm and watched the goose bumps dance across her skin. He cradled her head against his chest, needing her close, wanting her closer. "What kind of wacked out code is that?"

"It's father-daughter code," she said softly. "My dad has always called me Pumpkin Pie. I guess, in the middle of all this mess, he wanted me to know he loved me."

"Huh." Maybe the old bastard wasn't such a bastard after all.

She lifted her head and looked at him and even though he was exhausted, he suddenly felt energized. "God, Mack. We did it."

"Yes, babe. We did. Let me look at the back of your head." When she turned, he saw the dried blood. Gently, he felt around. "You've got a good goose egg there, but it doesn't look too bad. The blood's dried." It could have been worse. A whole lot worse. "We'll get a doctor to look at you when we land."

"It's not necessary."

"Yes it is, babe. I know about concussions. We get you checked out, and someone will need to be with you for the next twenty-four hours. Around the clock."

She grinned. "Someone?"

He lifted her chin. "I'm not leaving your side. Get used to it."

She opened her mouth to say something and closed it again. A flash of indecision passed over her face. What in the hell was going on in that beautiful brain? It scared him. Was she having second thoughts about them already?

He got up. "I'm going to break out the MREs. Want one?"

"Let me help you."

He knelt and dug through the food supply cartons, trying not to worry about what would come next. After they landed and went back to their homes, Jenna wouldn't need him anymore. And he'd be back to work. DEVGRU was his life. Wasn't it?

"Everyone needs to eat. And drink. What can I get you, Mrs. Harmond?" he asked.

"You mean there's food in those little bags?" Anna asked.

"Cool!" Jacob said. "I've never had food out of a bag before."

Jenna came up behind him, putting a warm hand on his back. "The pasta is sort of like Chef Boyardee's spaghetti and meatballs."

Jacob and Anna blinked at her. "Huh?"

"Don't tell me you've never had Chef B food." Jenna opened an MRE and handed it to Jacob.

He shrugged. "I don't think so."

"Okay. Completely deprived childhood. How about Hamburger Helper? Sloppy Joe?"

"Why would we eat anything by some sloppy guy named Joe?" Anna asked.

Jenna's mouth dropped. "Wow. This was the kind of food I lived on growing up. By the time I was eight, I did all the cooking in my house. None of us would have survived if not for Raviolios and Sloppy Joe."

"We have a private chef who cooks all of our meals. I want the kids to eat organic foods. Nothing processed," Marcella said.

Mack snorted. "Well, you're out of luck here. It's all processed, and I doubt seriously if anything is organic. If you want to eat, you'll have to pick an entrée out of the carton and heat it up with the heater."

"Oh, of course. We'll eat anything you have, Lieutenant Commander. Thank you." To prove the point, Marcella dipped her hand into the carton without looking and pulled out an MRE for herself and one for Andrew. "Go on, kids. You're hungry. Eat!"

Jacob held his pouch to his chest and grinned. "I'm gonna eat like a Navy SEAL."

Mack ruffled Jacob's hair. "Yep. Who knows, kid? You might just get hooked on MREs and have to become a Navy SEAL."

"Could I?" Jacob's eyes gleamed.

"Get good grades in school, learn how to swim, run and do proper pushups, and then I don't see why not."

"We'll talk about this later, Jacob," his dad mumbled.

Sure they would. Andrew probably had an office window in the bank already picked out for his son. But Mack knew all too well that some people were not cut out for behind-the-desk work. Some people were the hero types. He let his gaze touch each and every buddy inside the helo and was grateful he knew men with gigantic balls who would risk their lives for country, justice and each other. His gaze fell on Jenna. Her head was cocked, trying to determine what he was thinking. She had an uncanny knack for reading him.

He grinned. Some women were the hero types too. Thank God he'd found one of the best.

"Oh! I forgot to call Kat. She must be worried sick." Jenna dialed her cell. "Kat! Yes, it's me. We're okay. All of us are okay. We're coming home."

Mack could hear the cheering coming through the phone.

"I know you were. CRAF guerrillas took my phone. I couldn't call you back. I was...detained for a bit. I'm okay, a little banged up, but… Kat! Are you crying? I thought only your crazy stressed out boss was allowed to do that." Jenna swiped at her own eyes. "Thank you, that means a lot to me. But none of us would have survived without you and Senator Tonell. Please give him the great news and my deepest gratitude. And tell Duncan Fitz we need to have a memorial for…" her voice choked. "… for our teammates who didn't make it. When I arrive in Quito, I'll call Roberto's family and…all the others."

Hell, no. She was trying to be responsible and brave. She didn't need to be.

Mack leaned closer and said into the cell, "Your boss can handle that. You're injured and need your rest."

She blinked at him. "You're right. It is Duncan's responsibility. Go home and get some rest, Kat. When will I be in the office?" She cocked her head. When her eyes met Mack's, he saw a boat-load of promise, questions, and wonder. He also saw heat, lots of sexy heat. "Not sure. I'll have to let you know. Bye."

Mack couldn't stop staring at her lips. "Kat's okay?"

"A little shook up. When she didn't hear from me, she expected the worst. She watched all the explosions on the satellite feeds and told Fitz I had to be dead."

Jenna shivered.

She must have had a flash of how close she had come to it being true. It shook her up. Guys who came off the battlefield always believed they were strong enough to cope with the strange disconnect of fighting bloody war one moment and stepping back into real life the next. It was like being sucked into the Twilight Zone. Everyone needed time to adjust. Everyone. Even tough Navy SEALs. He'd help Jenna get through it.

"Maybe she's after your window office," he joked.

She grimaced. "After this trip, I'm starting to think she can have it."

"Trip, huh? Is that what you kids call it these days?"

"I still can't believe...well, any of it." She opened her MRE and started eating the peanut butter and cracker first.

"Um, you've got a little something right there." He took a towelette out of his pouch and cleaned her cheek with it.

"Peanut butter?" She licked her lips.

"Nope. Camouflage paint and dirt." Not to mention blood, scrapes, and bruises. He wanted to kill that honcho all over again for hurting his girl. Gently, he swiped her other cheek and ran the towelette over her nose. It came back completely green. "Looks like we're going to need a bigger towel."

She closed her eyes and let him clean her face. A soft sound came from her throat as if she was in heaven. As if he was giving her a naked full-body massage. Oh, he was going to give her one of those too as soon as they were alone. His body responded to the idea, and he wished for alone time right now. He wanted to love his girl and never stop.

When he was done cleaning her skin, her brown eyes sparkled like in days of old.

"There she is." He grinned. His beautiful, sexy admiral's daughter was right there before him. He itched to reach out and pull her onto his lap.

"Lieutenant Commander?" A voice interrupted his good thoughts and pulled him back to the present where he was surrounded by a family and his buddies. He wasn't alone with the woman he loved.

"Lieutenant Commander?" Andrew repeated. His voice was strained as if it took all of his energy to speak. Clearly, the man was exhausted. Had the guerrillas tortured him after they shot him?

"Yes, sir?"

"I know we got off on the wrong foot. It was mostly my fault," Andrew said.

Mack raised an eyebrow. Mostly?

"I wanted to thank you and your men for saving us."

"You're welcome. It's what we do. But none of this would have happened without Jenna Collins."

Andrew nodded. "Agreed. I'll tell Duncan Fitz how grateful I am for her help."

"Pardon my candor, but you can sure as hell do better than that," Mack said. "If you had listened to Jenna in the first place, she wouldn't have had to hire a group of SEALs to save your sorry ass."

"Mack!" Jenna said.

Mack put his finger to her lips. "Shh, babe. I've got this."

"He's right," Andrew said.

"Yes, he is," Marcella pitched in. "We owe Jenna more than a good word with her boss. She saved our lives and risked her own, sweetheart. Surely, there is something more we can do."

"What would you suggest, darling?" Andrew directed at his wife.

"I'm no darling, but I would like to suggest that the Fitz dude give Jenna a raise. A big whopping jump in pay grade. She deserves it."

Andrew's lips hitched. "Fitz owes me. I'm sure a jump, maybe even two jumps in pay grade can be arranged."

"Wow that would be wonderful. I think Kat deserves something too. She helped us on the outside and worked with Senator Tonell—" Jenna began, but Mack wasn't finished.

"And Jenna needs time off. A month, no two months, of paid leave for R&R in San Diego."

Jenna leaned into his shoulder. "San Diego?"

"Yes, babe. Coronado to be exact. I still have the condo there."

"You want me to stay with you?" Jenna's voice was so soft he barely heard her.

He tipped her chin up and gazed into her eyes. "Forever. If that's what you want."

She blinked the tears welling in her eyes. "Oh, Mack."

Oh, Mack? What did that mean? One thing he did know was that she didn't say yes. The absence of that one little word tore a chunk out of his heart.

He released her. "We can talk about it later." Was he letting her off the hook or protecting himself from an internal beating? Probably both.

"Is there anything else?" Andrew asked.

"What do you think?" he whispered in Jenna's ear. "Do we stop there?"

"That sounds pretty good to me." She thought for a second. "One more thing. EXtreme Adventures should provide two free trips for Charlie and Willy Handly to take their mother to the vacation spots of their choosing. I'm pretty sure Duncan Fitz will authorize it, but just in case we might need a little Harmond clout. Thank you, Andrew."

He closed his eyes. "You're welcome, Jenna. I'm going to close my eyes now, okay?"

"Yeah, you rest. Maybe you all want to take it easy. You've gotten more adventure than you bargained for." Mack took the empty MRE pouch from Andrew's hand. "Let me know if there is anything else I can do to make your ride more enjoyable."

Jacob raised his hand as if he was in school. "Can I go up front and watch the pilot?"

"Sure. There's a seat up there for you. If you ask real nicely, Ty might even let you steer."

"Suhweet!" Jacob jumped up and raced to the cockpit.

"He's not tired at all, is he?" Mack asked.

"No, but Lord, I am exhausted." Jenna yawned.

"All that adrenaline rush finally caught up with you. Come on, babe. Put your head on my shoulder."

She smiled and let her gaze travel the length of him. "The last time I had adrenaline issues was on the jet. Gosh, it feels like months ago. You worked real hard to calm me down."

Mack knew exactly what she was thinking. "I did. But I can't exactly do that here. We've got kids, for heaven's sake." He kissed her nose.

"I can wait until later as long as you let me look at you, touch you, and for all that is holy, kiss you." She reached up, grabbed his neck, and said against his lips, "All in a hot way."

Shit, he wasn't sure he could wait after that little tease. "You are one, wicked, wicked woman."

"But you love me."

"Babe, I always have."

He kissed her like he meant it. Hell, he kissed her like he meant it forever. If it were up to him, he'd kiss her with toe-curling passion every minute of every day for the rest of their lives. But he understood it was up to her to decide what she wanted. It always was.

Jenna sighed and leaned against his chest.

Gently, he moved so that her head could rest in his lap. He lifted her hair and let it run through his fingers. In her sleep, she snaked her arm around his waist. He smiled and closed his eyes. Sleeping would be easy now that Jenna was safe and wrapped around him. Tomorrow would still be tomorrow. They'd work things out then. He gave in to the exhaustion that had been dogging him since he left San Diego.

CHAPTER TWENTY

As Jenna rested with her head in Mack's lap, she worried about what would come next. Mack loved her. But was it enough? Would he choose the Navy over her again like he did before? Would she be able to live with that choice?

Eighteeen months earlier, they'd been stretched out across her sheets cooling down after making deliciously hot love. She had been on her belly melting into total bliss while the man of her dreams gently scratched her back.

"Babe, I wish you could see yourself in this light. You're so damned beautiful." His deep voice was reverent. He ran his finger down her spine, sending prickles across her skin.

She looked over her shoulder at him. "You're just saying that because I rocked your world."

He grinned. "That you did. Give me a couple of minutes, and we'll do it again."

"Mmmm. Sounds like a plan. A little lower, please."

Scratching her lower back, he continued south, slowly raking over her ass.

"Oh, I didn't mean...mmm, never mind. Seems like you've got this well in hand."

On cue, he brought his hand underneath her, cupping her sex. "Like this?"

Every nerve-ending she owned lit up like an electric parade. The man knew exactly what he was doing. She lifted her hips to give him better access. "Oh, yeah."

"We can stay in bed…" Leaning over her, he nibbled on the back of her neck, sending delicious shivers across her skin. That hand of his moved slowly back and forth, making her wet and aching with need. "…all day. Tomorrow too."

It sounded like heaven. She began making plans to call in sick the next day when Mack's cell rang.

"Shit." His hand stopped moving.

"Let it go on the recording?" she begged.

It rang again.

"Sorry, babe. I'm on call." He pulled his hand free and scrambled to answer the phone. "Riley here. Hey, Charlie, this had better be good."

Chill bumps rose on her skin.

"When? How many?" The softness drained like warm sand from his face and cold, hard steel seeped into the crevices. "Not Daniels. Are you sure? Dammit to hell! Are you sure they said Daniels?"

His feet hit the floor, and he planted his elbows on his knees. He didn't feel the small circles she rubbed on his back, but she kept on, hoping he knew she was there for him.

He listened for a long hard minute, his muscles bunching as if bracing himself against the news. She wanted to throw the phone against the wall, drag him into her arms, and shield him from this pain.

"Those bastards! Daniels had a newborn baby. He was going to be out of the Navy in three months." His head rested in his hand as if it was suddenly too heavy. "Shit, yes, I want to go! Tell the CO I'm in. No way am I going to sit this one out. I'll see you at the funeral. Thanks, Charlie. Sorry, buddy."

The man who hung up the phone was not the same man who'd been scratching her back and pleasing her in all sorts of delicious ways. This man who raised his shoulders and set his jaw was a battle-weary soldier. Hurt, anger and thirst for vengeance had hardened his features. Her Mack was gone.

"Three guys," he growled. "Three really good guys were killed today by a friggin' IED buried in the sand. Damned cowards won't even fight like men."

"I'm so sorry, Mack."

"I've known Daniels since BUD/S. One of the best guys you'd ever meet. He wanted to be a teacher when he got out. Imagine that?" His voice hitched. "Sons of bitches."

"Oh, Mack..." She reached for him but he pushed up off the bed. Away from her.

"Don't worry. The SEALs will take care of this." His eyes flashed, furiously. "I'll make 'em pay for Daniels."

Her heart hit the floor. "You're going?"

"Got to, babe." He raked his hand over his short hair, realizing as if for the first time what that phone call meant to her. To them. He had the decency to look sad about it. "It's my job and the guys need me. The Commanding Officer needs a sniper to...eliminate a problem area."

Naked, she faced him, pleading with everything she had. But her Mack had already left the room. And the man who stood before her at that moment couldn't wait to rush into the heat of battle. Lieutenant Commander Mack Riley had made his choice and it didn't include her.

There was only one thing to do. Mack would be furious if he found out, but she had to try and block his orders. She'd fallen deeply in love with him. Rock his world? He'd shaken her whole universe. Faced with losing him, she realized she couldn't live without Mack. Dammit! Hadn't the Navy taken enough from her already? No, she wasn't going to stand by and let this happen. It killed her to have to beg the great Admiral Collins, but she'd do anything to save Mack. Besides, Daddy owed her big time, and he had better pay up.

She drove straight to the base.

"Dad?" Her voice seemed so small in his office. Why did she feel the need to tiptoe?

"Pumpkin Pie! Come in." He used that cheesy nickname she used to like as a child. She could feel a headache coming on.

"Hi, Dad."

"What a pleasant surprise. Is it Thanksgivin' already?" Her dad rose from his humongous leather desk chair and stepped toward her. He nodded to the guard who'd escorted Jenna in. "That'll be all."

She went to him and he rounded the desk with those long legs and met her halfway.

"Darlin', it's good to see you." He kissed the cheek she offered and turned her to face him. "What's wrong?"

She smiled, or at least tried to, but her face hadn't been cooperative since Mack had gotten that call. "It's important. Do you have a few minutes?"

He led her to his deep leather couch. "For you, Pumpkin? I've got a lifetime."

She willed herself to do the one thing she vowed she'd never do after Mom died—ask Daddy for help. "I'm scared. There's this man...more than a man...he's..." Pressure built behind her eyes. She blinked hard. No way in hell she'd cry in front of the admiral. "I'm in love, Dad. Oh, God, I love him so much. I don't know how it happened."

Her dad fell back against the couch as if she'd pushed him. Recovering quickly, he sat forward and took her hand. "Well, Pumpkin, that's good news, right? Nothing to be scared about. Love happens to the best of us. Who's the lucky fella?"

She studied him. Was his smile forced? Jenna had learned long ago that her dad had a tell. Normally, when he smiled deep creases formed around his lips. She saw the beginnings of those same creases in her face. When he hid something from her, his smile went a bit wonky. The crease on the left side of his face didn't pop out as much as the right.

At that moment, the left crease was nonexistent.

"His name is Harry Bob Baker, a tree-hugging, pacifist who protests against the use of guns and despises the Navy. We're going to run off and live in Antarctica."

He dropped her hand. "That's not funny."

She tossed her hair out of her eyes. "You know who he is, don't you? I should have known that nothing gets past the admiral."

"Well, darlin', I'm your dad. It's my job to know what's going on in your life and protect you."

No. He'd given up that right years ago, but she hadn't come to argue. She'd come to beg.

"Then protect me. Don't let Mack go. Give him a desk job, something safe. Please, Dad, I've never asked for anything. I need this. I need him."

He stopped the fake smile. "Jenna, men like Lieutenant Commander Riley don't do desk jobs. He's a trained fighter, one of the best. You tie him to a desk, and he'll end up like one of them chained up pit bulls, angry at the world, and biting the hand that pets him. He'll hate you too, sweetheart. It's not the right thing to do."

She bit her lip. He hadn't told her anything she didn't already know. "What choice do I have? I can't let him go, Dad. I won't."

"Because you love him."

She nodded.

"How does he feel about you? Has he told you yet?"

Not in words. But when she closed her eyes, she could still smell and feel his gentle touch on her skin. The way he looked at her? Oh, God, no one looked at her like that. And when he whispered her name and filled her so perfectly… Who needed words?

"Mack loves me."

"Have you asked him to stay?"

She blinked and an unbidden tear dropped off her eyelashes. "It's his duty to go, and he doesn't have a choice. But you do. Change his orders. Please, Dad."

He let out a deep breath. "Listen, Pumpkin, there's something you need to know about Lieutenant Commander Riley. He's not who you think he is."

Anxiety twisted in her stomach. "What do you mean?"

"The man is well-trained to be who the Navy says he is. We send him deep undercover into the field for months at a time. He blends in like one of the locals and acts the part. He's good at it. One of our best."

She crossed her arms. "Are you saying he's acting like he loves me?"

"Maybe he's not acting. But how will you know the difference?"

"That's crazy! And paranoid. Why would Mack do that? We've been dating for months now. There's no way he could be acting all that time." *And loving me like no man ever has.* "I don't believe you. Nobody does that. Besides, what reason would he have for leading me on?"

"Ask him."

"No, I'm not going to ask him that! I trust him."

"I'm not sure that's the right move. Trust your life in his hands, yes. Not your heart. He'll only break it." He reached out to pat her leg. "I don't want to see my little girl get hurt."

The way Dad set his jaw meant that he was telling the truth. Was it possible? Did he know more about Mack than she did? Oh, God. It had to be something bad.

"Oh, no." She stood, towering over her seated father. All the blood went to her feet. "No, no. You have something on him."

"Sit down, pumpkin. Let me explain."

Anger boiled her soul. She shook her finger at him. "Stop calling me that! What do you have on Mack? Whatever it is, get rid of it. Bury it! Expunge his record, or whatever you need to do. He's a good man."

"I didn't say he was a bad man. Just not the man for you."

"Why?"

"He doesn't love you, sweetheart. He used you to get to me."

She sunk back into the couch. "Impossible."

"His friend was in the brig. Lieutenant Commander Riley thought that by being sweet to you, he could convince me to release his buddy. It worked, you know."

"I don't believe you."

"Sorry, pumpk…I mean, Jenna. But it's true."

Her insides shook. Was it true? Had Mack faked his feelings for her? She remembered the day they met. She'd sensed then he was playing her, or trying to. But after that? He'd seemed so sincere and loving. Had his amazingly rock-hard body and the beyond-her-wildest dreams loving clouded her judgment? Was she blind? Stupid?

He'd been so willing to go to war. To leave her.

She pressed her palms to her eyes.

"Oh, sugar. Don't cry."

She wasn't going to cry. She wanted to strangle Mack first and her dad second. "He doesn't have to love me." She lifted her head. "It doesn't matter." *I still love Mack and there's no changing that.* "Give him that desk job, Dad. Please. Don't send him into battle."

He stood too and put his hand on her shoulder. "You've always had a mind of your own. I'll talk to him."

She lifted up on her tip toes and kissed him on the cheek. "Thank you, Dad."

"I always look out for my little girl."

"I know."

She left her dad's office in a hurry as emotions flooded her. Tears puddled on her cotton shirt. Her heart was a shredded mess, and she suspected it was only going to get worse.

Oh, Mack.

If he hadn't loved her before, he'd hate her for getting him benched. Loving a SEAL wasn't part of her original plan, but saving him was the new plan. It was the one thing she could control.

Or so she had believed eighteen months ago.

Little had she known the great admiral had a plan of his own up his decorated sleeve. Whether he'd thought he was protecting his little girl, or simply thought he needed Mack more than she did, her dad hadn't any intention of benching Mack.

And she lost the man she loved.

CHAPTER TWENTY-ONE

About twenty minutes later, the helicopter hit a patch of turbulence. Jenna stirred and Mack woke up.

"What the hell, Ty? Folks are resting back here," Mack grumbled.

"Sorry, Mack."

Mack closed his eyes again.

"Hey, Mack. Now that you are awake, you can help us come up with a name." Charlie came and sat down by him.

Mack didn't open his eyes. "I'm asleep."

"No, you're not." Willy was on the other side of him. "You're lips are moving, and sound is coming out."

"Watch it, boys. Mack's been known to throw a few jaw-breaking punches in his sleep. You might want to scoot back a little." Tavon joined in.

"Just help us with the name," Willy said.

Mack cracked open an eye. "What name? Numbskulls? Pains in the ass?"

"No. For our group! We can't really be the recon Black Pirates anymore or the premier assault team Gold Knights. We need a new name. Something that shows how totally badass we are." Willy cocked an eyebrow.

"Willy's right, we can't be our old SEAL group names, or our DEVGRU name. It has to be different," Charlie agreed. "And totally badass."

"The mission's over. Why do we need a name at all?" Tavon asked.

Mack raised his hand in agreement. "Exactly. Now let me sleep."

"No. Think about it, if Jenna ever wants us to rescue a billionaire from the top of Kilimanjaro, or a sexy fair maiden tied up in the galley of a Somali pirate ship, or two sexy, sexy maidens strapped to the back of a camel in Bagdad, we're there, man." Willy bounced like a kid in his seat. "Saving clients, kicking major butt, and looking beautiful while we do it. But dude, we need a team name, or it just doesn't have the same badassedness."

"I don't think that's a word," Charlie corrected.

"Since when have I cared what you think?" Willy replied.

"How about the Black Warriors?" Ty spoke up from the cockpit.

"Seriously? You're in on this too, Whitehorse?" Mack shook his head.

"A team has to have a name, Mack."

Jenna sat up. "What about the Black Blades? You know, to match Willy's tattoo. Or what is yours, Charlie, a black raven?"

"Sorry these goofballs woke you," Mack said. "Do you want me to beat some sense into them?"

"Wouldn't work with Willy. No matter how hard you beat him, he doesn't get any smarter," Charlie said. "And I'm amazed you noticed my tat, Jenna, I had it covered most of the time."

"I'm working on my recon skills." She stretched, popping her back. "Or...oh, I've got it. How about the EXtreme Team?"

"EXtreme Team," Mack repeated.

"That's not too bad. It's like that television show I used to love—the A-Team."

"Did they have a woman on that show?" Charlie asked.

"I think they had a lot of women on that show, just as I fully intend to do in real life." Willy wiggled his eyebrows.

Charlie socked him. "That's not what I mean. We've got Jenna on our team. She really nailed that one guy. Perfect kill shot. With a little target practice, she'll be great backup."

"Two guys. One without the use of the iPad." A shudder rolled through her.

She had not processed it yet, and Mack knew from experience that the first kills could be really difficult to live with. Mack also knew he could help her deal with it. Hell, she'd been tied up, beat up, and blindfolded by guerrillas. His girl had been through a lot and she continued to amaze him with her strength.

Willy spun around to face Tavon. "And look! We have our own Mr. T."

Tavon gave his infamous mad-dog growl. "That's Big T. to you, puny man."

"I'm cool with that! As long as I get to be the hot guy who gets all the chicks," Willy said.

"Right. I'll buy the getting chicks part. Not sure about the hot guy stuff. You're more of the dense character who gets the girls in spite of your stupidity, and no one knows why," Charlie said.

"I'm cool with that. As long as they all end up in my bed. Naked. Oh, and we all know why." Willy hefted his own package.

"Enough! We've got women and children aboard," Mack admonished.

"Sorry," Willy said, but with that mischievous grin, it was hard to believe him. "I'll leave you all with that rather endowed image in your minds. Call it the King Kong of images. The great kahuna of all things large." He stood up and moved toward the cockpit.

Charlie shook his head. "Yeah, I don't claim him. Mother must have found him in a trash can."

Tavon laughed and rose too. "Okay. EXtreme Team it is. Go ahead and get some sleep, Mack."

"Like I could now," Mack grumbled.

"Uh, Jenna. Can I speak to you?" Charlie's voice was suddenly serious.

Her eyebrows crinkled. "Sure. Can you give us a minute, Mack?"

Mack didn't like it. Not one bit, but he rose and followed Willy.

***

"What's up?" Jenna didn't like the way Charlie was having trouble meeting her gaze.

"I wanted to apologize."

"For what?"

"I was supposed to be watching you, protecting you, and keeping you out of harm's way. It was a direct order, and I blew it. Those guerrillas stole you away right from under my nose. If it takes a hundred years, a thousand, I promise I'll make it up to you."

Wow, Jenna did not expect that admission at all.

"Charlie." She put her hand on his arm. "You have nothing to apologize for. They used Jacob as bait to trick me. I was stupid. Really stupid. I wandered away from you to rescue him. It wasn't your fault!"

"If anything had happened to you—"

"It would have been my own fault, not yours."

He hung his head like a kid in trouble. "I let you down."

"No. You didn't. You were the one who shot the CRAF's leader back there in the cabin. You saved my life. And you were amazing."

He grinned. "I did get the goober, right between the eyes. That was a righteous kill shot. You were very brave to give the signal and duck like that. How did you know I was there?"

"I heard the snick of the door cracking open. When I was blindfolded my hearing became more acute. No one else heard you. But I did."

He nodded. "Awesome."

"So Charlie…" She moved a little closer. "Would you mind if I gave you a little kiss for your heroism?"

He blinked. "You think Mack will kick my ass?"

Mack's voice came through the headsets. "Copy that. Hard and swiftly."

Charlie's dimples sunk and his pearly whites flashed. "Well then, by all means, pucker up. I'm sure it will be worth it."

Jenna laughed and leaned in to kiss his cheek. Her lips barely grazed his stubble when he turned quickly to face her. She ended up planting a kiss square on his lips. Jenna pulled back in surprise.

Charlie shrugged. "If I'm going to get an ass-kicking, I might as well go all the way. Hey, Mack! I got to first base."

Whistling, he jumped up and took the seat Jacob had vacated, doing his best to steer clear of Mack.

***

Mack made his way through the crowded helicopter and sat beside his sweetheart. "Hey, pretty girl."

"Pretty? If I hadn't witnessed first hand what a great shot you are, I'd say you need glasses, big boy. I feel like I've been run over by a truck. I'm sure I look it too."

"Nah. You're beautiful." He leaned in and kissed her lips, gently, lovingly. "You've been through a lot these past couple of days."

She pressed her hand to his chest and reveled in the rise and fall as he breathed. Feeling his heart beat so surely under her palm was more beautiful to her more than any music. She'd almost lost him. "Oh, my God. It's been crazy."

"That's the understatement of the year. How are you holding up?"

She let out a long breath. "I'm trying to process everything, but it's hard. I killed a man. Two! Dead. By my gun."

"I know. You did good."

"But it doesn't feel good. I keep seeing the first guy fall forward. He was this strange man, someone I'd never met, and I killed him. He could have been someone's father. He could have been just like my father, fighting because his boss told him too. Maybe his heart wasn't really in it. Maybe he wasn't a terrible man at all. How will I live with that?"

He rubbed her arm, making slow comforting circles on her skin. "On the battlefield, there is no choice. If a man is pointing a gun at you or your buddies, you take the shot. You don't have the luxury of worrying about the bad guy. He wouldn't worry about you. Or me. Or the team. You take the shot because if you don't and the bad guy takes his, you'll spend your life worrying about the shot you didn't take. If your buddies die because you didn't pull the trigger? That shot not taken is far worse than the one that hit its mark. Trust me. You did good."

She shivered. "I don't want to talk about it anymore."

"That's fine for now. But you are going to need to go through it eventually. It's not good to bottle that crap up, or it might explode on you when you least expect it."

She nodded. "I'll talk to my therapist next week."

Therapist? He had no idea Jenna had one. "That's a good idea."

"I've been through lots of crappy days in my life, but this stuff was really hard. I don't know how you guys live with the stress. But you're good at it, Mack. You were amazing out there.

Maybe I shouldn't have been so scared when you were deployed." She blinked. "Well, I'd still be scared out of my mind, but at least I'd understand a little better."

He pressed his forehead to hers. "You were really scared, huh? I couldn't comprehend that fear, hell, I had no idea how crippling the terror could be until the guerrillas captured you, babe. I felt like I was dying. I never, ever, want to go through something like that again. I wouldn't survive it."

She caressed his cheek. "That's how I felt, Mack. When you chose to leave me."

Suddenly, the drive to re-up wasn't pulling him so hard. He was good at what he did. DEVGRU fit him like skin. But how could he put Jenna through this crap again? It wasn't fair. He couldn't hurt her. And he didn't understand any of that until this engagement.

"Wait. I chose to leave you? You dumped me, babe. Hard. On my ass. Flat out."

She sucked in a breath. "Not really. I let you go. You couldn't wait to go. You loved the rush of battle more than you loved me."

He shook his head. "Bullshit."

She leaned forward until they were eye-to-eye. "Don't deny it. I tried to get you benched. I went to my father to have you transferred to a safer job. Away from the field so we could be together. I pleaded with him. I begged. He told me that you were just using me to get your friend out of the brig."

Tavon's voice rumbled through her headset. "Say what? No, brother, you did not do that."

Mack rubbed the back of his neck. *Shit.* "It wasn't like that. Okay, in the beginning, maybe, for about ten minutes. But after that? Everything I said, did, was real. You've got to believe me. I fell in love with you the minute you climbed on my Harley and drove."

"I believe you." Her voice was heavy, sad. "But it wasn't enough, was it?"

"It was, babe. I swear it was."

"My father gave you the choice. You chose to go and leave me behind. And Mack, it terrifies me that you always will."

It was as if someone had kicked him in the balls. The past, the way she saw it, came into focus.

"That day the admiral called me to his office? It was because you asked him to bench me?"

She nodded.

Shit. "And you thought I gave you up to go fight for Daniels and the other guys who were killed."

"You did. My dad gave you a choice, but you said that you didn't do desk jobs. And Mack, I didn't want to do alone." She tried to laugh, but it didn't work. "And here I am, still alone."

The blinding truth bit him in the ass. For all those months, he thought Jenna was a cold-hearted bitch, but wasn't he the bastard who'd used her to get to her dad? He never knew how hard she had fought for him to stay with her. And how easily he had walked away. She'd left him a note saying she was shipping out too. She'd requested a trip to Hong Kong with her travel agency. She was sorry to leave so abruptly, but she hated good-byes and didn't want to cloud the good times they'd had. In the letter, she'd said that it was better this way as his team would be leaving in the morning. He'd made his decision to leave, and she made hers. She'd signed it "take care."

Take care? He loved this woman, more than he dared admit to himself, or anyone else for that matter. *Loved, dammit!* But it had been too late. She'd left him.

Mack ran his hand over his short hair. "I wish you had given me a chance to tell you how I felt before you flew off to Hong Kong."

"Well, you were flying off to war." Her brown eyes scoured his face. "How did you feel?"

"I wanted to marry you, Jenna"

"Then why didn't you ask? You never even said you loved me."

"Are you shitting me? You didn't even propose to her? I thought she had said no," Tavon growled. "Jeez, Mack."

"I thought she left you at the altar," Charlie said.

"I thought she wised up and found someone better." Willy wiggled his eyebrows. "There's still time."

"Shut up! This is between me and—" He looked around. All eyes were on him. "And the woman I love with all my heart. I'd never loved anyone until I met you. You're the one for me, babe."

"Oh, Mack."

He faced her. "If I'd asked back then…"

"I would've known that you really did love me, at least as much as you loved going to war. And I would have had a choice, Mack. Not yours, or my dad's. My choice."

"Got it. I'm sorry I didn't ask, babe. I was an idiot."

"Yes, you were."

"He still is," Willy said. "There's still time to trade up."

Charlie snorted. "Up?"

"Yeah, Mack, you're a total idiot," Jacob added.

Mack narrowed his eyes at the boy. "You're not helping me here, kid."

"Well, you are. If I loved a girl that much, I'd give her a present."

"Agreed," Anna said. "Something sparkly."

"No, something she really wants like a lizard that shoots blood out of his eyes. Who wouldn't want a pet like that?" Jacob nodded.

Jenna smiled. "Absolutely, unless they are endangered."

Willy laughed. "Little man, you know more about women than I do."

"Seriously, a lizard knows more about women than you do," Charlie joked.

"I'm all out of reptiles at the moment, but I might have something almost as good." Mack used his Swiss Army knife to cut the seam out of his beloved camo pants.

"Mack! What are you doing?"

"Dude, just because you love those dirty pants doesn't mean a girl would want a piece of them," Charlie said.

"Hold on..." He cut the strings inside his pocket. "I've been carrying this around hoping...hell, praying that you'd accept it one day."

Jenna gasped when he held the ring up so that she could see it.

"Will you marry me, Jenna Collins?"

She blinked quickly and tears sprung off her eyelashes. "Oh, Mack."

He rolled his eyes. "Shit, Jenna. I don't know what that means. I'm a man. Is it a yes, or a no?"

"Yes!" She kissed his chin. "Yes!" She nibbled his jaw. "Yes!"

He kissed her so deeply that it took a second to realize that a commotion had erupted on the helo. Everyone on board was cheering. Mack grinned and continued the most important business at hand—loving his girl.

"There goes your sweetheart, Charles." Willy said.

"You win some, you lose some." Charlie said.

"You never had that one, my friend," Ty said.

"Nah, those two were made for each other," Tavon agreed. "She has been through a lot and could use a little TLC."

"Ah, Tavon, I didn't know you were such an old softie." Willy made kissy noises with his lips.

Tavon punched him in the arm.

"Ow, dude! That hurt," Willy rolled his shoulder. "You might have broken it."

"Not too soft, eh, William? Tavon doesn't punch like a girl named...let's just call her Willy."

Willy drove Charlie back into his seat.

"Hey! Don't make me turn this helo around," Ty said.

"Boys," Mack whispered against Jenna's lips. "Can we have more?"

She pulled back. "Little Mackies or EXtreme Team members?"

"Why not both? But I was thinking more along the lines of little Jennas. Sweet and as beautiful as their mother."

"Oh, Mack," she said again.

He still didn't know what it meant. But he liked it.

CHAPTER TWENTY-TWO

Ty landed the helo in Quito without any problems. The kids jumped up and waited by the door. Willy and Charlie helped to lift Andrew Harmond to his feet and Marcella followed close behind.

"Nice and easy," Mack warned.

They all exited the Knighthawk and gathered around it. Mack kept his weapons in the cases by his feet.

"Welcome to Ecuador." An official approached them. He was a little guy with dark skin and an apologetic expression. "My name is Alejandro Lopez. I am in charge here. The Ecuadorian government has asked me to express our regrets for the trouble that you have been through. CRAF guerrillas are a huge problem. Please accept our deepest apologies. Let us help you receive the care and service you need. The ambulance is here."

"Good. My husband needs to go to the hospital," Marcella said.

"I would suggest that you all go to the hospital, as well. Just to make sure you are okay. You will receive the finest care." Two paramedics approached. Señor Lopez spoke to them in rapid fire

Spanish. "These men will get a stretcher for you, Mr. Harmond. They will take you by ambulance to the hospital."

While the EMTs lifted Andrew into the stretcher, Jacob ran over and gave Jenna a big hug. "Thanks for saving us. I'm sorry I lost your gift in the jungle."

She eyed him. "Was it a penguin?"

"Nah, nothing alive." He looked down sheepishly. "I'll try to get you something else. Maybe for Christmas."

"You don't have to. But that would be nice." She gave him one more squeeze. "You guys take care of one another, okay?"

"We will." Anna gave her a hug too. "Mom says no more trips for a while. Maybe next summer we'll go somewhere, but probably not quite so exciting."

Jenna nodded. "I get that. Bye, guys."

As Andrew was carried toward the ambulance, reporters rushed him.

"Mr. Harmond! Are you okay? Tell us about the daring rescue! How did you get out alive?"

Andrew pointed toward the team. "We got out with a little help from our friends."

"That's it for now. My husband's been shot, and we need to get him to the hospital," Marcella said.

"You were shot? Mr. Harmond tell us more about—" the reporters voices were cut off as Andrew and his family were taken inside the ambulance. The reporters raced to their cars to follow behind.

"Talk about ambulance chasers," Tavon said.

"Yeah. That's sick. No one stayed back to interview us!" Willy complained.

"Is anyone going to hang out and wait for the B-2 bombers to come back and buy us drinks?" Charlie wanted to know.

"Hell, yeah! Hey, Señor, can you point us to the Pilot's Bar?" Willy asked.

The man's eyebrows lifted. "I am surprised you know of it. It is very small and quite...well, I would not call it clean. And the *policia* are called there frequently." He leaned forward and whispered, "Lots of fights."

Willy pumped his hand in the air. "Perfect!"

The man frowned. "It is around the corner. Not too far."

"You coming, Whitehorse?" Willy asked.

"Of course. Sounds like my kind of place," Ty said. "Tavon?"

"Yeah, all right. Not too often I get the chance to drink an Air Force Bomber crew under the table. How about you, Mack?"

"No. You guys go without me. My fiancé and I have unfinished—" He stopped short, his gaze raking over her.

She felt her face burn. Was he really looking at her like that in public?

"Business, brother. The end of that sentence is business." Tavon's deep rumbly laugh rolled over her. "Okay, you two. Go. Get a room for a change."

Mack grinned. "Sounds like a great plan."

He wrapped his arms around the Handly brothers. "You boys stay out of trouble."

"Us?" Willy blinked innocently. "How is that possible?"

"It isn't. Trouble is what we do," Charlie said.

"That and women." Willy laughed. "Sometimes at the same time."

"Watch yourselves! Make sure you know who the trouble is and where her daddy lives," Mack said.

"That's a lot to ask, Mack," Willy said. "How am I supposed to keep all that straight? It's too much, right, Charles?"

"For you, William, yes. It is two whole things. He's better remembering one thing at a time, Mack. Or a partial thing."

"I can't help it. God gave some guys big brains." Willy shrugged. "Ladies like what I've got better."

"I give up." Mack slapped them on the backs. "You've got my number if your asses land in jail."

Jenna stepped forward. "I want to thank you guys again. If we need to mobilize the EXtreme Team again, I'll give you a call."

"You better." Willy lifted her into the air and swung her around.

"Take care of her, Mack. If she gets tired of you, tell her to look us up," Charlie said.

Charlie had a crush on her. She might have one on him too if there was no blazingly brilliant man named Mack Riley. Next to him, no man could shine as bright in her eyes. Mack was…hers.

Mack didn't sock Charlie, which was a first. "See you around, numbskulls. Stay away from the CO's daughter!"

"Ah, man. Do we have to?" Willy chuckled.

"You better. He'll shoot you if he catches you in bed with her again."

Ty extended his hand and Mack shook it. "This was fun. Hope to see you soon, Mack."

Mack chuckled. "Yeah, it was fun. You pulled off some amazing helicopter maneuvers out there. I always feel safe with you at the controls. Except for that time in Kosovo."

"Kosovo?" Jenna asked again.

"You don't want to know, and we can't say." Ty pulled Mack into his arms and pounded his back. "It means a lot that you feel that way, Mack. Are you re-upping?"

"I'm not sure. I'm still thinking about it."

Ty dipped his head sagely. "It's not going to be the same without you, my friend. But there is something to be said for ending on a high note before crossing over to greener pastures. And those pastures—" he pointed in Jenna's direction. "Are pretty sweet."

"You're a smart old Apache."

"I'm younger than you, old man. But I'll take smart. See you around." Ty followed after the Handlys.

Tavon hung back. The big man acted as if he did to not want to say good-bye.

Mack strode over and hugged him. "Be good. Don't snap anyone in half without me."

Tavon lifted Mack off the ground. "See you on Thanksgiving?"

"I'll be there. You deep frying the bird again?" Mack ground out as if his ribs were being broken.

Tavon put him down. "If Alyssa will let me. We had to get extra fire insurance the last time. So...we'll expect the two of you." He cocked his head toward Jenna.

"Sure. If she still loves me by then."

Jenna curled her arm through Mack's. "We'll be there. Let me know what I can bring."

Tavon nodded. "Think hard about re-upping with the SEALs, Mack."

"I will," Mack answered.

But in truth he was leaning hard in the opposite direction. For the first time since he became a SEAL, he'd frozen in the field. Terror had seized him when the bastards took Jenna. He'd made mistakes. He hadn't been as sharp as he should be, rushing ahead when he should have held back. He'd been a mess out there, and he knew why. Jenna. It was hard to focus with her sweet body nearby. But it was more than that. He knew what it felt like to be afraid for a loved one in battle. He didn't want to make Jenna feel that scared again. It was torture.

He gazed at his friend's big head. Tavon was the big black brother his mother didn't give birth to. But they were brothers all the same. He was going to miss Tavon fighting beside him, always protecting his six.

"How about you, Big T.? All this adventure change your mind about retiring?"

"Nope. It pounded home what is important. I like working with my guys, but I miss my woman and those snotty kids back home. I'm done with the Navy and the eight months on duty. It's too long to be away. But I'll be there if we have more private gigs like this one. The eXteme Team." He chuckled. "I sort of like being Mr. T., and the time away from the family is doable."

"I get it." Boy, did he get it. It would be hard enough to leave Jenna behind for months on end, but if he had kids? No way. It would be damned impossible. "Give Alyssa and the kids a hug from me."

"Will do, brother." His dark gaze slid from Mack's face and over to Jenna's. "Oh, Ms. Collins? I need to speak with you. Privately. Mack, go get the gear."

Mack frowned. He didn't like the serious tone. "What's this about?"

"You don't need to know everything, Riles."

"Like hell, I don't."

"Go on. It's EXtreme Adventure business. I'll catch up with you," Jenna said, though she had no idea what Tavon wanted.

They watched Mack go back into the helo, grumbling as he went.

"It's about my money..." Tavon began.

"Ah, yes. Can I write you a check for the twenty thousand?"

He put his huge hand on her arm. "You keep it. I will pay you to watch Mack's back when I'm not around. Do a good job of it, or we're going to have a talk, boss." He motioned between himself and her. "You don't want to have that conversation. Are you feeling me?"

"Copy that, Mr. Sting." She smiled. "Don't worry. I love him."

"Yeah, I know." He patted her shoulder. "Be sweet." And Tavon walked away.

Jenna had a deep sense of sadness watching her guys leave. She'd grown attached to each one of them. They were her guys. Her team.

"What was that about?" Mack's whisper in her ear sent yummy shivers up her spine.

"Mmm. Nothing. So, sailor..."

"Yes, babe?"

She weaseled in so that she was pressing up against his rock hard chest. "EXtreme Adventures will put us up at any five-star hotel we want to stay in."

"Hmmm." He wrapped his arms around her back. "That sounds accommodating."

"And I was wondering, Lieutenant Commander..." She ran her hands from his wide shoulders down his back.

"I'm listening."

"What I mean to ask is ..." She grabbed his gloriously beautiful ass. "Mack, do you want me..."

He let out a deeply sexual growl, and she instantly went wet.

"To make hot, passionate, dirty..." She pressed herself against his hard cock and slowly rocked.

"Oh, babe." He gripped her hard, his warm fingers digging into her back. "You'd better slow down."

"Slow down? I was asking if you wanted me to make love to you. All..." She was breathing heavily now. "...night...long?"

"Yes. Please, Jenna."

She loved that they were re-enacting the first night that they'd made love. It felt so right to be starting over from here with her in the driver's seat.

"Let's hurry, or I'm going to throw you down and take you right here."

She grinned. "Would that be so bad?"

"Damned right it would be. I'm dying to see you naked! I want to take my time licking, kissing, and sucking every last inch of your sweet body."

She toyed with his earlobe. "Oh you will, Mack Riley. I promise you. You will."

He ran his hands up her sides, and then locking his fingers with hers, lifted her arms over her head. He kissed the air right out of her lungs, and Jenna Collins gave up control. Her knees buckled and she held on, knowing Mack would be there to catch her.

Her SEAL was back where he belonged.

ACKNOWLEDGEMENTS

First, I would like to humbly thank all the men and women in the military. What you do to protect me and my family goes beyond words. I am very grateful.

Lots of kisses to my loving hubby and sons. Bless you for supporting me in this crazy adventure and not squawking too loudly when the house gets messy and we eat out more than we should. I love you guys!

Thank you to my parents and sis who have been cheering me on from day one. I wouldn't be here without you.

C.C. Wiley, Anne Marsh, Cynthia Appel, Gia Alden, Sandra Troutte, Lisa Deon and judges of the Utah RWA Chapter all read and improved Mack's story. Hugs all around ladies! Romance Divas help me every day. Thank you Divas for your gentle guidance and support.

Georgia Woods was a fabulous editor and Kim Killion rocked the cover.

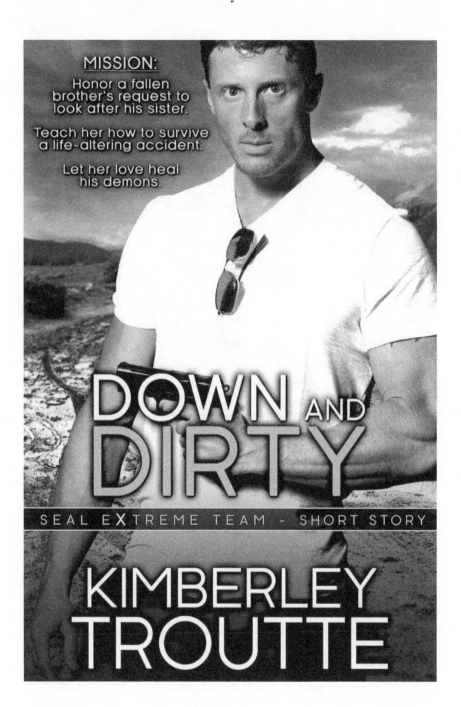

MISSION:
Honor a fallen
brother's request to
look after his sister.

Teach her how to survive
a life-altering accident.

Let her love heal
his demons.

DOWN AND DIRTY

SEAL EXTREME TEAM - SHORT STORY

KIMBERLEY TROUTTE

DOWN AND DIRTY
SEAL EXtreme Team Short Story
by
KIMBERLEY TROUTTE

Final request...

SEAL Lieutenant Commander Nick Talley keeps promises, but taking care of a teammate's sister is a vow he should've made. How can a man tortured by the past, help a woman fight a tough future?

Broken dreams...

Ironman qualifier, Jill Connors, is counting the days until her brother brings handsome Nick home with him. But a buried IED takes her brother's life and a drunk driver steals her competition hopes. Will Nick want a woman with one foot?

Love has a way of healing the wounded...one muddy step at a time.

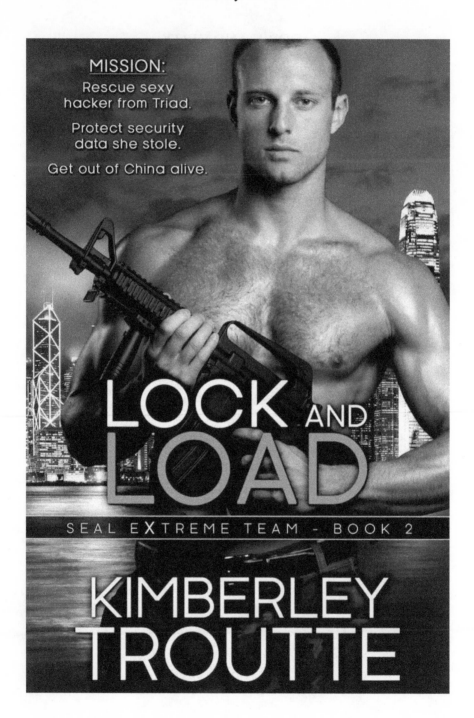

MISSION:
Rescue sexy
hacker from Triad.

Protect security
data she stole.

Get out of China alive.

LOCK AND
LOAD

SEAL EXTREME TEAM - BOOK 2

KIMBERLEY
TROUTTE

LOCK AND LOAD
SEAL EXtreme Team Book 2
by
KIMBERLEY TROUTTE

Dodge the bullets…

A Chinese gaming company tricks Amber Fitz into hacking the U.S. Department of Defense to extract weaponry secrets. In a panic, she steals the only copy and runs. Can she trust a newly-formed SEAL team to get her out of China and protect the secrets in her hands?

Solve the puzzle…

Communications Expert Charlie Handly loves a challenge and Amber is one sexy puzzle he'd like to solve. Is she a traitor or an innocent? Why does she remind him of the woman he's been searching for? The only woman he wants for himself.

Get out alive…

Amber needs one SEAL to help her escape. Charlie makes it clear he wants to protect and hold her close. But his brother and explosions expert, Willy, wants her too…and he's willing to share.

Excerpt for Book 2
LOCK AND LOAD

Amber was sure she was going to die.

One of the guys who had dragged her from Mr. Lee's shop barked at her in Cantonese, "Where did you hide the data?"

She was inside a yacht, tied to a chair, scared out of her mind.

"I don't understand! I am American." She yelled in English. "What do you want from me?"

Another man stepped forward. He had a red dragon tattoo peeking out of his white tank shirt and spreading all over his arms. He slapped her across the face. The sound resonated in the cabin and rang her ears. Her eyes dripped tears.

"Where is it?" The first man bent over until they were eye-to-eye. Was this the leader? King bastard of the 14K?

Amber blinked, trying to feign ignorance. "What? I don't know what you are talking about. You have the wrong—"

Slap. The other cheek got it, even harder than the first. Stars filled the room. Amber wiggled her jaw. Not broken, yet.

"Tell me where the data is," the man growled. "And I will make your death swift."

Fast or slow, it didn't matter. They'd have to kill her. She wasn't giving these bastards national security data. She tossed her hair back and glared back. "Go to hell, dickhead."

A guy in the corner stepped forward. He had a dragon tattoo covering his neck. He also had a pistol aimed at her head.

"Not her head, *gau*. How will she talk with her brains all over the cabin?" Dickhead said in Cantonese.

Amber shuddered.

"Shoot her kneecaps first. One and then the other."

The muzzle was pushed against her left knee. "Tell us where you hid the data."

"Please. I don't know what you are talking about! Don't hurt me."She squeezed her eyes shut.

An explosion went off. It took a second for Amber to realize that she had not been shot. She opened her eyes to see the surprised faces of the men in the room.

"What in the hell was that?" Dickhead yelled. "Go!" He shoved dragon-neck guy out the door. "Find out."

Footsteps pounded outside the cabin. "Yang! Something has happened."

"No shit! Find out what it was," Dickhead, who apparently was named Yang, demanded.

Two more explosions followed the first. The yacht lurched forward violently. The men stumbled. Yang was knocked to his knees. Amber was thrown forward, but the ropes held her to the chair.

"We're under attack!" Yang proclaimed, grabbing the other man's leg and pulling himself up to standing "Get the lifeboats ready."

"What about the girl?"

Yang cast one quick glance toward her. "Let her drown."

***

The blast rocked through the water. Willy cheered and did his famous "Got you suckers!" underwater dance. Charlie rolled his eyes and they all swam closer to the yacht.

Three large holes in the hull were sucking water out of the harbor. The behemoth would be resting on the bottom within the hour. There was no time to waste. Mack took the lead. They surfaced and studied the chaos on the already listing ship. Men raced out of cabins and scrambled on deck like incensed fire ants. Yelling, they cinched up their vests. Two lifeboats splashed into the water and men fought each other to get aboard. There was no woman in sight.

"One, two, three, execute," Mack whispered.

Away from the lifeboats, the team climbed the ropes and silently landed on deck. Their weapons were ready, fingers on the triggers. Charlie motioned to a door. The last time he'd heard her voice on his microphone it had come from this quadrant. He hoped to God that she was still alive.

One dude with dragon tats covering his chest and arms opened a door and ran straight for them. Bad mistake. "Keep cool, man, we don't want to hurt you—" Mack began.

The hostile was the mother of all dumb shits. He opened his mouth to scream and alert his buddies that SEALs were aboard. Mack took him out.

The guys silently followed Mack inside the hall.

***

Amber's chair started to slide. The yacht was clearly listing. After all she'd been through, this was how it was going to end? She couldn't believe the bastards left her like this! She struggled to wiggle out of the ropes, but her feet and arms were bound too tight. She couldn't budge the ropes. Damn the 14K. Drowning? That was not on her list of potential last seconds of her twenty-four years. Sky diving or speeding motorcycle accidents were always top on the list. Added today was being shot by a Chinese Triad while protecting the United States. But sinking to the bottom of Victoria Harbour? That was not going to happen.

She fought as hard as she could to pull her arms free. Her wrists burned like fire.

The door opened and four dripping men stepped inside. They wore wet suits, were fully armed and all business. The first thought that ran through her mind was that the military guys from the Ho King Shopping Centre had found her. Crap! How many bad guys were after her memory card?

"Stay away from me!" She yelled. "I don't have it."

"Quiet down, lady," the first guy said. He had piercing blue eyes and wore a take-no-shit expression. "We're getting you out of here. Willy, you and Charlie guard the door."

"Like hell you are! I told you. I don't have it and I'm not telling you were it is. Touch me and I'll scream."

The man rolled his blue eyes. "We don't have time for this. Tavon get her and let's go."

Tavon was the biggest man Amber had ever seen. "Copy that, Mack."

Amber opened her mouth and Tavon clapped his massive hand over it. "Listen, lady. We can do this the hard way. I'll make you pass out. Not kill you, but you'll have the worst headache of you life when you wake up. Do you want that?"

She shook her head slowly.

"Right choice." He removed his hand from her mouth and cut the ropes with his knife. "Are you walking out of here, or am I carrying you?"

She stood up, but her legs gave out beneath her from stress and being bound for so long. She fell back into the chair.

"Fine." Tavon scooped her up and threw her over his shoulder. "Carrying you it is."

The two guys by the door—Charlie and Willy?—went first to make sure the coast was clear. Apparently, it was because Mack whispered, "Move out."

They pushed her along the edge of the yacht toward the railing. Gunshots rang out.

"Behind me!" Tavon put her down and shielded her with his massive frame. When Tavon ligfted his weapon, she was able to peek through a crack between his elbow and side.

A guy was shooting at them from the top deck. "Let her go!" He yelled in Mandarin. "Or I'll—"

Charlie—or was it Willy?—put a bullet between the man's eyes before he could finish the sentence.

Terrified, Amber huddled behind Tavon and waited for the next set of gunshots. The 14K was full of arms dealers, for heaven's sake! She'd never get off the yacht alive.

"Okay, let's roll," Mack ordered and they were on the move again.

Apparently, he wasn't worried of a 14K ambush. And then she saw why. The Triad had abandoned the sinking ship. They were jetting around it in lifeboats, pointing and yelling at each other. Tavon all but dragged her to the other side of the yacht. The other guys were putting their masks on.

Diving gear? "Wait. Where's your boat?" she asked.

Mack had his breathing thing in his mouth already so he pointed to a typical Chinese wooden *junk* out in the water.

Um, no. That couldn't be their boat. If the U.S. military had come to rescue her, wouldn't they arrive in a Navy ship, or at least a speed boat? A *junk*? How stupid did they think she was? These guys weren't good guys. They had to be working with Director Lau to recover the data and there was no way in hell she'd go with them. She'd take her chances with the sinking ship.

One of the guys tapped his communications thingy by his ear. "We've got to move. I'm picking up chatter. The 14k boats are coming back around. They've spotted us."

"Everyone in the water," Mack said.

Willy put a life vest over her head, cinching it tight around her waist. "There you go." His hands remained on the vest too long, and too high. Her breasts were underneath all the bright orange fabric. "Safe and sound."

"Bite me." Amber crossed her arms. "I'm not jumping."

Willy's eyebrows hitched up. "Maybe later, sunshine. For now we all jump."

Mack spit the breathing device out. "We'll dive until it's safe. Charlie, give her your rebreather once we're in the water."

"Sure, Mack, but we need to go now," the communications guy said.

"Jump!" Mack ordered.

She held her ground. "No flippin' way."

Mack glared at her. "Tavon!"

"On it." Tavon grabbed her.

"On no, you don't! Let go of—" she started. Before she could finish she was sailing overboard and splashing into the cold sea.

She came up spluttering and choking. Dammit! The life vest popped her up to the surface where she buoyed like a cork in the water. She glanced up at the yacht she'd just been tossed off of. The bow was much lower in the water than the stern. Maybe it was a good thing that she got off that sinking ship. But she wasn't about to trust the men who threw her overboard.

Charlie swam up beside her. He took off his mask and handed it to her. "Put this on. I'm going to give you a quick and dirty diving lesson 101."

"No." Treading water, she stared at him. What was it about his voice that sounded familiar?

"Are you afraid of diving? Don't worry. I'll be right beside you. Trust me."

His voice drove her crazy. She knew that deep, teasing tone from...where? A dream? She'd never met this guy treading water beside her. She'd remember those dimples and sparkling green eyes. And no, she wasn't going to trust him. He just killed a guy back there. Bam, one bullet between the eyes. He'd do the same to her once he got what he wanted.

"Stay away from me." Her teeth chattered from the cold water.

Surprise registered in his big green eyes. "Why? I'm trying to rescue you."

Rescue her from the triad and then torture her for the data, all the same to him, right? Her gaze fell on his full wet lips. She imagined a few sweet ways that he might be able to get her to talk. A chuckle of insanity bubbled up her throat and she choked sea water.

"You're laughing?"

"I've lost my mind." It had been a freaking stressful twenty-four hours. She shook her head, but she couldn't stop laughing.

"Stress. Let's get to the *junk* and—" He reached for her.

The giggles shut down in a hurry. "Don't touch me!"

"Okay." He floated backwards, hands up. "Relax."

"Relax? I'm treading water in Victoria Harbour while every low-life dickhead in Asia is after me." She eyed him. "Who knows what *your* deal is." If she hadn't seen him in action, she might not believe he was deadly. A surfer, maybe, a trained killer, no. But then again, she hadn't been the best judge of men lately. Jacques was a perfect case in point.

"My deal is to save your life." He lifted an eyebrow. "Have we met before?"

She rolled her eyes. "Nice try. Save your pickup lines for some girl who cares. I'm not going with you. Who knows what you and your muscle-men friends will do to me."

"Amber, we're on your side."

"Right. Why don't I believe you? Oh, I know. Maybe it's because you shot a guy back there without blinking an eye and the Incredible Hulk just threw me off a ship."

He laughed. "Tavon is pretty incredible, but he's a softie. Your father hired us to bring you home. We're Americans, not part of the Chinese Triad."

"Dad?" Her eyes burned. "Called you?"

"Not me personally, but yeah. Come on, Mack can explain things once we get out of here. Aren't you tired of treading water? We've got food and dry clothes for you on the *junk.*"

For a moment her resolve melted. Maybe Charlie was telling the truth. She really, really wanted to trust him. To trust someone. She was tired. Not to mention hungry, cold and scared. But anyone could say that her father sent them. It wouldn't take much digging to find out that she was Duncan Fitz's only daughter.

A speed boat went by and the waves splashed into her face. While she was swipping the water out of her eyes, Charlie grabbed her. "Gotcha."

Big mistake. After the day she was having, she never wanted to be manhandled again.

"Let go!" She fought to get away.

She kicked as hard as she could and her boot slammed into him. By the way he grunted and doubled over, she'd hit the primary target. Ooops. It was her best chance to get away.

If she could swim for help...

The nearest boat was about a hundred yards away. A man and woman onboard probably didn't see her in the water. They had their backs to her and were focused on the sinking ship. It wasn't everyday that a billion dollar yacht sunk to the bottom of Victoria Harbour. When she got closer she'd yell. Putting her face down in the water, she swam as fast as she could with that stupid life vest on. She probably couldn't beat her best high school free-style record being fully clothed, but she was eager to give it a try.

Seventy-five yards.

She was panting for a breath. Her boots were full of water and so damned heavy, but she kept swimming as hard as she could.

Fifty yards.

The sound of a powerful, fast-moving speedboat hummed nearby. The 14K? She couldn't stop now. Keeping her head down, she windmilled her arms past the vest, and pulled through the water, while kicking her heart out.

Twenty-five yards.

The couple on the boat looked like Americans. Surely, they'd help her. She lifted her exhausted arms out of the water and forced them to wave. "Hel—!"

Strong hands gripped her vest and spun her around. She found herself nose-to-face-mask with Charlie. Dammit. She didn't hear him coming. The bastard wasn't even breathing heavy.

He pulled the breathing thingy out of his mouth and took the mask off. "What are you doing?"

"Gettting away from you."

"Not happening," he growled. "Be a good girl and put this mask on. We've got to dive. Now."

News for you handsome. That's not happening, either. But she might still have a chance to get away if the couple on board saw she was in trouble.

"Help—! She began again, but to her great surprise, he shut her up.

Not with his gun, nor his fists.

Charlie's full lips smothered her cry.

Kimberley Troutte

If you enjoyed COMING IN HOT,

you will love Anne Marsh's:

SMOKING HOT

On sale now!

Read on for a sneak peek...

Katie should get to drive. After all, it was her bucket list —
or, rather, Kade's. And Kade was her sort-of fiancé. They slowly
moved down the runway, the Segway rolling smoothly over the
asphalt as Tye drove like a little old grandma.

"Some speed would be good."

He didn't take his eyes off the runway. "You want to go
faster?"

"There's no *faster* about it," she grumbled. "We'd have to
actually be going *fast* first."

He chuckled. "You've got a thing for speed, don't you?"

No. She just didn't have a thing for *slow*. Life had a habit
of passing by unless she reached out and grabbed it with both
hands. She'd learned that the hard way. She eyed the speed
setting.

"This is turtle mode."

"Uh-huh," he agreed. "Enjoy the scenery."

The problem was, this scenery was all too familiar. They'd
started close to the Donovans' big metal hangar and now they
were putting down the runway, past a DC-13 and a chopper.
She'd seen these planes before. She'd seen this tarmac. Riding a
Segway was supposed to be exciting. Different. Something more
than this slow, sedate glide. When they hit the halfway mark on
the runway, she wiggled herself into position by his side. She
liked doing this better *with* him. Otherwise, it felt too much like
he was driving.

Which he was.

Darn alpha male.

She leaned back against Tye, feeling the tension in his
hard body. Since she was apparently just along for the glide at the
moment, she looked up at his face. And... *merde*. He had his eyes
focused on the horizon, a SEAL on a mission. This was supposed
to be fun. Kade had always had plenty of fun and lots of laughs.
There wasn't a bar where the man wasn't welcome and no one he
couldn't win over. Tye looked like he was planning on storming
an insurgent stronghold at the end of the runway.

That needed to change. Tye needed to have some fun. She slid her hands out from underneath his and slapped her palms over his fingers. There. Now she had a shot at being in control. "My turn."

He hesitated, his fingers tensing beneath hers. Then he let go. Not happily, she knew, and probably not for long, but she'd take it. She promptly adjusted the speed setting, because this beginning mode wasn't what she wanted. Not, she thought, that "standard" was much better. Apparently the makers of Segway were anti-speed too. There wasn't a "fast," "furious," or "go, baby, go" setting anywhere to be seen. The Segway picked up speed, though, and she'd bet they were going all of twelve miles an hour.

They hit a bump. Okay. She steered them straight through a pothole. That was the truth, plain and simple. Tye's arm snaked around her waist and he cursed. *Not* in French. Nope. She understood what he said perfectly well.

"Eyes on the road," Mr. Grim Reaper demanded in her ear.

"You always play by the rules?"

"When my team's safety is at stake? Absolutely." His jaw tightened and he wrested control of the Segway from him.

"I don't like playing by the rules," she informed him, turning to face him.

"You do today." He steered them left, making a tidy circuit of the landing strip behind the jump hangar. Katie counted two more planes parked on the runway and a half dozen pick-up trucks fanned out in a semi-circle. The place was peaceful and quiet. *Boring.*

Then he stopped fast and that move threw her against his chest, because she hadn't been holding on. Nope. She'd been letting go big time.

She finger walked up his chest. "Penalty on the play."

He eyed her. "That's the worst sports metaphor I've ever heard."

"Suck it up." She nudged his sunglasses up.

Danger, danger, Will Robinson. Tye had old eyes, like she'd thought the first time she'd seen him, but there was something else there now, something she couldn't help but respond to. *Heat.*

For *her*, Katie Lawson. She'd never been a *femme fatale*. Despite her man problem at the bar that had made Kade pony up his faux fiancé services, guys tended to see her as the fun friend. The girl they played with on the softball team and chatted up while they went after girls like Laura and Abbie. Tye, however, looked at her like he could eat her up.

And she liked it.

Which was so, so bad of her.

Instead of turning around or getting off the Segway or doing any one of a dozen practical things, she slid her hands up his arms. His shoulders were as hard and powerful as the rest of him as he brought the Segway to a gentle halt. Good. Causing an accident wasn't on *her* bucket list.

"I've got worse metaphors," she promised and his lips quirked.

"Can't wait for the show-and-tell." He stood there, less than an inch of space between them and that slightly amused look curling his mouth. Her whole body was shrieking *oui, oui, oui* while her head countered with *C'est impossible!*

"First base," she whispered and, when he ducked his head to catch her words, she kissed him. Which was all his fault, she decided. He looked so hungry, what else was she supposed to do?

Her mouth pressed against his, her lips slightly parted so she could catch his lower lip between hers. A soft, sipping kiss, just tasting him the slightest bit because he was probably—okay, definitely—off-limits and at no point had she asked him if this kissing business was okay. But he tasted perfect. She ran her tongue over his bottom lip just to make certain. Yup.

He tasted perfect.

ABOUT THE AUTHOR

Kimberley Troutte is a Southern California girl, born and raised. She lives with her amazing hubby, two awesome sons, one old dog, a wild cat, four very large snakes and various other creatures the man/kids/dog inevitably drag in.

Kimberley has been an accountant, substitute teacher, caterer, financial analyst for a major defense contractor, real-estate broker, aerobics instructor and a freelance writer. With a B.A in Business Economics and a M.S. in Systems Management, she was destined to write romance.

For inside scoop, ARC requests, and giveaways subscribe to the newsletter by visiting the website: www.kimberleytroutte.com.